I0612523

C.H.B. (CLIFFORD HENRY BENN) KITCHIN was born in Yorkshire in 1895. He attended Exeter College, Oxford, and published his first book, a collection of poems, in 1919. His first novel, *Streamers Waving*, appeared in 1925, and he scored his first success with the mystery novel *Death of My Aunt* (1929), which has been frequently reprinted and translated into a number of foreign languages.

Kitchin was a man of many interests and talents, being called to the bar in 1924 and later amassing a small fortune in the stock market. He was also, at various times, a farmer and a schoolmaster, and his many talents included playing the piano, chess, and bridge. He was also an avid collector of antiques and *objets d'art*.

Kitchin was a lifelong friend of L.P. Hartley, with whose works Kitchin's were often compared, and was also a friend and mentor to Francis King, who later acted as Kitchin's literary executor. Some of Kitchin's finest works appeared towards the end of his life, including *Ten Pollitt Place* (1957) and *The Book of Life* (1960), but though they earned critical acclaim, Kitchin was bitterly disappointed at their lack of success with the reading public. Kitchin, who was gay, lived with his partner Clive Preen, an accountant, from 1930 until Preen's death in 1944. C.H.B. Kitchin died in 1967.

FRANCIS KING (1923-2011) was the friend and literary executor of C.H.B. Kitchin and was also the author of fifty books, six of which—*To the Dark Tower* (1946), *Never Again* (1947), *An Air That Kills* (1948), *The Dividing Stream* (1951), *The Dark Glasses* (1954), and *The Man on the Rock* (1957)— have been republished by Valancourt.

Cover: The cover is a reproduction of the jacket design by Ben Feder (1923-2009) for the American first edition, published by Appleton-Century-Crofts in 1961.

BY C. H. B. KITCHIN

Curtains (1919) (poetry)

Winged Victory (1921) (poetry)

Streamers Waving (1925)

Mr Balcony (1927)

Death of My Aunt (1929)

The Sensitive One (1931)*

Crime at Christmas (1934)

Olive E. (1937)

Birthday Party (1938)*

Death of His Uncle (1939)

The Cornish Fox: A Detective Story (1949)

The Auction Sale (1949)

Jumping Joan, and Other Stories (1954)

The Secret River (1956)

Ten Pollitt Place (1957)*

The Book of Life (1960)*

A Short Walk in Williams Park (1971)*

C. H. B. KITCHIN

THE BOOK OF LIFE

With an *introduction by*
FRANCIS KING

VALANCOURT BOOKS

The Book of Life by C. H. B. Kitchin
Originally published London: Peter Davies, 1960
First reprinted by Valancourt Books, January 2009
Second Valancourt Books edition, January 2014

Published by Valancourt Books, Richmond, Virginia
Publisher & Editor: JAMES D. JENKINS
20th Century Series Editor: SIMON STERN, University of Toronto
http://www.valancourtbooks.com

ISBN 978-1-939140-82-1 (trade paperback)
Also available as an electronic book.

Set in Dante MT 11/13.6

INTRODUCTION

ONE morning in 1967, soon after my seventy-two-year-old friend and Brighton neighbour C. H. B. Kitchin had died, an excited reporter from the *Brighton Argus* telephoned me in my role of literary executor. Was the rumour true, he asked, that Kitchin had left millions? I replied that, since probate on the will had not yet been granted, I could not name a figure but that he had certainly left (as I then put it) 'a million or two'. Nowadays a million or two might just cover the price of a house in one of the more fashionable districts of London. But in those days to leave such a sum meant that one was truly rich. 'That puts him in the Somerset Maugham bracket!' the reporter exclaimed. 'I never knew that he wrote best-sellers.' I had to explain that, with the exception of his detective story *Death of My Aunt*, sold in large numbers all over the world, Kitchin had never written a best-seller in his life. His fortune derived partly from family legacies but chiefly from a careful reading of *The Financial Times* over breakfast every morning, followed by a telephone call to his broker.

In a preface to Kitchin's last, posthumously published novel *A Short Walk in Williams Park*, the novelist L. P. Hartley, his lifelong friend from their shared schooldays at Clifton College, declared that Kitchin 'was the most talented man that I have ever known'. His talents, I soon discovered after my first meeting with him, extended far beyond the writing of books and gambling on the stock exchange. He had been a promising barrister, thus no doubt obtaining a hoard of information about crime and punishment, subsequently to be of invaluable help in his writing of detective fiction. He had also been a successful farmer, even though, patrician and exquisitely dressed in the manner of an old-fashioned dandy, he certainly did not look like one. He used to play bridge to championship standard with former Prime Minister Herbert Asquith and his redoubtable wife Margot, and was also a briskly efficient winner at chess. At parties, if a piano were available, people would enthusiastically urge him to play for them. He would then ask for the name of a composer, any composer from Bach to Gershwin and from Chopin to Liszt, and would at once effortlessly improvise in that style. In his later years, soon before I had met him, he took up photography, buying not one but a number of cameras and setting up a dark room, with a huge battery of expensive equipment, in one of the two houses that he had knocked together in prestigious Montpelier Square in Knightsbridge.

Throughout his life he was a discriminating collector of pictures and antiques, as one of his best novels, *The Auction Sale*, indicates. On one occasion, when I needed a sideboard for my recently acquired Brighton house, he handed me a generous wad of bank notes with the words 'See what you can get with that.' What I got at the next auction sale held in Brighton was a Georgian sideboard, with which I was delighted. But when I showed it to him, he muttered 'Oh, dear!' 'Don't you like it?' I asked. He frowned, hesitated. Then: 'Didn't you realise that it's a made-up piece? Most of those brass fittings are not the original ones.' I still have the piece despite his disapproval and I still think it elegant, made-up or not. For a period he owned a racehorse and near the close of his life greyhounds, taking me with him to races on tracks in London and Brighton. Inevitably, when we made our bets, he won money and I lost it. During the depressing time when he was slowly dying of a heart condition that today might well have been cured by a bypass operation, he took up the study of higher mathematics. In explanation of this new and surprising interest he told me: 'I was always the top boy at algebra at Clifton.'

Like Hartley, Kitchin was the sort of old-fashioned homosexual who was punctilious in concealing his proclivities at that period when to reveal them might well lead to blackmail or a prison sentence. The great love of his life was a well-to-do accountant, Clive Preen, with whom he enjoyed what he told me was a 'blissful' relationship from 1930 to 1944. They were sharing a double bedroom at the best hotel in Liverpool, the Adelphi, when Preen suffered a massive heart attack and died. Kitchin realised that he must not give any indication of the intensity of his shock, horror and grief, for fear that the hotel staff and the ambulance men might conclude, rightly, that the couple were sharing a bedroom for some reason other than the desire for companionship or the wish to save money.

During part of that period Kitchin lived in a large mansion flat in Great Ormond Street with the celebrated bibliographer Richard Jennings, also a homosexual, and Lord (Ken) Ritchie, later happily to combine marriage with the acquisition of a handsome guardsman lover and to become chairman of the stock exchange. When T. S. Eliot's marriage to his first wife broke up, the three men offered him hospitality. Kitchin told me how, after dinner on most evenings, Eliot would first paint and powder his face and then sally out for what he would call 'a little stroll'. This convinced Kitchin that it was her husband's latent homosexuality that had mentally unbalanced the first Mrs Eliot and had resulted in the collapse of the marriage. Years later Ritchie showed considerable courage in his support in the House of Lords of a bill to legitimise homosexuality, even though some members of the Stock Exchange made ostensibly jocular but in fact hostile comments on his advocacy.

When I met him, Kitchin appeared to be unattached. But I used to speculate that perhaps there was some handsome university student or some brilliant financial whiz-kind whom he wished to keep secret from me. Then one day he invited me to the capacious residence in Knightsbridge. After I had rung the bell, it was not Sidney who opened the door with his usual tottery flourish, followed by an extravagant parody of a bow, but an elderly man in grey flannel trousers, a tweed jacket and carpet slippers trodden down at the heels. He preceded me to the door to the drawing room, where, with his usual courtesy, Kitchin struggled, despite my protest, to get to his feet to greet me. Then he said: 'Oh, Francis, I don't believe you've ever met George.' George, clearly from a class far removed from his own, was, I subsequently realised, his lover. I was amazed and touched that a man as remarkable as Kitchin should be so besotted with someone so totally unremarkable in looks and intelligence—and as old as himself. For George, his wife and daughter, Kitchin eventually bought a house in Brighton when he himself had moved there. Sadly, George eventually decided that he must spend all his weekends with his family. Kitchin found this deprivation hard to bear.

Unlike Hartley, demonstrative and sometimes even effusive in his solicitous, twinkling, ever-smiling manner, Kitchin was often thought to be chilly because of his reticence and shyness. But of the two Kitchin was essentially the more warm-hearted and the more constant in friendship. When it was clear that, by now spending more and more of his time in bed, he was unlikely to last for more than a few weeks, I informed all his old friends, many of them distinguished in the worlds of books, academia or finance, that if they wished to see him again they had better come quickly. They then descended on Brighton, sometimes from far afield, to say their goodbyes. The only exception was Hartley. 'Oh, heavens! Poor fellow! I'd no idea things were so bad. I have such a busy week ahead of me with so many engagements that I simply cannot put off. But I really will make the effort.' Hartley never made the effort. He had a manservant who could easily have chauffeured him in his large and comfortable saloon car door-to-door from London to Brighton. He could also have afforded to travel first-class on the one-hour rail journey. But it was clearly too much trouble for him. Kitchin would say: 'It's sad he hasn't been to see me. I think that he must be ill. It's so unlike him.' But it was all too like him. Although so close for so many years, I always sensed a certain rivalry between the two men. Hartley envied Kitchin for the power and purposefulness of an intellect that not merely propelled him to read the whole of Balzac's vast œuvre but also enabled him to remember even minor details of it. Kitchin envied Hartley for the social charm and ease that earned him the close friendship of at least half-a-dozen duchesses.

Kitchin was convinced that our meeting had been somehow foreordained. When I was living in Finland, I had written him a fan letter—something that I rarely to do to fellow writers unknown to me—about a novel of his, *Ten Pollitt Place*. Four or five days later I received from him a letter telling me how much he had enjoyed a novel of mine, *The Man on the Rock*. At first I thought that he was replying to my letter, but then realised that that was an impossibility in such a short space of time. An examination of the date of his letter revealed, amazingly, that our two letters had been despatched on the same day.

Our initial friendship eventually extended to all our family. He was particularly fond of my now dead brother-in-law, John Rosenberg, an American film and television producer who also wrote novels. He was also devoted to my mother, whom he loved to tease—'Oh, Clifford!' she would cry out, 'you are naughty!' when he had produced some absurdly extravagant compliment on her looks or her clothes. Every year on December 26 we would eat a second Christmas dinner as his guests, first in Montpelier Square and then in the resplendent London flat, into which, now a neighbour of Rebecca West, with whom he never got on, he had moved. The meal would be lavish, with his drunken manservant Sidney staggering about in attendance, and the presents would be costly. Our problem was always what we should give him, so fastidious in his tastes, in return. On one occasion I bought, at considerable expense in Bond Street, a supposedly antique French paperweight, since he had amassed a collection of such objects, which he displayed in a cabinet devoted solely to them. When on a subsequent occasion I peered into the cabinet, my present was nowhere to be seen. Clearly the antique dealer, in the fashion of so many antique dealers everywhere in the world, had misled me about its antiquity and value.

Kitchin had enjoyed financial success with his detective stories and critical success with his novels. His first literary novel, *Streamers Waving*, a book that might have been the result of a collaboration between Saki, Ronald Firbank and Aldous Huxley, was so much admired by his friends Virginia and Leonard Woolf that they accepted it for publication by their Hogarth Press. His second novel, *Mr Balcony*, a disquietingly mysterious and innovative work, unlike anything else that he was to write in the years ahead, also earned much admiration. But by the time that I met him, his fate was that of many elderly, once famous writers in England. Instead of lead reviews, he now got two or three paragraphs at the bottom of a page. Increasingly critics would apply the dread word 'veteran' to him, much to his annoyance.

When Kitchin published *The Book of Life*, Hartley had recently published the best known, most admired and most successful of his novels, *The Go-Between*, subsequently made into an outstanding film from a script by Harold Pinter. Each of the two books was to a large extent autobiographical and each had as its theme the passionate, painful passage of an adolescent from innocence to experience, when exposed to a sexual trauma that neither of them can fully comprehend at the time. Kitchin once told me that he had thought of calling his book *Coming to Terms* and had then changed his mind. I wish that he had retained that original title since, with insidious subtlety, the novel shows how the young Francis (so called after me, Kitchin told me) is prematurely forced to come to terms with both the grown-up world and his own nascent sexuality. Kitchin thought that the book would crown his achievements as a novelist. Reviewers certainly praised it and I myself told him, in total sincerity, that I thought that it was the best thing that he had ever written. But it didn't, as he ruefully put it, 'set the Thames on fire', as some of his earlier books had done.

I doubt if *The Book of Life* will set the Thames—or the Mississippi or the Seine or the Rhone—on fire now. But I hope that it will draw many more readers to the enjoyment of the delicate but enduring artistry of a writer who still deserves to be admired and cherished.

FRANCIS KING
London
February 3, 2008

THE BOOK OF LIFE

To

Roderick Meiklejohn

CONTENTS

I. SEPTEMBER 1909

I CAN'T have been more than four or five years old—it may have been even earlier than that, while my father was still living—when I first gathered that Grandfather Froxwell had a Book of Life. I chose that it was a book of magic spells and that my grandfather, who must be a wizard, kept it on a brass lectern in his bedroom, with a gold-tasselled marker hanging down on either side.

I had to abandon this pleasant fantasy one day when he was ill in bed with bronchitis and I was taken in to pay him a visit. He certainly looked old enough to be a wizard—of the jovial type, well nourished with human blood—but I could see no trace of either lectern or Book. This was a sad disillusionment for me and even the small packet of bull's-eyes with which I came out didn't quite console me. However, I felt sure that the Book must be somewhere not far away and decided that my grandfather had hidden it in a huge mid-Victorian wardrobe that took up almost the whole length of the north wall in his bedroom.

It was my cousin Cedric Froxwell who enlightened me. I happened to be alone with him in the library—I think I was then about seven and a half—when he suddenly pointed to the middle drawer of the flat-topped kneehole writing-table and said casually: 'You know Granddaddy keeps the Book of Life in there? If you give me a ha'penny I'll show it you.' Much as I longed to see the Book, I had to confess that I hadn't a ha'penny, but I promised faithfully that I would pay him the following Saturday when my weekly twopence was due. Perhaps he saw the hint of an embarrassing tearfulness in my eyes, or perhaps he regretted having asked me for money—there was no meanness in his character—but he said: 'All right, I'll show you for nothing,' and pulled open the drawer, which to my great surprise was unlocked.

I had a quick glimpse of a very large book indeed, bound in red

5

leather. Then some sound in the hall made him shut the drawer hurriedly and sent us both scampering to the window. When no one came in and we had recovered from the shock, I asked: 'Have you ever seen what's inside it?' and he answered: 'Yes, once, but not properly—just some funny words I didn't understand and lots of figures. Aunt Sophy says it's something to do with the money we're all going to get if we're good. When I asked Daddy, he shut me up and told me it wasn't a thing a boy of my age ought to think about.' I pondered. No doubt, Cedric's father, my uncle Augustus, who was a clergyman, would disapprove of any kind of wizardry. I said: 'So perhaps it is magic, after all.' But Cedric gave a snort of contempt and replied: 'Magic—what rot! I bet you've been reading fairy-tales for girls!' I had, and was too ashamed to question him further.

It wasn't surprising that Cedric should be better informed than I. Apart from being nearly three years older, he was much more familiar with the ways of my grandfather's house, which he could visit almost as often as he had a mind to, his father's parish being only four miles from Whitgate, while I, who lived with my aunt Mary Hemming near St Albans, only came to Whitgate for a fort-night in the late summer, when we stayed at the Hydro.

I realise now how little she could have enjoyed those holidays and how overwhelming she must have found the multitude of her Froxwell-in-laws—Uncle Egerton, Uncle Augustus and Uncle Seymour, all with their families, and my bachelor uncle Deme-trius—and, far more formidable than any number of uncles, my spinster aunts Letty, Sophy and Diana, all firmly fixed in their varying niches in my grandfather's house at Six, Albert Terrace, and clannishly cold-shouldering outsiders.

I suppose it was out of loyalty and affection for Aunt Mary that in those early and slowly passing years I felt myself to be much more of a Hemming than a Froxwell and consequently came near losing the good opinion of my three Froxwell aunts, who hardly bothered to hide their view that my father had married quite a long way beneath him. I remember one day—this was two years after I learnt the true whereabouts of the Book of Life—when we were having a family picnic at South Whitgate Sands, Aunt Letty came up to me as I was building a castle near Aunt Mary's chair, put her hand on my head and turned it southward to the sunlight, bent down and studied my face short-sightedly, then straightened herself and said, over my head, to Aunt Mary: 'Yes, he has all the Hemming prettiness, but with boys I'm afraid prettiness doesn't last.' As usual, Aunt Mary blushed and said nothing, but in my eagerness to be credited with some kind of supremacy I couldn't help asking: 'Do you think I'm prettier than Frobby and Ceddy and Claude?' Aunt Letty looked round at her three other nephews, who were playing with a ball nearer the sea, and said: 'You'll never be as handsome as Frobisher. Cedric is at a fat stage and one cannot see much promise in him, but Claude will have looks, though they may not be quite ours.' By 'ours' she may have meant English; for Uncle Seymour, as part of his general naughtiness, had married a Frenchwoman. But more probably she meant 'like the male Frox-wells.'

The female Froxwells had no claim to beauty. Aunt Letty had a long, thin, tight-lipped face, with an expression half imperious and half scared. Aunt Sophy's face, though somewhat plumper, had a strange, lop-sided look, as if some of the muscles had been distorted by a stroke. Aunt Diana's, which might once have shown traces of a classical perfection, was marred by premature lines and a pasty complexion which she took no steps to improve. Grand-mother Froxwell had died a year before my mother—that is to say, a year before I was born, for my mother died in giving birth to me—but even the artist who painted her portrait in the eighteen-sixties had been unable to turn her into a beautiful woman. She looked a 'lady', but a very plain one. Poor thing, it must have been difficult for her to fit in the sittings between her perpetual accouchements.

It was the male Froxwells who had the good looks. My grand-father, though he was over eighty, had a thick crop of white hair and still suggested a handsome, blue-eyed lion. My father, whom I can only judge by photographs, since he died when I was three, was perhaps the least attractive of the sons, but my uncles were tall fine men, each with a well formed head, blue eyes set wide apart, a nose that was firm without being in any way aggressive, a big whimsical mouth, strong jaws and chin. As soon as I learnt the existence of the god Apollo—which I did surprisingly early, since Lemprière's Classical Dictionary, which I came across in the big bookcase in the library, provided me with some of my holiday reading—I saw him in the likeness of Uncle Demetrius.

I think Aunt Letty must have told Aunt Diana about our little conversation on South Whitgate Sands, because the following afternoon—the last day of my Whitgate holiday for that year—when I arrived to say goodbye to my grandfather, Aunt Diana caught me alone and said, out of the blue: 'You know, Francis, we never thought your father was the kind to marry. He must have been thirty-four when he met your mother, and he had never seemed to look at a girl before. Your mother was a *very* pretty girl. He certainly plucked the rose among the thorns.' This was a play upon words, for my mother's name was Rose. But I am fairly sure Aunt Diana hoped I should pass on her remark to the surviving thorns in my mother's family—Aunt Mary, Aunt Violet and Uncle Giles—when I rejoined their circle in St Albans. It was with the same wish to put the Hemmings in their place—behind the counter—that my Froxwell aunts, especially Aunts Letty and Sophy, would sometimes exclaim what a tragedy it was that my grandfather had sold his lovely seat in Sussex to a linen-draper. The seat in Sussex—Walsingly Place, near Lewes—was far from being an ancestral property. My grandfather had bought it only five years before my grandmother's death. I gathered from Uncle Demetrius that she had it in her to be the squire's lady, though she may have been a shade too literary to go down well with the 'County', but that my grandfather was by no means cut out to be the squire. He was too close with his money, too much inclined to regard the estate as a business proposition, too old to take any pleasure in bloodsports, which he thought a waste of time. His interests still centred round Whitgate, where he had settled in early middle-age, and where, through skilful dealings in property and local investments, he had made a good part of his fortune. A few months after my grandmother's death, when Six, Albert Terrace, became suddenly vacant—he had built the terrace some thirty years before and still owned the freehold—he decided to sell Walsingly Place and move back to Whitgate. My three aunts, who professed themselves heart-broken at the thought that their father was now living on a par with some of his tenants, must, I am sure, have been secretly delighted to exchange the damp fringes of a Sussex wood for the smooth asphalt of Whitgate promenade.

The linen-draper to whom my grandfather sold his estate was a very successful one by all accounts, for already Oadby's Outfitters had begun to festoon the south coast with a chain of shops. But for all that, Josiah Oadby, though he later received a knighthood, was definitely a shop-keeper, while the Froxwells had never been that—unless, of course, you insisted on going back to the eighteenth century, when who knows what might not have happened.

My mother's family were also linen-drapers—not alas in the grandiose fashion of the Oadbys—but they had two shops in St Albans, one at Hatfield, one at Hitchin, and in their heyday two or three others besides. The heyday had passed some years before I was born and Uncle Giles Hemming wasn't the man to revive it.

I am glad to think I had the good sense or the decency to pass on very few of these and other thrusts to Aunt Mary, even after I had become so thoroughly a Froxwell that I too regarded the Hemmings as a lesser breed.

The ceremony of saying goodbye to my grandfather was that year quite a notable event. Apart from me, my cousins Lavinia, Esmeralda and Oenone, Uncle Egerton's children, and Claude and Nicolette, Uncle Seymour's, were also leaving Whitgate the next day; the former group were to have a further ten days' holiday with their mother's family, while the latter were returning to Uncle Seymour's home near Bordeaux, and our combined departures somehow involved Uncle Augustus's children, Frobisher, Cedric and Millicent, in the general leave-taking.

We were to go into the library one by one at Aunt Letty's direction. Lavinia, the eldest grandchild, went in and came out first, while the rest of us waited in the long dark hall for our turn. When Cedric saw her emerging, he hissed at her: 'How much is it this year?', but she only murmured: 'Don't be a greedy boy!', as she flounced by. Frobisher's turn came next, but Cedric knew better than to tackle his elder brother and waited for Esmeralda, who

was a few weeks younger than Frobisher. She said: 'Only six bob—
same as last year. I don't suppose you'll get more than four. The
piles left on the table look very small.' Then Aunt Letty suddenly
appeared among the shadows, tapped Cedric smartly on the
shoulder and said: 'You are next, but if I heard what I think I heard,
I am inclined to advise our father to give nothing to such very
mercenary grandchildren.' Cedric blushed a deep scarlet and I
began to fear that Aunt Letty might carry out her threat, but when
he came out and Oenone took his place, he gave me a cheerful,
condescending nod, as if to say, 'I've done all right! Of course, I
know nothing of what *you* may get.' Oenone's visit only lasted
about a minute—I thought she looked rather sulky afterwards—
then came the turn of Cedric's little sister Millicent, who was two
months my senior. She had a demure and precociously lady-like
expression which made me long to empty an ink-bottle over her
flaxen ringlets.

'Now, Francis, remember, if you speak up well, our father may
catch what you are saying. In any case, be sure to nod and smile
when he speaks to you, to let him know you've understood.'

I answered, 'Yes, Aunt Letty,' and went in. My grandfather was
sitting in his wheeled chair by an octagonal table covered in red
plush. On the top of it Aunt Letty had stacked nine piles of silver,
though now only three remained, one for me and one each for
Claude and Nicolette. The room faced the back of the house, away
from the sea, and the early autumn sun struck through the small
panes of coloured glass forming the lower part of the bay window
and threw overlapping polychrome lozenges on to the more than
usually hideous William Morris anaglypta wall-covering between
the big bookcase and the window-recess. I found those shafts
of coloured light so entrancing that I had for the moment little
thought for the amount of silver waiting for me on the table and
still less for my grandfather, who sat expecting me to give him a
bow of greeting. Indeed, I don't think I really looked him in the
face, till he recalled my strayed attention by making a loud guttural
noise which he was in the habit of using to overawe a listener and
sometimes to mark a pause in his own thoughts. At all events,
this explosive, throaty 'Aha!' had something disciplinary about it,

which could bring to heel even the most wayward members of his family, my uncles Seymour and Demetrius.

'Aha! So, my boy, your summer holiday is over, though I suppose your life is still for the most part one long holiday. Aha! You will not always find it so. I hope you and your good aunt Mary have enjoyed your stay at Whitgate?'

I nodded and smiled, then shouted in my piping voice: 'Yes, thank you, Granddaddy, very much indeed!'

He gave me a pleasant smile in return and went on: 'I hope also that you have derived some benefit from our fine sea air. There is no better air than that of Kent . . . aha! . . . and Whitgate is the Kentish coast at its best.'

I nodded my agreement, though I couldn't bring another smile to my face, finding nothing funny in the Kentish climate. During the short pause which followed, I turned my eyes, though not my head, towards the money on the octagonal table-top, but my grandfather was instantly aware of this; for before I had begun to estimate how many sixpenny-bits there were in the tallest pile, he said: 'Aha! This has been a costly afternoon for me, my boy, bidding goodbye to so many grandchildren. Indeed, I was tempted to economise over you younger ones and send you away with a small packet of bonbons. But, Francis, I do not forget that you are the only son of my eldest son. If I were still one of the landed gentry, you would be the heir to my estate. As it is, aha! . . .'

He broke off and looked round at the writing-table drawer which Cedric had opened when he showed me the Book of Life. I felt full of guilt at having seen the Book, and something in my expression must have betrayed me; for as soon as my grandfather looked up at me, he said: 'I see you know the secret of that drawer, though you are hardly of an age to understand it, however clever you may be at figures. Aha! Well, as you may have been told, I leave this drawer unlocked. I have never made a secret of what God in His generosity has been pleased to give me. A man should be ashamed of his debts . . . aha! . . . but I see no reason why he should be ashamed of his money, provided he uses it with a prudent frugality. Have you seen the Book?'

I trembled with dismay and, forgetting that he couldn't hear

me, began to stammer: 'I promise . . . I only saw the outside of
it,' but to my enormous relief he continued: 'Open the drawer
and bring the Book to me—the big ledger with the red leather
binding.'

He took it from me and laid it on his lap, while I peered over
his shoulder. The first page was headed, in his firm, slanting hand-
writing, *Miss Laetitia Froxwell*. My grandfather let me study it for
a moment, though the entries, which consisted of words, for the
most part abbreviations, followed by figures arranged in columns,
meant nothing to me. Then he turned to page two, where the
heading *Maximilian Froxwell* had been altered to *The Late Maximilian Froxwell's Trustees*. He said: 'This is *your* page, my boy, or
will be, if events take the course they should. You see the first
item? Great Southern Junction Railway four and a quarter per cent
preferred ordinary stock—two thousand eight hundred pounds.
The present quotation is round sixty-seven, but as I bought the
stock at fifty-two and a half . . . aha! . . . you cannot complain!
North-west Midland three per cent Annuities—four thousand
two hundred pounds. A somewhat less successful investment this,
though I think there is no case to cut a loss. However, as I told
you, these details can mean nothing to you as yet. Here is page
three, your Uncle Egerton's. It is the same as yours in all respects.
Page four, the Reverend Augustus Froxwell. Page five, your Uncle
Seymour. He still has his page, though there was a time when . . .
aha! . . . Page six, Aunt Sophia. Page seven, Diana. Page eight,
Demetrius. Page nine was poor Beresford's, but you see it has been
struck through, with the result that one eighth part of each item
appears on each of the pages I have shown you. Page ten—these
are references to my personal ledger, which . . . aha! . . . you will
not find in this drawer. Would you like to have one more look at
your own page?'

I nodded vigorously, while he obligingly turned to it again. On
my second inspection, it meant no more to me than before, except
for one item towards the bottom of the long column. This read,
'One eighth share, Land at South Whitgate (say) £3,000.' I pointed
to it and looked at my grandfather with interrogative eagerness.
He chuckled and said: 'You are a shrewd young man! That entry

may well, one day, form quite a considerable element in your fortune.'

There was a tap on the door; Aunt Letty poked her head into the room and then withdrew. My grandfather must have seen her reflection in the mirror, for he shut the Book with a snap and gave it to me to put back in the drawer. Then he said: 'We are keeping Claude and Nicolette waiting too long, not to mention your good aunt Laetitia.' He slewed his chair round, stretched out an arm and took my pile of silver from the table, and went on: 'Here, my boy, is something for you to take away with you. Lay it out wisely and be sure to remember that if you are a credit to the name of Froxwell, you will some day inherit much more than this. Open your hand. You have a very small hand for a Froxwell—unlike your cousins Frobisher and Cedric—but you have our hair and our eyes. Look! Here are ten sixpences. When I was your age, my pocket money was one halfpenny a week, but . . . aha! . . . life has grown dearer since then. Be sure to write and tell me what progress you are making with your studies.'

I cried: 'Oh, thank you very much, dear Granddaddy,' once more nodding my head and trying to smile. Then his cold fingers closed round my hot ones and after the handshake I scampered to the door.

Aunt Letty was waiting outside and said, as soon as she saw me: 'Frobisher and the other two are walking up and down the Terrace road. I told your Aunt Mary they would go back with you and say goodbye to her. But you might like to say goodbye to Uncle Demetrius first. You will find him upstairs in the smoking-room. I shall be seeing your aunt and you in the morning. Now, Claude . . .'

The smoking-room was reserved for my Froxwell uncles. It was immediately above the library, though rather smaller, since the drawing-room, reserved for my Froxwell aunts, took up more space than the dining-room below. When I went in, Uncle Demetrius was standing with his back to me, searching in the top shelf of a book-case. He was the tallest of all the Froxwells and must have been over six-foot-two. When he heard me, he turned round and said: 'Hello, have you been borrowing my Nietzsche?' I asked: 'Your what, Uncle Dimmy?' 'My Nietzsche,' he said, 'N-i-e-t-z-s-c-h-e—a

German philosopher. But that was a very silly joke to make. Let's forget it. I hope you did well out of our father this afternoon.'

My Froxwell uncles and aunts always referred to my grandfather as 'our father' even when speaking to me, but Uncle Demetrius contrived to put a mock sanctimoniousness into the two words, as if he hoped they would suggest the opening of the Lord's Prayer. I murmured non-committally and he went on: 'Well, what can I do for you?' I answered: 'I've come to say goodbye to you, Uncle Dimmy. You know I'm going home with Auntie Mary tomorrow.' He laid his hand on my shoulder and I raised my face girlishly for him to kiss. 'Surely,' he said, 'you're too old for that kind of thing now. Men don't kiss boys'—his voice was affectionate and he gave my shoulder a squeeze as he spoke—'and you're much too old to call me Uncle Dimmy any longer. You must call me Uncle Demetrius, for the next fifteen years, at least. After that, you may say Demetrius without the Uncle. Our father and mother doted on pompous names and we've all got them, but I think mine's the best of the bunch. Do you like it? And, much more important, can you spell it?'

I began, 'D-i-', but he interrupted me. 'No, D-e-. That's what makes *Dimmy* so awful. D-e-m-e-t-r-i-u-s.' I spelt it after him, and added: 'Uncle Demetrius, who was Demetrius?' He said: 'Oh, there were several. I can think of at least three. There was the rather wishy-washy Demetrius who would fall in love with the wrong girl in Shakespeare's play *A Midsummer Night's Dream*. There was a Greek called Demetrius Poliorcetes—a bit of a bully, I fancy—and of course there was Demetrius the silversmith of Ephesus, who had a row with St Paul.'

I savoured the phrase, which was one that no Hemming could have uttered. My mother's family, having formerly been chapel-goers, had joined the Church of England a few years before I was born—I fear, because they thought it was socially superior—but they were still apt to be shocked by the sight of a surplice. If pressed doctrinally, they would all have declared that they believed in the literal inspiration of the Scriptures, though their natures had a frivolous, pleasure-loving side which contrasted oddly with such a simple faith. My grandfather Froxwell was a firm sup-

porter of the Established Church in its broadest form, disapprov-
ing equally of Evangelical fervour and Romish antics, and Cedric's
father, Uncle Augustus—the fool of the family, as Aunt Diana once
naughtily described him—had cemented the alliance by becoming a clergyman. My other Froxwell uncles, and my father too, I
gathered, were more or less free-thinkers, though they were dip-
lomatic enough to conform on occasion. I don't think my grandfather ever quarrelled with them on the score of their scepticism,
though Uncle Seymour, who was in the French wine-trade and had
married a Frenchwoman who was a Roman Catholic, had nearly
lost his page in the Book of Life. Indeed, you could see where it
had been struck through in pencil, though the line had since been
erased. Of my Froxwell aunts, all three of whom went to church
every Sunday morning, Aunt Letty may have been a fairly conven-
tional believer, but Aunt Sophy openly professed a religion of her
own, or rather several religions, since there were so many incon-
sistencies in her tenets, and I doubt if Aunt Diana had any religion
at all.

Uncle Demetrius looked at me steadily with his blue eyes, as if
he were studying my reactions, his head bent forward and slightly
on one side, with a lock of gingery-chestnut hair waving effemi-
nately across his broad, high forehead. Then he said suddenly, in
a different tone: 'Don't you think you might spend more of your
time here? I don't mean staying with Aunt Mary at the Hydro—she
must find Whitgate far too full of Froxwells—but here with us.
Aunt Diana was very fond of your father and I'm sure she's very
fond of you. You could have the small bedroom on the second
floor. It mightn't be a bad thing for you to see more of our father.
He has great ideas of the family, and you are the son of the eldest
son, you know.'

I said excitedly: 'That's what Granddaddy told me this afternoon.'

'Oh, did he! Well, there's no knowing that some day he mightn't
do something rather special for you. I don't see why Augustus's
boys should make all the running. Claude, of course, is here as
little as you are, and our father can't forget he's half French. Do
you think you would like to come and visit us by yourself? Would
you like Aunt Diana to suggest it to Aunt Mary?'

I said nothing, swayed by conflicting loyalties and self-interest. My uncle went on: 'I don't mean, of course, that you should leave Aunt Mary. Your father appointed her to be your guardian and I'm sure she has given you a happier childhood than we could have given you here. But now that you're old enough to take life a little more seriously, I think you may find that the Froxwells have something to give you. No, this time I'm not thinking of money. You'll understand later what I mean, if you don't now. We wouldn't hurt Aunt Mary's feelings for the world, but as your Aunt Violet'—she was my mother's youngest sister—'has had those twin babies, Aunt Mary will have some other outlet for her maternal instincts. You see, when you're a little older, she's bound to find you a bit of a handful from time to time.'

There was a sharp knock on the door—my Froxwell aunts had somehow been trained never to enter the smoking-room without knocking first—and Aunt Letty came in to say that, if I didn't hurry, Frobisher and the other two wouldn't have time to see me back to the Hydro before they cycled home. I looked at my uncle questioningly and he said: 'I'll see Francis back. As he hasn't a bicycle, the others would have to wheel theirs all the way to the Hydro, and however well Frobisher might behave, Cedric and Millicent wouldn't enjoy that at all.'

'But I told Mary they would be calling to say goodbye to her.'

'My dear Letty, you can't think Mary really wants to see them, can you?'

'I don't see why she shouldn't. However, if Francis will make it clear that *you* changed the plan, I don't suppose it will matter. I'll tell Frobisher that they needn't wait about any longer. You had better come with me, Francis, so that you can say goodbye to the three of them.'

I gave Uncle Demetrius a quick look of gratitude—I vastly preferred his company to that of my cousins—and followed Aunt Letty downstairs, a little surprised that she had given in so easily. Perhaps she didn't like to think of her three favourites having to wheel their bicycles, while I walked unencumbered beside them. When we reached the front door, we saw them cycling up and down the private road which belonged to the Terrace. Cedric was taunting the other two with their inability to keep up with him, but they paid no attention—Frobisher, because he considered cycle-racing unseemly, and Millicent, because having only recently learnt to ride, she didn't yet feel at home on her machine. Aunt Letty waved and they joined us at varying speeds. When she explained that there was no need to escort me to the Hydro, Cedric said: 'Hurrah! Thank goodness for that!', while at the same moment Frobisher was assuring her that it would have been no trouble at all. He was, as Aunt Letty said, a very handsome boy, in the style of Uncle Demetrius, and I might easily have hero-worshipped him, had it not been for something cold and priggish about him that repelled affection. A few months previously he had announced his intention of becoming a missionary as soon as he left school and, despite the amused incredulity of his uncles and aunts, the sarcasm of his worldly cousins, Lavinia, Esmeralda and Oenone, and Cedric's open jeers, he remained unshaken. Perhaps he was the only one of us who had in him the stuff of which martyrs are made. Millicent's comment was: 'Oh, I do hope Miss Hemming won't think it wude of us not to say goodbye to her. You will explain to Miss Hemming, won't you, Fwancis, that we should have loved to come wound.' I think she knew that her grown-up way of saying 'Miss Hemming' instead of 'Aunt Mary' infuriated me. I replied savagely: 'I shall tell her that you ate so much for tea that you were sick and had to be taken home.' Cedric roared with laughter at this and said: 'My word, that's a good one!', but his brother looked at me with prim disapproval, as if I had committed a breach of the moral law. Then we all said goodbye, Cedric mounted his bicycle and did a few fancy swerves, while Frobisher and Millicent pedalled away in a leisurely fashion, and Aunt Letty went indoors, leaving me with Uncle Demetrius, who had just joined us on the threshold.

We had only walked a few steps together in the direction of the promenade, when Cedric came hurtling back and shouted at me as he passed: 'Don't forget to write if you get anything fresh for the Loo-list!' I knew he hoped that I should have the embarrassment of being questioned by Uncle Demetrius as to what we meant by the Loo-list, which was, in fact, a collection we were forming

of the names inscribed on the pans of water-closets. I blushed so
deeply that Uncle Demetrius must have noticed my confusion,
but he ignored Cedric's remark and said: 'I suppose this is the last
term you'll be going to your tutor?' I answered gloomily: 'Yes, it
is,' and he went on: 'Well, you mustn't let the prospect of taking
the plunge spoil your Christmas holidays. After all, the spring term
is the shortest of the three, so it's the best one to start with. It's a
little like dying, of course, for people like us. But we get through
it all right . . . and once it's over . . .' He paused and I murmured:
'But public-schools are far worse than prep-schools, aren't they,
Uncle Demetrius? Cedric says they are.'

'How does he know? He hasn't been to one yet.'

'Well, Frobisher told him the awful things they do to some of
the boys.'

'I shouldn't pay much attention, if I were you, to Cedric's
version of what Frobisher may or may not have told him. In any
case, it doesn't do to try to peep too far into the future. Of course,
you'll always find these wretched games a nuisance. They go on
being a curse till one gets into the Sixth at one's public-school.
After that, one can simply ignore them, if one wants to. Have you
settled whether you'll go to Oxford or to Cambridge?'

'Oh, Cambridge, like you and Daddy.'

'I'm not sure Seymour didn't have a better time at Oxford. Our
father thought he had far too good a time. Most of my friends
at Marlborough were going to Oxford, and I asked if I couldn't
go there too, but our father wouldn't hear of it. We were never
allowed to forget that Seymour went down owing forty pounds
to his tailor. But this really is looking too far ahead. So much will
happen in the next ten years. We may even have a war. That would
be the worst horror of all, I think—being forced to join the army.'

'Forced, Uncle Demetrius? They can't force you to join the
army, can they? Did they do that in the Boer War?'

'No, indeed they didn't, or we should all have been in the nasty
business. But war with Germany would be a very different matter.
Even now, in peace time, on the continent they have what they call
conscription. Every able-bodied man has to serve in some branch
of the forces for a year or so.'

Filled with panic, I exclaimed: 'Oh, how I wish I'd been born a girl instead of a boy!'

My uncle looked at me closely, then smiled and said: 'They have their troubles, you know. I'd rather be what I am than be Aunt Letty or Aunt Mary . . . or Millicent.'

We were just turning out of Harbour Road into Marsden Road, which leads away from the sea up to the Hydro, when I heard the sound of a motor-car behind us. Motors had passed the experimental stage, but they were still something of a rarity, and people stared at them in the provinces, even though Blériot had flown the Channel that very year. The previous summer, Uncle Seymour had brought a motor over from France and taken us all for rides in it. It was slow, noisy and smelly. He soon sold it, partly because it was always giving trouble, and still more to curry favour with my grandfather, who, though he had always maintained a carriage and pair for my grandmother, thought it grossly extravagant to run a car.

There was a toot on the horn and, as I turned round to see what make of car it was, to my great surprise it drew up beside us, slowed down and stopped. The driver was a man rather under middle height, wearing a dapper brown suit, a tweed cap and the usual goggles. On the seat next to him was a youngish woman in a silver-grey dust-coat and heavily veiled, after the fashion of most female motorists. The woman said: 'Oh, Mr Froxwell, I thought I recognised you. I simply had to stop and show you my new toy. This is Captain Goodrow, who is kindly teaching me how to drive it.' While she spoke, she fumbled with her veils and raised the outer one up to her nose, so that one could see her big, white teeth emphasising an artificial smile. There was something a little odd about her voice, or perhaps I should say her accent. My Froxwell uncles and aunts all had deep, melodious voices and spoke with a slightly donnish deliberateness. The Hemmings spoke more excitably and, when they let themselves go, their vowel-sounds had a suburban quality of which I was later to become ashamed. But at least there was nothing unnatural about them, as there was about the way this woman pronounced certain words. Her voice, too, kept varying in pitch, and when she wished to stress a syllable, which she did far too often, one never knew whether it would rise to soprano shrillness or drop down to the most full-bosomed contralto.

Needless to say, I didn't take all this in during the first few minutes. I was far too excited about the motor-car. My uncle raised his straw-hat and said: 'Good afternoon. This is indeed a surprise. I hope your instructor isn't letting you take any risks.' She laughed brightly and replied: 'Oh no! Captain Goodrow is exceedingly careful. Is this one of your nephews, Mr Froxwell?'

'Yes, this is Francis, my eldest brother's son. I'm sorry to say he's leaving us tomorrow. I am taking him back to his aunt at her hotel.'

She gave me a gracious and provocative smile, and I managed to take my eyes off the speedometer—it looked like a fat alarm-clock attached to the dash-board with a length of thick brass tubing that ran into the engine—and gave her a timid smile in return. 'Good after*nune*, Francis. I'm so *glad* to have met you. Have you ever driven in a motor-car?'

'Yes, last year, twice, in Uncle Seymour's. But it was a lot smaller than yours and couldn't get up Harbour Road.'

'Oh, we can do that at fifteen miles an hour. We don't even have to change *de-own* into bottom gear. Do we, Captain Goodrow?'

He gave a little twist to his twirled moustache. 'Well, that rather depends on what sort of a start we get, you know. I don't recommend *you* to try it in anything but bottom, for the present.'

She laughed again and said: 'You see how cautious he is with me! To tell you the *tre-uth*, I haven't done *much* driving in the *te-own* yet. Do you think your nephew would care for a spin, Mr Froxwell? We could drive him home. Captain Goodrow will drive, of course, if you two could manage in the dickey-seat. There's a little screen-thing that would stop you getting *ble-own* about too much.'

She put her head on one side and gazed at my uncle, while her large greenish eyes twinkled through the grey mesh of her veils. He said, with a trace of awkwardness: 'Oh, I don't think we ought to trespass on your kindness like that.' Then he paused and looked at me, and though I knew he didn't wish to go in the car, I couldn't resist interrupting: 'Oh, but, Uncle Demetrius, I should love it so. And you said we mustn't be late for Aunt Mary.'

The woman said: 'Then it's absolutely settled. Ne-ow, if you'd both go re-ound to the other side, Captain Goodrow will help you to tuck yourselves in. I'm afraid you won't find very much room for those long legs of yours, Mr Froxwell.'

My uncle didn't reply, but, as if to demonstrate the length of his legs, only used one of the three steps by which one was supposed to reach the dickey-seat. Then he put out a hand for me, while Captain Goodrow gave me a shove from behind and asked: 'Where shall I take you?' Uncle Demetrius answered rather shortly: 'To the Hydro. It's less than half a mile along this road.' The woman exclaimed quickly: 'Why, that's no distance at all! We shall have tame for a tany drave first and Captain Goodrow can show you what we can do. Where shall we go for a ten minutes' spin—somewhere where you can put the throttle right de-own?'

Captain Goodrow suggested a route, then went round to the front of the bonnet and cranked the engine, while the woman said: 'That's the one thing I dread—startin' up—especially when she's cold. But they say there's very little risk of her back-firing— and if you're careful, it doesn't matter if she does. There, you see he-ow easily it's done!'

Captain Goodrow got into the driver's seat and we began to move, with far less of a jerk than Uncle Seymour's car used to give. Uncle Demetrius had to hold his hat in his hand and his hair was blown backwards by the wind. I was small enough to crouch snugly behind a glass screen that wobbled on two supports fixed behind the front seats. I didn't spare a single glance for the view of the town we had left below us and gave all my attention to the speedometer needle, which quavered up to twenty, then twenty-five and even beyond. When, for a moment, it passed the thirty mark, I screamed with excitement, but the wind was whistling round us so loudly that I doubt if even Uncle Demetrius could hear me.

Then, all too soon, the car pulled up at the entrance of the Hydro. When we got out, I was so dazed that I could hardly bid my hostess goodbye, let alone thank her for the ride, but my uncle, instead of reproving me—as Aunt Mary would have done, by saying 'Now, Francis, remember manners!'—remarked solemnly:

'You have made a life-long friend of this young man!' The woman replied archly: 'Of *be-oth* young men, I *he-ope!*', gave my uncle a languishing smile, then shrouded her whole face once more in her veils.

While we were waiting in the lounge for Aunt Mary, I asked: 'Who was that lady, Uncle Demetrius, and that gentleman?' He answered: 'I've never seen the *gentleman* before. All I know about him is that his name is Goodrow. I know very little of the lady, either. I met her two or three times last winter, when I was out with the Thanet and Canterbury. She's a good horse-woman. And she played in the Whitgate tennis tournament last July. I saw her there from time to time. She doesn't play tennis anything like as well as she rides. What did you think of her motor?'

I told him at such length that I forgot to ask again for the lady's name. But already I regarded her as an enemy.

II. THE CHRISTMAS HOLIDAYS

(1)

Monday, 3rd January, 1910.　　　　The Vicarage,
　　　　　　　　　　　　　　　　　　Broadforsters,
　　　　　　　　　　　　　　　　　　　Nr. Whitgate, Kent.

Dear Francis,

Thank you for your Xmas card and the stamps. I've got the one with the monkey and the one with the croccadile but they'll come in for swops. Aunt Letty gave me ten bob, jolly deacint of her, five more than last year. Aunt Diana five—same—and only one bob and some mouldy sweats from Aunt Sophy, mean pig. I heard Mummy and Daddy saying Uncle D. may be going to get marred to a Lady Lucy something which apprently would be a good thing for the family. Frobby has been in bed ever since Xmas with bronkitis, so shall be glad when you come to number 6 as it is pritty dull with onely Millie about. O she says will I thank you for the hanky you sent, I suppose it was really Aunt Mary's kind thoucht. No luck with the Loo-list. Thoucht I should get a new one when we went to the pantomime at Margate but it was onely a Cascade like the one at Prince's Hotel. Wat a long letter, write soon, your affectate cousin Cedric.

I had already formed the habit of hoarding every letter I received. To have destroyed one would have seemed to me the annihilation of some part of my ego, as if I needed the support of documents to convince me that I was a real person with a real past. So this letter of Cedric's joined the rest of my correspondence in a big cardboard box on the bottom shelf of my toy-cupboard.

My reply, which I wrote at once, was somewhat as follows:

23

4th January, 1910.   Palmyra,
                                   Throngley Avenue,
                                   Oatingford Park,
                                   Nr. St Albans.

Dear Ceddy,

Thank you for your letter which I hasten to answer because I have some wonderful news for you about the Loo-list. I've found a new one and what *do* you think it was called? The LAETITIA! It seems too good to be true. You won't believe it but I garantee it. It's in the Horseshoe Tearooms where we had tea yesterday. You go up some steps from the second floor. Oh, thank you very much for your Xmas card and the postcards, but I have dessided to give up collecting them now and take to stamps like you.

Is it quite true what you say about Uncle D.? I don't think it would be at all a good thing. I shall try to stop it. I am looking forward to coming to Whitgate next Friday as it's rather dull here as Aunt Mary keeps going over to see Aunt Violet's babies. And she seems sad about something but I can't think what. She says she'll miss me when I'm away but I don't think it's that.

                              Your affectionate Cousin Francis.

Not only was Cedric three years older than I; he was twice as big and five times as muscular. At one time he was a little inclined to bully me, but I was shrewd enough to find out one or two of his weaknesses—which included a morbid fear of insects—and had no scruple in trading on my knowledge. One day, when he had made me cry, which I did only too readily, as I fear will be seen—I think he had threatened to make me swallow some frog-spawn—I put a grasshopper into an empty match-box and offered it to him with a feigned humility. He must have thought it was a kind of Danegeld, for he took no precautions when he opened it. When the insect jumped out into his face, he almost had hysterics. A year later I had a greater and more creditable triumph. He had somehow got himself dirty from head to foot and Aunt Letty ordered him to go and have a bath. When he was about to turn on the water, he saw a huge spider crawling near the plug. I was in the small bedroom on the floor above—the bedroom which was afterwards to be allotted to me—when I heard frantic howls and cries of 'Help!' from the half-landing below. Hearing me running downstairs, he came out and seized my hand, dragged me into the bathroom and shouted: 'Kill it, kill it! It's crawling up the side. It's poisonous, I'm sure it is!' Then, without waiting to see how I fared, he darted out again. I bent down calmly over the bath, cupped my hands, scooped up the spider as gently as I could, put it out on the window-ledge and shut the window. Luckily Cedric had plucked up courage to watch this last manœuvre round the edge of the door. After that, I could always hold my own with him.

This was just as well, because there were many things about me which might easily have made him want to torment me. He was stupid at school-work and already I knew more French, Latin and arithmetic than he did, nor was I tactful enough to hide the fact. I was hopeless at any kind of outdoor game, couldn't catch, however softly a ball was thrown to me, flinched if a football suddenly came my way, and, if I did contrive to kick it, sent it unfailingly in the silliest direction. I never scored a single point at ping-pong and couldn't even make my diabolo spin properly, let alone throw it up into the air and catch it on the string, a feat at which even Millicent and Claude excelled. On the other hand I had an aptitude for card games and nearly always won at 'noughts and crosses' and draughts. At chess, I could beat all my cousins and Aunt Sophy. Unfortunately, till one is over twenty, successes such as these don't count for much. One powerful swipe to the boundary on the cricket-field brings more prestige than a dozen victories in a spelling-bee.

I had no cousins on the Hemming side, except for the two four-month-old twins, and never made friends of the few boys who went to my tutor at St Albans. But I rubbed along fairly happily with Cedric and became a good deal more attached to him than I realised, even though, as a rule, I preferred the company of adults to that of my contemporaries.

He was a thoughtless, good-natured, greedy boy. I was thoughtful, sentimental, rather than good-natured, and greedy too, though my greed took more subtle forms than his. Like nearly all children, we were both egoists.

(2)

When I reached Whitgate on the seventh of January, it was a great blow to me to find that Uncle Demetrius was not there. He was by far my favourite uncle and I felt towards him all the emotions which a dutiful son is supposed to feel towards his father, with a mixture of others which are not normally filial.

He had been a junior partner in my father's somewhat obscure publishing business. I think that, so far as practical matters were concerned, he must have been much more capable than my father, who was too shy to go about in society and make useful contacts. Indeed, I gathered that my father spent all his spare time—and also time which he ought not to have spared—collecting material for a great work to be called *A Synthetic History of Philosophy*, in which he hoped to embody all the constructive teaching of the various schools and, ignoring their efforts to demolish one another's theories, to weld it into some kind of a unity. It was the sort of book which, had it been written by a professional philosopher at one of the universities, might have had a mild academic success. But though my father had acquired a smattering of the subject while he was at Cambridge, he was not qualified for the task and, even if he had been, he could never have written with sufficient authority to claim attention. When he died, his executors found six volumes of notes and the drafts of the preface and the first chapter. They also found an unsatisfactory muddle in the affairs of his firm. Uncle Demetrius managed to stave off disaster and struggled on for some years, just making both ends meet, but as soon as he had the chance of getting his and my father's money out, he took it and decided to read for the Bar, which doesn't really commit one to very much. Besides, it gave him the excuse for being in London whenever he wished, without being tied there.

There was a dilettante streak in all my grandfather's sons. In spite of his great carefulness over money, he had given each of them a splendid start—a good education and the capital necessary to embark on the career for which they thought they had a bent. I learnt later that he had even bought the advowson of Uncle Augustus's living. But his own dominating vitality seemed to have sapped all their initiative. It wasn't that they were wastrels—perhaps I should make a slight reservation in the case of Uncle Seymour—or mentally lazy, but they had no drive. They were not self-made and they couldn't make themselves. And indeed, why should they try? Had they not each a page in the Book of Life? For them, as for most of their friends and acquaintances, life without a Book of Life was unthinkable. To all their circle, the notion that work is a duty owed by the individual to society would have seemed morbid and unnatural. One worked either because one enjoyed it, after the fashion of artists, or to make money, and one made money in order not to have to work unless one wanted to. One's first obligation was somehow to acquire sufficient capital to enable one to live on the labour of others, and the most comfortable way of doing this—and perhaps the most creditable, since it spared one the reproach of being called *nouveau-riche*—was by inheritance.

Once one had a nice, fat Book of Life, all was well, unless one was a fool or a gambler. The cost of living was almost stable and the worst that any politician would dare to do would have been to raise the income-tax by threepence. Dividend-limitation, taxes on capital gains and capital levies were fantastic bogies that no level-headed man could take seriously. And after all, though great inequalities in the distribution of wealth might appear unjust to tender consciences, what other tyranny is so humane and flexible as the tyranny of money? Abolish it, and you pave the way at once for the slave-state.

Such at least were my grandfather's views. Though he considered himself to be a practising Christian, the terrifying parable of Dives and Lazarus or the moving account of the young man who had great possessions had no more influence on his life than they had on the life of his more sceptical children. Even Aunt Sophy, who, if the mood took her, could talk alarmingly about the conflict of good and evil in the world, never thought for a moment, as she gloated over a new entry in the Book of Life or the rise of her private balance at the bank, that she was delivering herself to the powers of darkness.

It wasn't only the absence of Uncle Demetrius that made me unhappy on my first evening at Six, Albert Terrace. I suddenly missed Aunt Mary very much. Ever since I could remember, her bedroom had been next to mine and I knew that if I felt ill or frightened she would come to me at once. It was true that Aunts Sophy and Diana had each a bedroom on my floor, but, however interesting I might find them by day, the thought of their nearness gave me no courage to face the terrors of the night.

There was something frightening about the tall, dark house, with its steep, twisting staircase that led past mysterious apertures and recesses, hidden, some of them, by thick, shabby, red-velvet curtains, and the strange tunnel-like passage on each floor by which the front and the back stairs communicated. The house had been built for gas-light—hence the high ceilings—and though, when my grandfather moved to it from Sussex, he installed electric lighting in the basement, ground floor and first floor, he hadn't thought fit to carry it up to the three floors above. The staircases were lit only by night-lights. So was the bathroom, on the half-landing between the first and second floors. If one wanted any brighter illumination there, one had to rely on candles.

I had never seen my bedroom by night before and was shocked by its bleak ugliness. The bed was a four-poster, with the curtains removed, though a pleated frill of some dingy material ran round the canopy. The wall-paper had a muddy design of cabbages in decay. It was probably thirty years old. When my grandfather took possession of the house, he had the ground and first floors redecorated, but left the bedrooms above just as they were. One might have thought that Aunts Sophy and Diana would protest. But, like all the Froxwells, they set small store by their material surroundings. For them a certain amount of display was permissible, even laudable, in the reception-rooms, but what did it matter what a bedroom looked like? The modern cult of the 'home beautiful' meant nothing to them at all.

In this respect I was—and still am—much more of a Hemming than a Froxwell. Aunt Mary lived in a jerry-built villa on a housing-estate, but she was as proud of it as if it had been a Queen Anne country house. She spent every penny she could afford, 'brightening it up'—repainting, changing the wall-papers and buying new curtains, cretonnes and ornaments. However deplorable her middle-class Edwardian taste may have been, there was an effect of cheerfulness and gaiety about her home, which was altogether lacking at Six, Albert Terrace. I couldn't help making comparisons, and one morning soon after my arrival, while I was having breakfast with my Froxwell aunts, I told them boastfully that Aunt Mary had given herself a Christmas present of a lovely new tea-pot, with tulips and daffodils all over it. Aunt Letty noticed that I had been eyeing distastefully the big brown earthenware pot which we were using and she asked sharply: 'How did the one she had before get broken?' When I told her it hadn't been broken, she said: 'Then it seems a very needless extravagance. This pot has served us for over twenty years and I hope it will serve us for another twenty.'

At Aunt Mary's we had high tea at half-past six, but the Froxwells had dinner at a quarter to eight. I wasn't considered old enough to sit up till that hour and had my evening-meal in the library, usually in the company of my aunts, who talked partly to me and partly to one another. My tray was brought in by Eglinton, my grandfather's manservant, who put it down on a late Regency sofa-table—which seemed to me outrageously old-fashioned, though now it might be treasured as an antique—and announced in a heavy, pompous voice: 'Your dinner is served, Master Francis.' I enjoyed this, but I was always frightened of Eglinton, perhaps because Cedric had once warned me that, if we misbehaved, my grandfather would order Eglinton to take us into his pantry and give us a flogging with his razor-strop, which one could see any day hanging up by the sink. I was all the more disposed to take this threat seriously because one day when, feeling starved for something sweet, I crept into the pantry and helped myself to two lumps of sugar, Eglinton happened to catch me in the act, and growled ferociously: 'Now, Master Francis, I warn you. If I find you at these tricks again I shall put you over my knee and give you half a dozen of the best. I have to account to Miss Froxwell for that sugar.' He was a big, square-headed, swarthy man, with a bright red complexion that went blue

where he shaved. When I read a potted version of *David Copperfield*
I at once saw Mr Murdstone in his likeness.

He and his wife had been with my grandfather for about twenty-
five years. Apart from his general duties, he had to act almost as
male nurse to my grandfather, of whom he seemed in great awe.
I can't believe his wages were generous, and Six, Albert Terrace,
wasn't a house in which the staff could get away with perquisites.
I think it quite possible that my grandfather had some hold over
him. Perhaps he had caught him trying to fiddle over the weekly
bills or accepting a commission from a tradesman. It would have
been a legitimate form of blackmail to say: 'I have decided to over-
look your offence, but if you leave me I shall be in duty bound to
inform anyone who applies to me for a reference.'

Mrs Eglinton was the cook, a very plain one, though no doubt
Aunt Letty's penurious catering gave her small scope for frills. I can't
complain of being starved at my grandfather's, but I found the food
a dismal change from what I had been used to at St Albans, where
Aunt Mary pampered me with my favourite dainties and planned
all our meals accordingly. Aunt Letty's view was that, if children
didn't eat what was provided for them, they could go without.

There were three other servants in the house—a house-parlourmaid, a housemaid and a between-maid. All three of them had
a scared, brow-beaten look. The house-parlourmaid on occasion
waited at table with Eglinton. One was apt to see the other two
emerging furtively from the back of the house, carrying jugs of
hot water and heavy pails. Aunt Sophy told me that at most of
the houses in the terrace the staff numbered seven at the least. Sir
Isaac Geldenmoser, the diamond-king at Number Twenty-eight,
even kept a pair of matched footmen—powdered wigs, knee-
breeches and all—when he was in residence. She added: 'It seems
an absurdly ostentatious waste of money.' I thought, 'If I were as
rich as Granddaddy, I should have a great many pairs of matched
footmen about the house.'

My first evening, before I went to bed, Aunt Letty asked: 'Are you
used to lighting the gas and turning it off?', and when I answered
doubtfully that I thought I could, though I'd never actually tried,

she said: 'Well, perhaps it would be safer if you relied on a candle to begin with. It won't tempt you to sit up too long in bed.' She gave me a pecking kiss on the forehead and went up to dress for dinner. A few minutes later, I went upstairs with my other two aunts. On the landing, Aunt Sophy gave me her goodnight kiss, just grazing the edge of my cheek with her lips. Aunt Diana followed me into my bedroom and looked round. When she saw my earthenware hot-water bottle in its pink woollen jacket, which Aunt Mary had packed among my things, she said with amusement: 'Our father would call that real coddling. Do you always have one at home—I mean at St Albans?' I said I always did in the winter.

'Do you fill it yourself?'

'No, Aunty Mary fills it for me, but I know how.'

'Well, I'm afraid we can't get any hot water now, as Aunt Letty is taking a bath before dinner tonight. We could ring for Jane to fill it downstairs, but why not see if you can do without it? Why, those are bedsocks! Now I'm quite sure you can. After all, when you go to . . .' She broke off before the horrid word 'school' and touched the hot-water jug, which one of the maids had left, swathed in a towel, on the marble-topped wash-stand. 'Yes, that's nice and hot. I hope you will sleep well. Sophy and I are only just across the passage. If you hear something clanking up above, it will be the skylight on the top floor. It makes peculiar noises in windy weather. Now I must go, or I shall be late for dinner. Goodnight, Francis.'

Her kiss was more affectionate than Aunt Letty's or Aunt Sophy's had been, but it was very different from the loving hug which Aunt Mary always gave me when she left me for the night. All the Froxwells were undemonstrative and shrank from any display of effusiveness. I didn't want to be hugged by Aunt Diana, but, when she had gone, I felt cold both in body and soul and almost cried at the thought of my snug little bedroom at Palmyra with the acrobats and clowns on the wall-paper and my toys in the white-painted cupboard. It was a long time before I fell asleep and, when I did, I dreamt that Aunt Mary had died and that I had a cruel step-mother who threatened me with a black stick and turned me out into the snow with a starving cat, which I followed into a dark forest, where Eglinton was lying in wait to kill me. And the next day, when I wrote to Aunt Mary and came to the words, 'I miss you terribly', I could hardly help adding, 'Please come and take me home.'

But I knew that, if I did ask to go back to Aunt Mary, the Frox-wells would never forgive me. I might lose not only my page in the Book of Life, but the good opinion of Uncle Demetrius—I find it hard to say which of these two considerations weighed with me more. Besides, if I found Six, Albert Terrace too Spartan, how could I hope to face the rigours of school? So I bore with my new life as well as I could and did my best to pretend I was enjoying it. Nor was it quite without compensations.

The Augustus Froxwells gave a small children's party at the Vicarage, and I had the good luck to win the treasure-hunt. Cedric seemed really glad to see me again and cycled over to Whitgate most days, as a rule contriving to leave Millicent at home. Frobisher was still too much of an invalid to be allowed out and it was even said he might not be well enough to go back to school when term began. How I hoped that such a fate might be mine, when my own holiday came to an end! Then the Egerton Froxwells gave a party, which in the ordinary way I should have loathed—there were far too many girls and I was forced to dance—but Cedric saved the situation for me by being sick in the middle of the room. Aunt Diana, who was in charge of him and Millicent and me, sent round for the carriage at once and took us home. Lavinia and Esmeralda, who had begun to regard themselves as young ladies, were prob-ably as glad to be quit of us as I was to be quit of them. Still, the evening had made a change from my plain supper in the library and early retirement to my chilly bedroom.

(3)

The next day brought an even greater change from routine. After breakfast, Aunt Diana followed me to the library and said: 'You know, we are having some visitors this afternoon—the Coun-tess of Brora and her daughter, Lady Lucy MacQuiggin.'

I was immediately agog and exclaimed: 'Oh, is that the lady Uncle Demetrius may be going to . . . ?' I didn't dare to finish the sentence.

My aunt laughed and said: 'What things you children pick up! Yes, it is. At least, we all hope they will make a match. She is certainly fond enough of him, but I'm not sure he is as fond of her. I'm afraid she isn't a beauty.'

I asked boldly: 'Is she very rich?'

'No, they're as poor as church mice. Her father always neglected his Book of Life and, when he died about a year ago, the estate couldn't even pay the Countess her jointure. A jointure is a kind of pension you may, or may not, get, when you're a widow. They're spending the winter in lodgings in Royal Parade. Uncle Demetrius came to know the present Earl, a pleasant young man, four or five years younger than Lady Lucy—I think he's perhaps a bit of a ne'er-do-well—when they were out hunting, and from that he came to know the family. We shall be having tea in the drawing-room today, and we thought it would be nice if you joined us. You won't be shy?'

'I'll try not to be, Auntie Diana. Shall I call the Countess Milady?'

'No, of course not. If you call her anything at all, just say "Lady Brora", and "Lady Lucy" to the daughter. But if I were you, I should avoid the names, in case you get them wrong.'

'What a pity Uncle Demetrius isn't here!'

'But we hope he will be. He said he had a luncheon engagement in London, but he's going to try to arrive in time for tea or soon after. He'll be staying with us here for three or four days. You'll be glad of that, won't you?'

I said: 'Oh, how lovely!', delighted to think that I should have him to myself for such a long time. Then suddenly I felt jealous. Perhaps he was coming to Whitgate not to see me, but Lady Lucy. As my aunt was going out of the room, I ran after her and said: 'Auntie Diana, why do you think it would be a good thing for Uncle Demetrius to marry Lady Lucy?'

She smiled teasingly over her shoulder and replied: 'Well, I suppose it is something to be able to claim an earl as one's brother-in-law. It might help Uncle Demetrius when he's a barrister, if he ever takes the trouble to pass the examinations.'

'And would it help us?'

'You mean, I suppose, would it help *you*? In a way, I dare say it might. Some of the boys—and still more, some of the masters—at your school might be impressed if they learnt you had an aunt who was the daughter of an earl. But it's not a thing ever to brag about. After all, the Froxwells, as they are, can hold their own with most people.'

At twenty past four, in a clean white collar and my newest suit, my hair brushed and smoothed down and my face specially washed, I presented myself in the drawing-room. Aunt Letty was wearing a dress of sage-green satin, heavily ornamented with tarnished gold braid. It had flouncy sleeves, a stiff whale-boned bosom and a big bulge below the waist at the back. Though I knew the style was ten or twenty years out of date, I thought she looked very majestic. By her side, Aunt Sophy who had gone arty in purple muslin, was mutton dressed up as lamb. Aunt Diana wore a pastel-blue velvet gown, which I thought beautiful, though it, too, was well behind the fashion of the day. If they felt excited, they showed no sign of it, and I couldn't help contrasting their calmness with the flurry my Aunt Mary would have been in, had she been about to entertain the aristocracy. Beyond putting on their best, they seemed to have made few concessions to the party. There were no flowers in the drawing-room, only the perennial palm in the big china bowl near the piano and the dyed pampas-grass in two crackleware vases on the chiffonier, such as nowadays one never sees except in a dentist's waiting-room. It is true that the silver tea-set had been brought out of the safe in Eglinton's pantry and that we were to use the Crown Derby service from the china-cabinet in the hall, and I was thrilled to find that the food was more lavish than usual. There were two kinds of sandwiches, a plum cake, a seed cake and a plate of queen cakes—all these made by Mrs Eglinton—and a dish of iced fancy cakes to which I looked forward with special relish. When the time came, though I ate two of them, I found them nasty and not a little stale. I think Aunt Sophy had bought them on the cheap at one of the poorer confectioners'. The hot scones, of course, only came up after our guests had arrived.

I was tuned up to a high pitch of expectancy. It wasn't only that for the first time in my life I was to meet two ladies of title, but I was somehow convinced that Lady Lucy would prove to be the owner of the car in which Uncle Demetrius and I had had a ride at the end of my summer holiday. It seems strange to me now, but, though I had told Aunt Mary all about it, I had never mentioned it to Cedric or my Froxwell aunts. I felt that, if it was Lady Lucy who owned the car, I could never possibly bring myself to like her. I became fidgety and kept getting up from my chair and darting to the window, where I moved the shabby brocade curtain aside, lifted the bottom of the blind and peeped out. Aunt Letty was talking to her sisters—'I suppose they'll come in one of Wastell's carriages; we must tell them we find Norris more reliable and his charges more reasonable'—when she realised what I was doing and called out sharply: 'Francis, come here! That kind of curiosity is extremely vulgar.' Shame-faced, I sat down.

The adults continued their talk. 'Our father . . . yes, he assured me he wished to see them, just for a minute or two. It might be as well, if you know what I mean. . . . But, Diana, he has no temperature at all. There's no reason why Eglinton shouldn't wheel him into the library. . . . I tell you, he asked to see them. . . . Ah, there they are! I do hope Lady Brora doesn't find our stairs too steep for her.'

Faint voices, the loud ticking of the drawing-room clock, slow steps on the stairs. Then the door opened and Eglinton announced: 'The Countess of Brora—Lady Lucia MacQuiggin.'

We rose—I alone with too much alacrity. Aunt Letty swirled slowly forwards round the tea-table, avoiding the cake-stands like a careful wave. 'How very kind of you to come and see us! Not at all. . . . We must apologise for our stairs, but our father has what ought to be the drawing-room. He suffers from an infirmity of the legs. . . . Your mother will be quite safe from the draught in this chair, Lady Lucy. . . . May I introduce our nephew, Francis, the son of our eldest brother Maximilian, who died seven years ago? We are expecting Demetrius any moment, but there may have been a slight fog on the line. . . . Ah, thank you, Gwen, put it here will you? Did you take a stroll in that little burst of sunshine after luncheon? Do you prefer Indian or China tea? They are both here.'

I noticed to my surprise that Gwen, the parlourmaid, had brought up an extra tea-pot, Crown Derby, matching the cups and saucers and plates. I was sitting next to Lady Lucy and, as soon as I heard her speak, I knew that she was quite unlike the lady who owned the car. She was very tall for a woman, with high cheek-bones and a long, pointed chin. She wore what Aunt Mary would have called a 'tailor-made' of striped grey tweed and a cream-coloured blouse. I was so relieved to find she wasn't the enemy that I felt I could almost welcome her as an aunt, if Uncle Deme-trius had to marry someone. She said: 'How lucky you are to live at Whitgate, Francis!' 'But I don't,' I answered, 'at least . . .' Aunt Diana, who was listening, came to my rescue. 'Poor Francis hasn't really got a home. You see, his mother died when he was born. He divides his time between us and his Aunt Mary, his mother's sister who has a house near St Albans. Do you think you may settle down at Whitgate?' Yes, Lady Lucy thought they might. The air suited her mother. Their landlady, Mrs Aitken, was so kind, and not at all a bad cook in a simple way. Since their brother had had to give up their old home, there was really nowhere special for them to go. At one time, she had longed to live in London, but, her mother's health being what it was, that was out of the question.

I decided that of all the women I had ever met, except for Aunt Mary and Aunt Violet, she was the least alarming. So far from trying to impress us with her rank, she gave the impression that it was a privilege for her to be admitted to our society. As she looked slowly round the dull, Victorian room, she said: 'You have such charming things about you. That sampler there . . . may I get up and see it close at hand?' Whether it was a most happy inspiration or amazing tact, she had picked out the only interesting object in the room.

Aunt Diana said, not without a touch of pride: 'It was our great-aunt, my grandfather's sister, who worked that. She was only eight when she finished it. Let me take it down and show it you. The two lines of verse underneath are not unamusing.'

The sampler, which was in an old-fashioned maple-wood frame, was attached to a cord suspended from the picture-rail below the frieze. Aunt Diana unhooked it and brought it to Lady Lucy, who laid it in her lap, raised a tortoiseshell lorgnette and read aloud: 'Laetitia Froxwell, aged eight, the first day of May, eighteen hundred and five.

> *This have I done, I thank my God,*
> *Without correction of the rod.'*

Then she exclaimed almost tearfully: 'Oh, the poor little mite! How brutal they were! Eighteen hundred and five, the year of Waterloo.'

Aunt Sophy, who was out of the conversation, since Aunt Letty was monopolising the Countess, leant across the tea-table and said loudly: 'No, Trafalgar. Waterloo was eighteen-fifteen.'

Lady Lucy continued simply: 'Yes, Trafalgar of course. I was always a duffer at dates. You know, it makes me feel quite faint to think that in those days they could beat a little girl of eight. I suppose she trembled over every stitch. It's a wonder they didn't take all the spirit out of her.'

But Aunt Sophy was still inclined to be provocative and said: 'I'm not sure that I quite subscribe to the modern theory that all suffering must be reserved for adults. Is it not fairer, perhaps, to the children themselves, to teach them that they cannot go through this life without pain? A taste of it early on may save them from a bitter disillusionment. Our father says that he used to receive the most savage beatings from his father's coachman—our grandfather injured his right arm in his youth, and the coachman did the family flogging for him. Yet no one could say our father's spirit was broken.'

I didn't take all this very seriously, for I knew already that Aunt Sophy was capable of arguing just as vehemently on the other side, if the whim had so taken her. Uncle Demetrius had once said, half to me and half to himself: 'There are times when I think Sophy completely mad.'

While the wrangle between Aunt Sophy and Lady Lucy was

still in progress, there was the sound of a cab stopping at the front door. Aunt Letty said: 'Ah, there is Demetrius. We must give him five minutes,' and they all made conversation to fill in the time, while I used it to study the Countess, who was sitting in a straight-backed wing-chair near the fire. She was very small and wore a black bonnet trimmed with jet, below which her face suggested a white mouse streaked with blue veins. I wondered if that was what they meant by blue blood.

Then he came in, wearing a black coat and sponge-bag trousers, and looking rather pale after his weeks in London. In his hand-someness there was something wistfully pleading and romantic, which hadn't struck me before. As he passed me, on his way to shake hands with our visitors, he put his hand on my shoulder and said: 'It's good to see you here, Francis.' I was almost raising my cheek for him to kiss, when I remembered that he now thought me too old for that kind of thing. Meanwhile, Lady Lucy's sallow complexion was coloured with pink and her eyes shone with excitement. The Countess nodded and smiled as she stretched out her hand. Aunt Letty rang for a fresh pot of tea. When it came, he said: 'I can't eat alone. Perhaps Francis will keep me company?'

Aunt Letty demurred. 'But Francis has already made a good meal. He'll be having his supper in a little more than an hour.' My uncle answered: 'I think, as a treat tonight, Francis might have dinner with us in the dining-room.' Aunt Letty knew when to yield and said to the Countess with an attempt at a laugh: 'You see who is the master in this household!' Lady Lucy replied: 'I'm delighted to find your brother doesn't seem to share Miss Sophy's views.' Uncle Demetrius asked what views those were, and they told him. Aunt Sophy tried to defend herself, knowing, I think, that they were all laughing at her, but not really caring, and the conver-sation soon turned to other subjects—I hardly know what, for I was busily eating my second tea. By the time I had finished, they were talking of motor-cars. Aunt Letty said: 'Our amazing neigh-bour at the end of the terrace, Sir Isaac Geldenmoser, has had his motor painted with black and white stripes like a zebra.' Lady Lucy asked: 'Do you own a motor, Mr Froxwell?' (In those days, only cads called motor-cars cars.) 'No, not I. Our brother Seymour brought one over from France and that was quite enough to deter me for ever.' Lady Lucy sighed and said: 'My brother's greatest ambition is to own one. But I fear there's very little hope of that.' The Countess added plaintively: 'Well, if he ever gets one, I trust he will not expect me to be a passenger.' Aunt Diana reported that Uncle Seymour, in his last letter to her, had announced his intention of buying another as soon as he could. They were making improvements in motors every day, he said, and there was no doubt that in a few years they would revolutionise our way of life. The Countess murmured: 'But I don't want my life revolutionised. I can remember when a railway-journey was a novelty.'

There was a pause and, wishing to draw attention to myself, I said with dramatic suddenness: 'Oh, Uncle Demetrius, have you had another ride in that . . .'—I was going to complete the sentence with the words 'lady's motor', meaning the one belonging to 'the enemy', when I saw Uncle Demetrius looking at me with a most strange expression on his face—a mingling of embarrassment and anger. I checked myself just in time and stammered 'in that . . . in that . . .', searching for something in which he could have had a ride other than the motor which for some hidden reason must on no account be mentioned. He was very quick to save the situation. 'I suppose you mean that contrivance in Paradise—I think it was called the Whirlicar, wasn't it?—that we went in last summer with Frobisher and Cedric.' Then he added for our visitors' benefit: 'It really was like a motor, in some ways, at least like my brother Seymour's motor. It hardly moved, but it gave one all the sensations of jolts and smell and noise.' Aunt Diana explained that Paradise was a kind of permanent fun-fair in a low-lying, squalid quarter of the town by the harbour. 'If, as we hope, you are at Whitgate next summer, you will hear the screeching of the roundabouts. In winter, of course, they shut most of the side-shows.' Uncle Demetrius looked at me and smiled. For a few minutes they all talked about Paradise. My blushes subsided and I felt convinced that my *faux pas* had been successfully covered up. But when the visitors were taking their leave of us and I noticed a puzzled frown on Aunt Diana's brow, I felt less sure.

(4)

For the next three days, the last three of my winter visit to Whitgate, I saw a great deal of Uncle Demetrius. He made no reference to my tactlessness and, though I longed to ask him why no one must know about the motor-drive we had had together, I wasn't bold enough.

He had brought me a fine stamp-album from London, with five maps, unlike Cedric's which had only one, and we spent some time looking into the windows of the stamp-shops—there were six in all at Whitgate, though Uncle Demetrius said that three of them were too advanced and expensive for a beginner—and making a careful purchase from time to time. I asked him if I should take my collection to school, much as I hated using that painful word. He said: 'Yes, take it. You'll find they nearly all collect stamps after a fashion. Be careful only to swap your duplicates. Never remove a stamp from your album, unless you are changing a poorer copy for a better. Your collection will be quite safe. Although nearly all schoolboys are detestable, they seldom steal.'

He went on to advise me, if ever I spent more than a penny on a stamp, to write the price in pencil underneath. 'It will help you to value your collection, and, if ever you sell it, to calculate your profit. And apart from that, it may give you some idea how to keep a Book of Life, when the day comes that you have one of your own. This is the kind of lesson our father would be glad for you to learn from me. There are other things I could teach you, of which he would not approve.' 'What kind of things?' I asked, but he laughed and said: 'Oh, you won't find me giving myself away like that . . . at least, yet awhile.' This hint of secrets that we might some day share gave me a great feeling of elation.

On the last afternoon of my visit, when I was sitting in the library, Aunt Sophy came in and asked me if I would go out for a walk with her. I had been hoping that Uncle Demetrius, who hadn't been with us for luncheon, would be back in time for me to go out with him. I murmured something about waiting for him, but she said: 'He's playing golf today, and as soon as he gets back he will want to have a bath and change his clothes. I should like to talk to you alone this afternoon. I have something to tell you which will interest you.'

I hurried at once to the cloakroom at the far end of the hall, to fetch my cap and raincoat. Aunt Sophy was wearing a seal-skin coat, which she had bought second-hand several years before. She hadn't looked after it, and it was now as mangy as the fur collar of a decrepit cabman. Cedric swore that one dark night Uncle Seymour had caught her among the bushes in Royal Parade Gardens and that, when he asked her what on earth she was doing there, she confessed she was getting rid of some underclothes, which she had worn to such tatters that she daren't offer them even to the charwoman. Whether this was true or not, her appearance was as a rule so bedraggled and slovenly that I was ashamed of being seen with her in public. Sometimes, when I went with her into a shop where she wasn't known, she met with that contemptuous negligence which is commonly the lot of the destitute. It is only fair to add that, as soon as she spoke, the shopkeeper was quick to change his tune.

I had hoped that she would take me down Harbour Road—I was fascinated by the old part of the town near the foot of it—or failing that, down Thanet Street past the principal shops. But she chose Uppercliff Road and Prince's Gardens, both of which looked quite dead on that cold, grey afternoon. For some reason she was set on pointing out to me all the property which my grandfather owned or used to own at one time or another. 'You see those six houses? There was a small field there, which our father bought. He sold it to a builder some years later, at a nice profit, I believe. There was another, larger field adjoining it. He built those houses, the last four in Clarence Road, on part of it and gave the rest to the Corporation so that they could continue Uppercliff Gardens, which in those days ended just about here. And do you see where the cliff becomes less steep and they've made those steps leading down to South Undercliff Road? He gave that to the Corporation too. He's done a great deal for Whitgate in his time and we feel that some day he should have his reward. He could have had a knighthood easily, if he had pulled a few strings. But there's nothing much in a knighthood; the title isn't handed on to the eldest son. It's not like a baronetcy.'

She looked at me intently as she spoke and added: 'If our father ever became a baronet, what do you think would happen to the title when he died?' I said I supposed it would pass to Uncle Egerton. 'No, Francis. It would pass to the *eldest* son—as you know, your father was the eldest—and if the eldest son were already dead, it wouldn't pass to any of his brothers, but to his *son*. And who is that, Francis?'

I answered excitedly: 'You mean me, Aunt Sophy! It's like what granddaddy said to me when I said goodbye to him at the end of the summer holidays—how his estate would have come to me some day, if he'd still had it. Oh, what a pity, what a pity he sold it!'

She smiled mysteriously. 'A baronetcy is better than an estate. The Earl of Brora, Lady Lucy's father, used to have enormous estates and what are they now? The present earl hardly dares to go near them; they're mortgaged to the last penny. But nothing can ever take the earldom away from them. Would you like to be Sir Francis Froxwell some day?'

I danced across the pavement with delight and said: 'Oh, I should, I should! But how do people get these baronetcies?'

'There are various ways. One of the easiest is giving money to the government. It is most unfortunate that these dreadful Liberals are in power at present, because I'm sure nothing would ever induce our father to give them a penny. He has always been known as a staunch Conservative. But . . . . will you promise not to repeat this to a soul? Otherwise I can't tell you.'

'I promise, Aunt Sophy. I do, honestly.'

'Not to Uncle Demetrius or Aunt Diana or Cedric or any of your relations on the Hemming side?'

'I promise really faithfully, Aunt Sophy.'

'If you break your promise, I shall never forgive you. Besides, it might spoil all your chances. Well, you know the new promenade on the South Cliff?'

I said I did.

'The Corporation want to extend it to the very end of South

Whitgate Road, but they can't as long as our father owns that big piece of land between the road and the cliff. They've approached him twice with a view to buying it, but he said the price they offered wasn't enough. You see, the King is coming to Whitgate next September to open the new Consumptives' Home, and the plan is that at the same time he should open the extension of the promenade. Now suppose our father were to *give* them the land . . . ?'

I said excitedly: 'They'd give him a baronetcy in return! But should we have to wait till next September?'

'Not so fast, Francis. The Corporation can't give baronetcies, though they can bring a good deal of influence to bear. No doubt they would have it in mind that our father is getting on in years and that it would be wrong to keep him waiting too long. If he gave the land here and now—and they'd want it some months before the King's visit, so that they could have time to build the promenade—everything might be settled in a few weeks. By the way, if Uncle Demetrius married Lady Lucy, or even if the engagement were announced, that might be quite a help. No one could say then that the Froxwells weren't a fit family for a title.'

I became thoughtful. Better a thousand times that Uncle Demetrius should marry Lady Lucy than the lady who had given us the motor-ride, but I wasn't sure that I wanted him to marry at all.

'What's puzzling you, Francis? Are you wondering how much the land is worth?'

'How much is it worth, Aunt Sophy?'

The Corporation have offered eighteen thousand pounds. Our father says the land is worth more than thirty. And there is another point to consider. If he gives away thirty thousand pounds, it means so much less in the Book of Life for each of us. There are eight of us. Eight into thirty, Francis?'

I taxed my brain to its fullest extent and answered slowly, 'Three thousand . . . seven hundred . . . and fifty pounds. Is that right, Aunt Sophy?'

'I don't know, dear, I can't do it in my head, but it sounds about right. If it is, it means that each of us would be three thousand seven hundred and fifty pounds worse off. From your point of view, of course, it would be well worth it. And I should think it was worth my while, too, to be the daughter of a baronet, and the aunt of one, when you come into the title. But the others mightn't be so accommodating. If the title could go to Uncle Augustus after our father dies, and then pass to Frobisher, I'm sure Aunt Letty would gladly give up her share, but I'm not so sure that she'd be as willing to do it for you. She and your father used to have terrible rows. The same applies to Uncle Egerton, who has no son, and Uncle Seymour, too, because even if anything happened to you, Uncle Augustus, Frobisher and Cedric would all come before him and Claude. Those are the three in the family who might be against it. Uncle Augustus is doubtful. Uncle Demetrius and, I think, Aunt Diana are too fond of you to stand in your way.'

I suddenly had a brilliant idea. Perhaps Aunt Sophy intended me to have it.

'But couldn't it all be taken out of *my* page in the Book of Life?'

'Have you any idea how much your page is worth?'

'No, not really. But Granddaddy did show it to me and there seemed to be thousands and thousands written down in it.'

'It's a good sum, I agree, but thirty thousand would make a very big hole.'

'Oh, I don't care, I don't care!' I said pleadingly. 'I shall be able to make some money when I'm older. And . . .' I broke off and blushed; for it had occurred to me that some of my uncles and aunts might leave me part of their share. Aunt Diana certainly might, Aunt Sophy might, and Uncle Demetrius, though I couldn't bear to think he would ever die.

Aunt Sophy affected to consider the matter, then she said: 'Well, of course, all the money, except for the little bits that have been made over to us, still belongs to our father. He has an absolute right to do whatever he thinks is best. But if I get the chance, I could suggest to him that you might be ready to forgo a good deal of what otherwise would be coming to you, rather than stand in the way of his baronetcy. Would you like me to let him know that?'

'Oh, Aunt Sophy, I should!'

'Then that's settled. But mind, in the meanwhile, not a single word to anybody about what I've told you. Now it's starting to drizzle. We must get home as soon as we can.'

Neither of us spoke a word while we were hurrying back to Albert Terrace, and I didn't see Aunt Sophy alone again before I left, the next morning, for St Albans. But when I said goodbye to her, she bent down and whispered in my ear: 'Goodbye, Sir Francis!' The others thought she was giving me a kiss.

III. THE SPRING TERM

(I)

IT may be a pity that I didn't remember how Uncle Demetrius had once said to me, 'There are times when I think Sophy completely mad'. On the other hand she had certainly done me a kindness for the time being. The thought of my baronetcy excluded all other thoughts, even thoughts of school. When I said goodbye to my grandfather—I had seen little of him during the holidays, since a cold and bronchitis had kept him mostly in bed—and he gave me ten shillings, exhorting me to make it last throughout the term, I almost begged him to keep the money and credit me with it in my Book of Life. My farewell to Uncle Demetrius lacked poignancy and my reunion with Aunt Mary seemed unreal. She said, 'You're in a very dreamy mood, Francis. However, you don't seem unhappy, which is the main thing. But you will miss me a little, won't you, when you're at school?' I reassured her, but less fervently than I should have done, had I not been sustained by visions of my grandeur.

The more I reflected on what Aunt Sophy had said, the more convinced I became that my title was almost in the bag. I began to invent corroborative details—a peculiar twinkle in my grand-father's eye when I left him, an unusual glance of respect from Eglinton, a notable obsequiousness in the manner of the porter at Whitgate station. While I watched Aunt Mary packing my playbox—that narrow little world which was all that I could call my own for the next eleven weeks—instead of struggling to keep back tears of misery, I was trying to visualise my page in the Book of Life and wondering how soon I should be allowed to learn stocks and shares, which now seemed the most essential part of my education.

I cannot pretend that I was anything but unhappy during my first fortnight at school, but my sufferings would have been far more acute if Aunt Sophy hadn't administered her sedative. I had somehow got it firmly into my head that the moment my grandfather acquired his title, he would find a way of handing it on to me. However great my loneliness and depression, I consoled myself by imagining that within the next five minutes a telegraph-boy would come speeding on his bicycle up the hated gravel drive that led to the school front-door, ring the bell with a violent urgency and deliver an orange-pink envelope to the headmaster. Then the school bell would be tolled and summon us all, masters, boys and servants, to class-room IV—the biggest of the class-rooms, where we had prayers—and the headmaster would stride through the green baize door which led from his private quarters to the school, dressed in his gown and mortar-board and red hood, stand on the little dais at the far end and make the following statement:—'I have just received the most important news. Froxwell has succeeded to a baronetcy. He is now Sir Francis Froxwell. We must all call him "Sir" and treat him with every possible respect. Sir Francis, will you please come with me to my study and discuss what I can do for your comfort?' And when we were together in the study—I should be seated in a big armchair, while the headmaster stood in front of me—I would say, 'Well, to begin with, I should like a bedroom all to myself—or if I must share one, I choose Morton Major to be my companion. Potter shall be expelled. As for your food, I loathe your fatty bacon. Instead, I should like . . .' There was hardly a limit to what I should demand.

(2)

February 2nd. [1910]   Palmyra,
                                            Throngley Avenue,
                                            Oatingford Park,
                                            Nr. St. Albans.
Darling Francis,
    I was very, very glad to get your letter and hear that you are

getting used to school. I know it must be dreadfully strange at first. I am glad the masters are all kind to you and that they have already moved you up a form for arithmetic, and that there are three or four boys you think you may become quite friendly with.

It seems very lonely here without you, as I told you in my last letter. Since I wrote it, Auntie Violet and the twins and Uncle William have come to stay here. I didn't like to tell you during the holidays, but there has been some trouble in the business and Uncle William has had a difference of opinion with Uncle Giles about something. I don't really understand it, except that Auntie Violet and Uncle William have had to sell their house and would have had to go into rooms somewhere, which would be very awkward with two babies and really too expensive for them, if I hadn't been able to have them here. These family quarrels are horrid and I do all I can to keep the peace, but Uncle Giles *can* be very difficult and I really think he ought to help Auntie Violet because Uncle William says that what happened was really all Uncle Giles's fault. He bought a business in Barnet without consulting Uncle William at all and things went wrong and the Bank asked for the money back and could have ruined Hemming & Co if Uncle W. hadn't agreed to do something which means he and Auntie Violet will have very little money for some time. Luckily, when your grandfather died—I mean *my* father of course, not old Mr Froxwell—your mother's share was paid out in full and part of my share was paid out to me. But the other part is still in the business and I am afraid I may not get any dividends on it, so I shall be badly off too, though not of course as badly as poor Auntie Violet, as she never had anything paid out to her but left it *all* in to help Uncle William. It's all very well for U. Giles, because Aunt Emma has money of her own—enough for the two of them to manage on—and no children.

You are very young to be told these things, but I thought I had better tell you, because I have had to put Uncle William in your bedroom. I do hope you won't mind this. He has promised to be very, very careful of all your things. I have locked the toy-cupboard. Of course, the moment the holidays come, he will have to leave. It's dreadfully worrying.

Hoping your next letter will tell me that you are really settled and *happy*, Your ever loving Auntie Mary.

(3)

9th Feb. [1910]   The Vicarage,
                                                  Broadforsters,
                                                  Nr. Whitgate,
                                                  Kent.

Dear Francis,

Thanks for yours. The first three weeks are bound to be a bit blody at a new school, specially a boarding-school. When I go to my public school they'll probably take it out of me for having been only a day-boy, but that was because of Frobby and the expence of sending us both away together. But of course I shall go as a boarder at my public school. We went skating this morning and I did rather well. I am in the first hockey eleven, so am now a 'blod'. Oh, last Sunday Uncle Demetrius hired a carriage from Norris's and drove the Countess of Broarer and Lady Lucy over to lunch with us. So you're not the only one to have met them! I heard Mother and Daddy talking about them when they'd gone and I went out of the room but left the door open on purpose so that I could hear what they were saying. When they thoucht I was out of earshot— we had that word this morning, in English, did you know it?—M. said, 'I'm sure *she's* more than fond of him, but I wish Demetrius were more a-pree'. (That's what it sounded like—the letter *A* then *pree*. Do you know what it means?) D. said, 'Yes, our father would throughfully approuve of the match. We are all rather concerned about Demetrius, but you know one can't talk to him'. Then the door gave a creek—I must have leant against it—and D. got up and shut it. He didn't see me, luckily.

The EVERGUSH is a good one. I never seem to get anything new for the Loo-list. That's the worst of not getting about like you. Hoping you have done some good swops, your affec. Cousin Cedric.

P.S. Do you play hockey or football in the spring term? Oh, I forgot to tell you, the King's visite to Whitgate is fixed for the 9th September, they are going to have fireworks at the end of the peer.

(4)

13th February, 1910   6, Albert Terrace,
                                                            Whitgate, Kent.

My dear Francis,

I was glad to find you more cheerful in your last letter—not just grinning and bearing it, in the awful way that seems to be expected of one. I don't think you'll find going to a public school quite so bad as the experience you have just had to go through.

I have had a letter from Aunt Mary about your half-term—the 25th. She would very much like to come and see you, but, as I have no doubt she has told you, there are so many difficulties in the way that it hardly seems worth while for her to make the effort for the sake of one afternoon.

Still, as we don't want you to feel that the family is neglecting you, I hope you will accept me as a substitute. I propose to call for you at 2 o'clock. Perhaps you will tell the headmaster, or whoever it is who ought to be told about that kind of thing. We could, if you like, spend the afternoon at the roller-skating rink—I hear you have a famous one at Eastbourne—and have tea there. I would suggest that you brought a friend or two with you, but I have something to discuss with you, and it is better that we should be on our own.

Your affectionate Uncle Demetrius.

I prized this letter so highly that I wouldn't part even with the envelope to a boy who collected crests and had noticed ours on the back. (*Amplo cum Spiritu*—a bull-frog inflating itself—*Frog-swell*—a pun on Froxwell. I am not sure that it was ever registered at the College of Heralds.)

Apart from my delighted anticipation of being with Uncle Demetrius again, of escaping from the school for an afternoon and seeing the skating-rink, I was convinced that something still more exciting was in store for me. I pictured my grandfather presiding over a conference in the library at Six, Albert Terrace, and addressing the assembled family. 'Laetitia, what are your views? . . . Yours, Egerton? . . . Yours, Augustus? . . . I have heard from Seymour and he says he will abide by our decision. Now, Sophia? . . . Diana? . . . Demetrius? . . . I think half and half will meet the case, half paid out of Francis's share and the other half paid by the rest of you. Of course, we must ask the boy if he agrees. Demetrius, will you be good enough to do so?'

And on Saturday I should be giving him my answer.

I hardly slept at all on the Friday night, and the next morning I had forgotten all the poetry which we were supposed to have learnt as part of our prep.

'*The woods decay, the woods decay . . . the woods decay . . .*'

'They only decay twice, Froxwell. Begin again.'

'*The woods decay, the woods decay and . . .*'

The rest of *Tithonus*, or rather the first ten lines, which were all we had to memorise, became a dreadful blank.

'Whatever is the matter with you today, Froxwell? You've never done badly like this before. Weren't you well last night?'

The sandy-haired little man came and stood over me and pinched my ear.

'Well? If you've no explanation, I'm afraid I shall have to keep you in this afternoon.'

The whole class was watching me, half of them hoping, in their charming, schoolboy way, that I should burst shamefully into tears, which I nearly did. Luckily the master realised this in time and said: 'Oh, I know what it is. Half-term, half-term. Relations coming down to see the young hopeful of the family and stuff him full of sickly cakes at Fullers'. If I had my way, there would be no half-term . . .'—he glared round the room—'No, not for *any* of you! They distract your minds from your work. All right, Froxwell. If you can recite those lines to me without a mistake after breakfast on Monday morning, we'll say no more about your lapse from grace.'

At ten minutes past two the second prefect, a tall, thin, spectacled boy called Betteridge, came into class-room IV where I was
waiting and told me off-handedly that I was wanted in the headmaster's study. I made my way there, through the green baize
door, with a nervous eagerness. When my uncle saw me, he said:
'Hello, Francis. I'm glad to see you look pretty flourishing.' Then
he turned to the headmaster and said with what I thought was
amazing self-possession: 'Well, Mr Dykes, we mustn't keep you
now. You'll be sick of parents by the end of the day. I'm surprised
you ever allow them on the premises.' Mr Dykes gave the special
double-edged laugh he reserved for occasions when boys and
parents were in his presence together. It was designed to extreme
affability to the parent without any diminution of his authority
over the boy. He said: 'Well, perhaps there may be something in
that idea. Goodbye, Mr Froxwell. It has been a great pleasure to
meet you. No doubt you will see that your nephew is back here
in time for supper at seven.' My uncle replied: 'Oh, I may want
to get rid of him long before that!' For one moment I thought he
was serious, then I knew he wasn't. Mr Dykes smiled, shook hands
with my uncle and gave me a friendly nod. Three minutes later we
were passing through the gates of the prison-house into the world
of freedom.

I had hoped my uncle would broach the great matter at once,
but he talked about this and that, put questions to me—none of
them was embarrassing—and seemed really interested to hear
my answers. We passed a stamp-shop on the way to the skating-
rink and he took me inside and bought me a shillingsworth. In
the ordinary way I should have wanted to loiter in the shop as
long as I could, but I hurried over my choices and we were there
for barely ten minutes. When we got outside, I could no longer
restrain myself and asked: 'Uncle Demetrius, didn't you say you
have something important to talk to me about?' He said: 'Yes, I
have, but I think it'll keep for tea.' Then, noticing my look of disappointment, he added: 'Or would you rather get it over now?' *Get it
over*—the phrase struck me as being ill-chosen, but I answered as
calmly as I could: 'Well, we might as well.' My uncle said: 'Then

we'll take a turn on the front and sit in a shelter out of the wind, if
we get tired of walking.' We walked two hundred yards in silence,
before he spoke again.

'What I've got to tell you isn't altogether pleasant. In fact it
isn't the kind of thing one would normally discuss with someone
of your age. But we feel it would be wrong to keep you in the
dark. It concerns you and Aunt Mary. I went over to see her in
St Albans the other day. She told me she had written to you to
let you know that she has your Aunt Violet and her husband and
the twins staying at Palmyra, and that she had explained to you
that there has been some trouble in the family and that—we hope
it's only for a short time—your Aunt Violet is now very badly off
and Aunt Mary herself may lose some of her income. What she
did *not* tell you, and I feel a bit shy about telling it you myself, is
that without the money she receives for your maintenance—that's
the lawyers' word for your keep—she would find it hard to go on
living at Palmyra.

'As you know, we should all be very happy for you to make
Whitgate your home. Your school-fees and bills for clothes and so
on would be paid out of the money your father left you, but there
would be no question of our father's requiring anything for your
board and lodging. That is to say, there would be a surplus of, say,
two hundred a year which your Trustees would invest and add to
your Book of Life. In other words, if you make your home with us,
you should be roughly two thousand five hundred pounds better
off when you come of age.

'Your Trustees, appointed by your father's Will, are Aunt Mary
and Uncle Egerton. Egerton, except when he's discussing the
occult with Aunt Sophy, is a dried up piece of parchment and looks
at everything from the standpoint of a lawyer. He and Aunt Mary
between them have a complete discretion as to how they handle
your affairs.'

I had been so deeply disappointed when my uncle began the
painful story that I had hardly listened to him, but I became gradually interested and did my best to follow what he was saying. I
asked: 'Suppose Aunt Mary says she *must* have the money, would
Uncle Egerton have to agree with her and let her have it?'

'No, far from it. They would either have to go to arbitration, or the case would be decided in court, and there's no doubt at all that the court would decide in favour of Uncle Egerton. But you mustn't think Aunt Mary has said she *must* have the money. She would never say anything of the sort. In fact, I know she thinks it isn't right for her to take it if she isn't providing you with a proper home.'

'But if I say she *can* have it?'

Uncle Demetrius smiled. 'Strictly speaking, *you* have no say at all. But your Trustees can be guided by your views, if they're not too silly. Uncle Egerton wants you to understand very clearly that if you make your home with us at Whitgate, you will, by the end of ten years, have put by quite a nice little sum for yourself.'

'Ten years! I may be dead!'

'We may all be dead.'

That settled it. If I could have had the extra money there and then, so that I could have contributed it to the fund which was to buy me a baronetcy, I might perhaps have ignored Aunt Mary's troubles—though, surely, once I was a baronet, I should only have to wave a wand and Aunt Mary's position would be quite secure. But to wait ten years, to live as long again as I had already lived, before I could enjoy the fruits of my selfishness, was idiotic. I said firmly: 'No, Uncle Demetrius, whatever happens, I want Aunt Mary to have the extra money, as long as she needs it.'

He answered solemnly, as if speaking to an adult: 'I am very glad to hear your decision.'

I had never been inside a skating-rink before. It was a huge building, got up in pseudo-Oriental style and lit with festoons of Chinese lanterns. An orchestra on a dais surrounded by palms played gay music loudly and continuously—the latest waltzes, hits from musical comedies interspersed with an occasional popular classic—while the close-packed skaters wheeled round the charcoal-coloured floor. At first we were content to sit and watch them from the spectators' gallery. I noticed among them a boy from my school, whom I didn't much care for. He was arm in arm with a girl and between them they executed many expert manœuvres. Uncle Demetrius said: 'Would you like to have a try? We could hire a pair of skates.' I asked if he would come too, but he said: 'No, I'm too old to make myself ridiculous. Besides, at my age, a tumble can be nasty. If Uncle Seymour were here, he'd show them a trick or two. But, you know, I think you really ought to have a go, just to say you've done it.'

I struggled round twice, for the most part holding on to the rail with one hand. Browne Minor swirled up to me and called out: 'Try not to look quite so miserable, Froxwell,' and the girl with him giggled. I hated them both and made for the exit as quickly as I dared. Evidently I was destined to be no more successful at skating than at cricket, football, hockey, ping-pong and diabolo.

When I rejoined Uncle Demetrius, he looked at his watch and said: 'How about tea?' I was quite ready for it. The afternoon, which should have been the highlight of the term, had somehow fallen flat. After all, what was a visit to a skating-rink compared with the prospect of a baronetcy? I kept telling myself that it didn't necessarily follow, because my uncle had been silent on this subject, that there was no longer any hope. None the less, I felt bitterly disappointed. Even when I asked: 'Is it true, Uncle Demetrius, that the Corporation want to build a new promenade as far as the end of South Whitgate Road?', he only replied: 'I'm afraid it is. Why can't they leave Whitgate alone? They seem to want to turn it into another Margate. If they do, Albert Terrace will soon become a row of boarding-houses.' Then the conversation dragged itself back to Aunt Mary, whom I thought we had disposed of. Uncle Demetrius said I should probably be getting a letter from Uncle Egerton and that I might have to answer it. This depressed me still more. I had never written to Uncle Egerton before and didn't like the thought of my letter being kept for years in a file of legal documents. I said: 'Can I send my answer to you first, so that you can see if it will do?' He laughed and answered: 'Of course you can, but don't worry.' Then he looked at his watch and said: 'Aren't you getting sick of that band? How about a short walk on the front before I take you back?' I agreed listlessly. The rink or the front— they were both equally dull. Even Uncle Demetrius was dull that afternoon.

As we passed the entrance of the drive that led to the Grand
Hotel, I noticed a green car standing empty a few yards inside the
gate. Filled with sudden excitement, I caught my uncle by the
sleeve and said: 'Oh, look, Uncle Demetrius, that motor, isn't that
the one we went out in at the end of last summer holidays, with
Captain Goodrow and the lady with all those veils?' He turned his
head towards the car, then looked at me as if I had done something
which annoyed him. 'What makes you think so? Is it the colour,
or do you happen to remember the number?' I confessed that I
hadn't memorised the number of the Whitgate car, and he went
on: 'Well, if you're only going by the colour, I suppose there are
twenty or thirty green motors in Eastbourne today. Look, there's
one over there, by the lamp-post.' I glanced at it, and said: 'No,
that isn't hers, but this one . . . oh, couldn't we go a little closer and
see what the speedometer is like? I'm sure I should know it. They
wouldn't mind, would they, if we walked just a little way inside
the drive?' He took my arm and pulled me almost roughly past
the entrance, while he said: 'Yes, they *would* mind, and so should
I, very much. I can't have my nephew peeping into other people's
motors like a street-urchin. Come along, or we shall be late.'

It was a relief to both of us when the gates of the prison-house
closed behind me once more.

(5)

Froxwell & Co	19, Jubilee Chambers,
Solicitors & Commissioners	Whitgate, Kent.
for Oaths	
28th February, 1910	

Dear Francis,

I don't suppose you have ever had a letter from a solicitor before,
but I promise you I shall try not to forget that I am also an uncle.

Uncle Demetrius has told me about the talk he had with you
when he took you out at half-term. He assures me that you fully
understand the situation and that you are eager that your Aunt
Mary shall not be deprived of any money she now receives for

providing you with a home, even though she now finds herself hardly in a position to do so.

I should be wrong to hide from you the fact that certain members of our family are not very happy about this arrangement. They consider that it is my duty to ignore this expression of your wishes and to insist that if your Aunt Mary cannot or is unwilling to give you value for your money, she should not profit by it at your expense. However, Uncle Demetrius has argued that your father would have given no support to this view. He has also made the point—which some of us are inclined to forget—that part of the capital we hold in trust for you is money which your mother left to your father, and that it is not altogether fair to allege that someone who is no blood-relation of ours is being maintained by *our* father's generosity. I agree with Uncle Demetrius that owing to the size of our father's household he will be put to no appreciable extra expense by reason of your living at Six, Albert Terrace.

Provided therefore you have it clearly in mind that you are depriving yourself of a sum of money which, at compound interest, may well have reached nearly three thousand pounds when you come of age, I am willing, for the time being at least, that your Aunt Mary shall continue to receive from the Trust what she has had ever since your father died. I send you herewith a short statement to this effect and shall be glad if you will be good enough to sign it and return it to me in the enclosed stamped and addressed envelope, unless of course you have now changed your mind, in which case please inform me at once. The document which I am sending for your signature has no legal force at all. It is merely a record. By the terms of your father's Will, the decisions of your Trustees cannot be questioned by anyone, even by you when you come of age. (My firm did not draw the Will.) Otherwise, I should never agree to the course which we are taking.

You will be glad to hear that Aunt Lorna, Lavinia and Esmeralda are all keeping well. Oenone has unfortunately contracted whooping-cough. Dr Sturgess has told me to take things more easily, which makes me feel an old man. We all look forward to seeing you in the holidays.

Your affectionate Uncle, Egerton Froxwell.

(6)

                                        6, Albert Terrace,
1st March, 1910   Whitgate,
                                               Kent.

Dear Francis,

There is no need for you to feel so disappointed. Uncle Demetrius would be the last one to know about certain arrangements
which I think our father has in mind. You see, Uncle D. is the
youngest in the family, now that dear Uncle Beresford is no longer
with us, and he is not so much in our father's confidence as Aunt
Letty and I are, or for that matter Uncles A. and E.

The King is definitely to visit Whitgate on the 9th September
and I hear he is to open the new promenade as soon as he has
opened the Consumptives' Home. So we must hope it will be a
great day for us!

Poor Oenone is suffering from whooping-cough and Uncle
Egerton has not been very well. Our father is much better and is
looking forward to getting out in his chair when the spring days
come. The rest of us, I am glad to say, are all well. I am knitting
you a pair of lovely blue socks and hope to have them ready when
you come to us. We shall all be glad to see you.

                        Your affectionate Aunt, Sophia Froxwell.

P.S. I know what Uncle D. went to see you about. I am not sure
that you decided altogether wisely—*in the circumstances*. You know
what I mean by that! Still, perhaps you are laying up treasure in
Heaven. And you can always change your mind, if you think fit.

(7)

Friday   Palmyra,
[4th March, 1910]   Throngley Avenue,
                                           Oatingford Park,
                                             Nr. St Albans.

My darling Francis,

I had a letter from Uncle Demetrius yesterday and today there is one from your Uncle Egerton. I don't know what to say to you, my dear boy, except thank you and may God bless you for your loving kindness to your old Auntie. Oh, I do hope that some day I shall be able to pay you back every penny. Your generosity means such a lot to me—and the sweet thought which prompted it. I keep crying as I write this, so had better stop! All love from your most grateful Auntie Mary.

(8)

16th March [1910]   The Vicarage,
                                                      Broadforsters,
                                                      Nr. Whitgate, Kent.

Dear Francis,

Thank you for yours. Yes, you much be longing for the end of term—not quite three weeks to go now, hurrah! I have sold my stamps to Hopkins Ma. for thirty-five bob. I shall want a new cricket-bat next term and I want to go in for breading pigins. Hopkins says those Borneo stamps I had with the animals on them are a cheat, they were sold off and postmarked just to please collectors, so they're hardly worth anything. His father is a very keen collector and told him that. There's been a good deal of talk about your family lately—I mean the Hemmings. They say an uncle of yours, I don't know which one, but they call him the C.J. when you're not there, has lost your Aunt Mary a lot of money. Lavinia told me this but she said I wasn't to pass it on to you. We had to go over to her school on Saturday afternoon, they were acting a religious play—it was very boring—and Lavinia had a big part and Esmeralda had a part too but not such a big one. Oenone has got whoaping-cough and keeps being sick. Serve them right for being so sniffy about the time I was sick at their blody party last Jan. There is a lot of whoaping-cough about and the two boys who sat next to me in class last week have both just got it. Just my luck if I get it directly the hols. begin. We haven't seen any more of the Countess of Broarer or Lady L. Uncle D. has been spending a lot of time in London and has given up hunting. Hope he gave you a good time when he went to see you in Eastbourne.

Oh, they're talking a lot about somebody they call the D.M. and another person they call the U.P. You know how they use initsiales, when we're there, wanting us not to find out what they stand for. But I shall, I expect, from Lavinia who thinks she's grown up and who they speak more freely in front of than us. At least, the aunts do. I have lost or miss-layed my Loo-list. If it doesn't turn up, will you send me a copy of yours? Nothing new for it. I managed to go at Lavinia's school, but it was only another CASCADE. Must stop now. Love from Cedric Froxwell Esquire.

(9)

Thursday   Palmyra,
[31st March 1910]   Throngley Avenue,
                                           Oatingford Park,
                                           Nr. St Albans.
Darling Francis,

Only another six days and I shall be meeting you at Victoria! You seem to have been away from me for ages and ages and I do wish you were coming back to Palmyra with me. However we will have a lovely lunch at Buszards' and then see the conjuring at the St George's Hall and then tea at Fullers' before I need put you on the train for Whitgate.

Do you know, in a way I'm almost nervous of seeing you again after all the unpleasantness there has been over the money. I shall feel in your debt, which is a horrid feeling to have, especially for somebody you love very much. I'm sure it was really Aunt Letty's fault and that she put it about that I couldn't give you a proper home now that I have Auntie Violet and the twins living here. But that isn't true. Uncle William can always go and stay with his brother, whenever you want your room. Of course I know that with two babies in the house, things can't be quite what they were like before, but I'm sure you would put up with them for my sake. Besides they are two dear little girls and very quiet, all things considered.

Sometimes I feel I almost hate Uncle Giles for all the trouble he's brought on the family, and giving the Froxwells such a hold over me. Your Froxwell aunts have always been unfriendly and tried to make me feel small, except Sophy sometimes, when she wanted to irritate the other two. The Froxwell uncles have been nicer, especially of course Uncle Demetrius. He is a kind, good man and I hope you will grow up to be like him.

Oh Francis, don't ever let any misunderstanding come between us. Your home is still at Palmyra and it's settled that you are to spend the last week of the holidays there. Those Froxwells shan't have you all to themselves.

Your loving Auntie Mary.

P.S. Auntie Violet sends her love too.

(10)

My General Report for the Spring term, which Uncle Egerton gave me to take to Aunt Mary, was as follows:

'He has worked well, and, were it not far too early to make predictions, one might be tempted to say that he has the makings of a scholar. His conduct on the whole has been satisfactory. He shows no promise at any outdoor games and seems to have an almost morbid dislike of them. He should try to overcome this, even if he can never hope to achieve proficiency. The chief defect in his character is at present a tendency to be too self-absorbed. We must hope that he will soon outgrow this and learn the meaning of *esprit-de-corps*.

V. O. Dykes, Headmaster.'

Esprit-de-corps! Team-spirit, playing for the side, bad form, community-feeling, the honour of the House, *Alma Mater*, 'a way they have at the Varsity', the tradition of the Service, group-solidarity, the wolf-pack instinct, the tribe, the state, compulsory gregariousness—even the enforced matiness of a club—I have always had a loathing for the lot.

IV. THE EASTER HOLIDAYS

(1)

I HAD fallen in love with a signal-gantry in the window of the toy-shop in Thanet Street. I longed, with that intense longing which in the young is perhaps an anticipation of sexual desire, to possess it and keep it on my bedroom mantelpiece or even in its box in a drawer.

I had managed to steer Aunt Letty past the shop, but the sight of the beautiful object didn't move her and, when I sang its praises, she turned a deaf ear. Aunt Sophy, when her turn came, was even worse; for she said: 'Eight and six for a toy like that! Anyone who buys it must have a good deal more money than sense.' Now I was making trial of Aunt Diana. Her comment was: 'I must say it's a most realistic model. But it would be very silly to think of buying it before you have an engine and some rails. As you know, there's nowhere you could set them out in our father's house, and it would be absurd to think of taking them to school.' And she hurried me on to the lending-library at the corner of Sussex Street, where she changed her book.

My disappointment made me reckless, and, not so much out of curiosity as with a wish to cause her embarrassment, I asked, after a minute or two of sulky silence: 'Aunt Diana, what does D.M. stand for? Do you know?' She looked at me good-humouredly and said: 'What very long ears you young ones have got! I admit I had them too, at your age. Well, I don't think there's any harm in telling you. D.M. stands for *demi-mondaine*.'

'For what, Aunt Diana?'

'*Demi-mondaine*. Don't ask me what it means or how to spell it, because I shan't tell you that.'

She had deliberately pronounced the word in such a very French fashion—*d'mee-morndenne*, with the stress on the last syllable—that it was not at all surprising I couldn't discover it in the dictionary.

Finding her more forthcoming than I had expected, I almost forgot about the signal-gantry, and resolved to see if I should have the same or better luck with regard to the other two abbreviations Cedric had mentioned in his letter to me.

'And C.J.?' I asked. 'What does that mean?'

She blushed a little and pretended to think, then she said, 'C.J.? Let me see, that was someone Aunt Sophy and I knew quite well. She was at school with us, but she fancied herself so much that we called her *Crown Jewel*—her surname was Jewell, you see. But I can't think how you ever came to hear of her.'

I knew from her manner that she was prevaricating. Besides, Cedric had told me that C.J. was what they called one of my uncles, when I wasn't there. This could only have meant Uncle Giles Hemming. However, fearing that if I pursued the matter I might find myself giving Cedric away, I let her think I was satisfied with her answer and said: 'Oh, and there's something else you sometimes say. "The U.P." What's a U.P., Aunt Diana?'

She was so relieved that she answered at once: 'U.P. stands for Unfrocked Priest.'

'Unfrocked? What do you mean?'

'Oh, it's just a saying. It doesn't mean priests wear frocks or have them stripped off when they do something naughty, though I think they used to, in the old days. Besides, the person they call the U.P. never was a priest.'

'Oh, do tell me who he is! Please, Aunt Diana.'

'He's the D.M.'s brother—or half-brother, I should say. They had the same father but different mothers.'

'But why do they call him a U.P.?'

'Well, he got into some sort of trouble and is now living on his sister's money. It's even said that he's blackmailing her.'

'Blackmailing? What's that?'

'Dear me, what a lot of tiresome questions you're asking today! Suppose you know that someone has done something very wrong and you say: "Unless you give me some money, I shall tell everybody." That would be blackmail. It's a wicked and cruel thing to do, because the blackmailer can always come again and ask for more and, if you're frightened enough, he'll slowly get all your money. Do you understand?'

'Yes. But if the U.P. did something wrong, why isn't the D.M. blackmailing him instead of him blackmailing her?'

'You should say *"his* blackmailing her" not *"him* blackmailing her." Don't ask me why, because I don't understand the rule. Well, there are two reasons why she isn't blackmailing him. One is that so many people know what he did, and the other, which is even more important, is that *he* hasn't got any money.'

'Is the D.M. very rich?'

'Well, she behaves as if she were. Her second husband left her a lovely house and all his money. Some people say she killed him and that's why the U.P. is blackmailing her. But that's simply gossip. There's probably no truth in it at all.'

'Is she pretty?'

'In a way. Yes, some people think her very pretty indeed.'

'Who was her first husband?'

'He was an inn-keeper. She worked behind the bar and then married him.'

'And the second one, Aunt Diana?'

'He was a silly young man of good family, who came into his money early in life and fell in love with her and ran off with her and married her when her first husband divorced her. You can divorce your wife if she runs away with another man. But no decent people will ever call on a woman who's been divorced, or even speak to her.'

'Is she very lonely?'

'Not at all. There are plenty of men flocking round her, and women, too, but not the type we should ever dream of knowing. She has a flat—that's a set of rooms all on the same floor—in London and she gives what they call "week-end parties" at her country house. It isn't very far from Broadforsters, but of course she never goes to Uncle Augustus's church, or to any church, so far as I know. She used to hunt when her second husband was alive, and went on after his death, but not long ago someone was very rude to her at one of the meets, and I rather think she's given it up.'

'Have you ever seen her?'

'Yes, once. I was walking with Aunt Lorna near the Grand Hotel and we saw the commissionaire helping a lady out of her motor. It was a bright green one and looked very smart, though it isn't as smart or as big as Sir Isaac Geldenmoser's. Aunt Lorna said she had seen the motor before and that someone had told her it belonged to the D.M.'

'And have you ever seen the U.P., Aunt Diana?'

'Not to my knowledge. However, that's quite enough about these undesirable people. Let us see if the tulips have begun to flower in Royal Parade Gardens.'

Two or three days later I learnt the real meaning of the third abbreviation—the C.J. My cousin Esmeralda, Uncle Egerton's second daughter, came to tea. We were left alone in the library together and somehow contrived to have a row. As a final thrust, she said: 'Anyway, *I* haven't got an uncle who's a C.J.'

I said provocatively: 'You don't know what that stands for.'

'Oh yes I do! It stands for counter-jumper. That means a linen-draper's assistant, like that little man at Roll's, who bows and scrapes as he measures out cloth by the yard. "Yes, Madam . . . No, Madam . . . Madam, please allow me to carry the parcel out to your carriage." That's what a counter-jumper is, in case you don't know.'

It was humiliating, but I disliked Uncle Giles Hemming too much to be distressed. He was a common, jaunty little man, and would probably have been much more successful touring provincial music-halls as a low comedian than he was as a linen-draper. He sang all the rubbishy 'hits' of the period, accompanying himself on the piano with, I must admit, an excellent touch. He could hardly speak without trying to say something facetious. I think he fancied himself as a lady-killer, a 'Gilbert, the Filbert, the Knut with a K'. His humour was sometimes a little too broad for my Hemming aunts, though they thought him amazingly gifted. His mere presence roused all my Froxwell fastidiousness. I would pretend to read a book when he began to hold forth and leave the room when he sat down at the piano. Aunt Mary told me that he had met two of my uncles, probably Uncle Egerton and Uncle Seymour, at some seaside resort and that they had done their best to cut him, and, when he made that impossible, to make him feel that he didn't belong to their world. As Uncle Giles was the only authority for this, there is no need to suppose that my Froxwell uncles were so lacking in manners, though I can well believe they were far from pleased when he came up and bumptiously claimed their acquaintance.

Not unnaturally, he did his best to get his own back by being unpleasant to me whenever we met. He would say, for example: 'How's your poor mouth today, Francis?' 'My mouth, Uncle Giles? It's quite all right, thank you.' 'I'm glad to hear that. I thought that silver spoon you were born with might be making it sore.'

As soon as I learnt the meaning of 'C.J.', I resolved to tell Aunt Mary and Aunt Violet at the first opportunity. But when I did, at the end of the holidays, thinking they would enjoy the joke, Aunt Violet said: 'What a very nasty thing to say!' and to my surprise Aunt Mary supported her. 'It isn't right of them to speak like that about an uncle of yours, whatever he may have done.' And I felt rather ashamed of myself.

(2)

Time was hanging heavily on my hands. Uncle Demetrius was taking a holiday in Paris, of which I gathered Aunts Letty and Sophy didn't approve. Cedric's sister, Millicent, had developed whooping-cough, and though neither he nor Frobisher had caught it so far, they were not allowed to visit Six, Albert Terrace, while I was there, nor was I allowed to go to the Vicarage. I used to go for walks with my three aunts and more rarely accompanied my grandfather in his wheeled chair, with Eglinton pushing it behind. Once, with the help of Eglinton, who had the knack of making him hear, I asked if we could go and inspect the site of the new promenade. My suggestion led, as I hoped it would, to a short conversation very near my heart. My grandfather said shrewdly: 'Aha! You would like to see the land of mine which our Corporation want me to make over to them. I fear the distance would be too great for Eglinton, but it shouldn't be too far for your young legs, when you next take a stroll by yourself.' Then I asked, again with Eglinton's help: 'Is the land worth a great deal of money, Granddaddy?' 'Yes, vastly more than they wish to pay for it, and certainly too much to give away without . . . aha! . . . the expecta-tion of a *quid pro quo*.' I didn't know what a *quid pro quo* meant, and didn't like to bother Eglinton a third time, especially as we were going up a slight incline and he was out of breath. But I trusted the phrase was the Latin for a baronetcy.

I walked to see the land that afternoon, but it looked just like any other land on the outskirts of Whitgate—a stretch of ill-mown grass with a few clumps of brambles and gorse dotted about it and enclosed by a tumble-down wire fence. There was no notice-board to proclaim that it was my grandfather's property or even to adver-tise it as being for sale. Perhaps this was a good sign and meant that negotiations were more advanced than my grandfather had led me to believe.

The next day I went for a walk down to the harbour, one arm of which served Whitgate as a pier. I loved that unfashionable part of the town to which I could so seldom tempt my aunts. I enjoyed peeping into the enclosure of Paradise, though it was not yet open for the season, and standing on the quay-side among the ropes and watching the boats as they rolled gently from side to side, lapped by the yellowish water. I liked the smell of the shabby kiosks which sold cheap shell-fish. There was an air of squalor about the whole scene which suggested adventure and made me feel strangely emancipated.

It cost a penny to go on the pier and, as I had only twopence in my pocket, I decided that morning to prowl about by the entrance and try the slot-machines, in case any of them worked without the insertion of a coin. I had no shame in this, because the whole place was deserted, except for a few seafaring men and dockers who were too intent on their business to notice me.

I had no luck in my search for free entertainment. The little rubber football never came up through its hole in the middle of the tin field, the fortune-teller never raised her hand, the witch never stirred her cauldron and the hangman never pulled the rope round his victim's neck. Then I came to a machine which I hadn't seen before. It was called 'The Master Printer', and consisted of a circular dial which bore all the letters of the alphabet, the numerals, a full-stop and a space. As one could see from a sample displayed in a cracked glass case above the instructions, it would print up to twenty letters—numerals, the full-stop and the space being reckoned as letters—on a strip of thin metal with a hole at each end, so that one could, if one wished, nail it on to a piece of wood. An impulse came over me to calculate what I could get in for one of my precious pennies.

SIR — space — FRANCI — that was ten — S — space — FROX-WELL. Exactly twenty, the permitted maximum. I couldn't resist, put in a penny, turned the S round to the pointer and tried to press down the lever. It was very stiff, and I was only just strong enough to force it down by using both my hands.

I had got as far as SIR and the space, when I realised I was being watched. A thick-set little thug of about eleven with a spotty face and a very dirty nose was standing beside me, almost elbowing me out of the way.

' 'Ere, let me do that!'

I longed to order him to mind his own business and leave me alone, but I was too frightened of him. Besides, my hands were already getting bruised. So I murmured something and turned the dial round till F was opposite the pointer, hoping that he would be content to press the lever and leave me to select the lettering myself. Having printed the F, he twirled the dial round and said: 'What next? You tell me and I'll do it.' His tone was less obliging than his words.

I said weakly: 'R', and all went well till he came to the end of FRANCIS. 'Now a space—that's the space, there.' He jerked the dial round, but to my horror, when he pressed the lever, a Z appeared.

I whimpered: 'You've spoilt it, you've spoilt it. I shouldn't have made a mess of it like that. Oh, why did you interfere?'

'So I'm interferin', am I, Mr Bloody La-di-da. That's all the thanks I gets for 'elpin' yer. Come on now, we might as well finish it. There's yer spice. Next letter?'

By now I was really in tears. 'You've ruined it now, you've really ruined it. My name won't go in. It'll be one letter too many.'

He said truculently: 'Then we'll start again. Give us a penny.'

'I shan't,' I screamed angrily. 'Next time I do it, I shall do it all by myself.'

'Oh, yer will, will yer! You come and try!' He stood right in front of the machine, put his hands in his pockets and, when I didn't move, took them out again and cocked a snook at me. 'Cry-byby, yer afride of me, that's what *you* are! Come and try! For two pins I'd give you a lovely black eye to take back 'ome to yer ma.'

At that moment a man came up from behind him, seized him by the nape of the neck, slapped his face three or four times, then released him with a kick on the bottom. The boy fled away howling, and my rescuer walked slowly towards me, as if he wished to give me time to pull myself together before he spoke to me. He was a square-built man in the late twenties, less tall than my Froxwell uncles, brown-eyed and swarthy—rather a gipsy type, except that he had a wide-nostrilled nose. He wore no collar or tie and his shirt was open to the second button, revealing a chest covered with thick black hair, which fascinated me. Perhaps Cedric was right when he said that the trunks of adult males were covered with hair. In those days both sexes kept their flesh most carefully hidden, with the sole exception of women wearing evening-dress, when for some reason they were privileged to make a display of their charms which by day would have been considered indecent. Even in the hottest weather one never saw a workman stripped to the waist, and sun-bathing was almost unknown.

I stood by the machine, blushing with shame that the stranger should have seen me so humiliated, but at the same time longing for him to speak to me.

'Were you printing your name?'

His voice was a great surprise; it was a little rough and lacked the refinement of my uncles' voices, yet it suggested a professional man, a doctor or a schoolmaster perhaps, and made me at once revise my estimate of him.

I said: 'Yes, but that boy spoilt it all.' Then suddenly I was filled with confusion, at the thought of the *SIR* which stood in front of *FRANCISZ*. I hurriedly pulled the release-handle, snatched the now odious metal-strip and crumpled it up as I put it into my pocket. If my new friend had read SIR FRANCISZ, he showed no sign of it, but asked: 'Would you like to have another try?' I told him I should very much. Then he said: 'I shall have to get change at the pier ticket-office. I've only got sixpence.' I offered him my remaining penny and he took it with the words: 'I'll pay you back in a minute. Now you turn the dial and I'll press the lever. Don't forget the spaces between your names.'

There was no hitch and FRANCIS FROXWELL appeared correctly spelt—though, alas, untitled. When he had read it, he looked at me and asked: 'Are you a grandson of old Mr Froxwell who lives in Albert Terrace?' I answered, not without pride: 'Yes, I'm the only son of his eldest son.'

'They say your grandfather owns half Whitgate.'

'Oh, not half, not nearly half, but he did build a great many houses and he has a lot of land which the Corporation want him to . . .' My tongue was running away with me and I stopped.

My new friend said: 'Would you like to go for a stroll with me on the pier? We can sit in one of the shelters, if you're tired.'

We went to the turnstile, he took a sixpence from his pocket and gave me one of the pennies from his change. I said: 'Thank you very much. I really ought to pay for myself, but I gave you my last penny. Will you tell me your name?'

'My name is James Waring. You can call me Mr Jimmy, if you like that better.'

I answered: 'Yes, I like it much better, Mr Jimmy. Will you call me Francis? Don't say Frank. I hate Frank and nobody calls me that. My uncle says he hates dimmy—dimmin—oh, I can't remember the word.'

'Diminutives?'

'Yes, I think it was that. It means pet-names and nicknames.'

'But Jimmy is a pet-name for James.'

'Well, I like it. James is a grumpy name. Somehow it reminds me of school.'

'I used to be a schoolmaster, but I've given it up.'

'You mean, you've retired?'

'Not quite that. I had a row at the school and they thought I ought to leave.'

I pondered. Then, recollecting, not without a glow of pleasure the violence with which he had rid me of my tormentor, I asked: 'Were you cruel to one of the boys?'

He said drily: 'No, I wasn't cruel to him.'

At the time I felt not a little proud of the way I kept my end up in this conversation, and now I feel not a little ashamed of it. Looking back, I realise—if I may use a phrase which in those days would have been meaningless—that I was putting on a Christopher Robinish act and simulating an ingenuousness which even at the age of ten was unnatural to me. I thought it was the quickest way to Mr Jimmy's heart. Perhaps I was right; for when we had found a shelter which faced away from the keen spring breeze, instead of saying: 'I think you're rather a horrid little prig,' he continued to draw me out with an affectionate interest.

'I suppose you're too young to have gone to a proper school yet?'

'No, I'm not, Mr Jimmy. I've been to a school in Eastbourne for one term. It's a boarding-school.'

'Do you like it?'

'Not very much.'

'Is it the boys or the masters?'

'Oh, it's the boys. I like some of the masters—Mr Smith who teaches me arithmetic, and Mr Robson. He's my Latin master.'

'How far have you got in Latin?'

'I've done all the declensions and regular verbs and *capio*.'

'And in arithmetic?'

'That's my best subject. I've got up to rule of three, but I haven't done stocks and shares. I want to do them so badly. Could you teach me?'

'Yes, I could. But most people think they're a very boring subject.'

'Oh, but they're so important—at least, they are for me. I want to know how much . . .' I hesitated, but this time my tongue did run away with me, and I went on: '. . . how much there is on my page in the Book of Life.'

'The Book of Life?'

'Yes. That's what we call the book that tells us how much we can expect when my Granddaddy dies.'

'Isn't that rather greedy?'

'I suppose it is, in a way. But I've a special reason for wanting to know. I can't tell you that . . . yet.'

'Will you tell me when I've taught you stocks and shares?'

'Perhaps. Yes, I will. When could we begin?'

'Not this morning. You'll have to be getting home for your mid-day meal.'

'Tomorrow, then? I've only got another four days at Whitgate, before I go to my aunt who lives at St Albans.'

'Are you allowed to come down here whenever you want to? Don't you often have to go for walks with your uncles and aunts?'

'Yes, I do, but if I told them I'd met you and you'd promised to teach me stocks and shares . . .'

'That's a thing, Francis, you mustn't tell them, if you want to see any more of me. I can't tell you why, but if they knew we were friends they'd forbid you ever to come near me again. If we should happen to meet in the town, when you're with your relations, don't give any sign that you know me, and I won't give any sign I know you. For both our sakes we must keep our friendship a secret. The Froxwells despise me for a lot of reasons. One of them is that I haven't any money. Apart from the three pennies in my pocket, I've got absolutely nothing till I go to the bank and draw the weekly two pounds my half-sister allows me. It's the least she can do, and I'm not ashamed to admit that I'm living on her charity. The only unfortunate thing is that she can stop being charitable whenever she chooses. Now we must go. I should like to buy you a twopenny bar of chocolate and spend my last penny having your fortune told.'

He bought the bar of chocolate at a kiosk just inside the pier, then he led me back to the group of automatic machines near which we had first met.

'Would you rather try the palmist or the witch?'

'Oh the witch! It looks more . . . more ghostly.'

He put in his penny and said: 'May this bring you luck! When is your birthday?'

'It's the first of May. When it comes I shall be ten.'

'Well then, turn this pointer to May and that one to number one. That's right. Now turn the knob here, and wish very hard.'

There was a whirring sound, the witch nodded her head and stirred the cauldron, the cat waved his long tail, a bat flew jerkily across the dark cave and a skeleton lurched out from behind a rock. There was a plop and a piece of cardboard a little bigger than a railway-ticket fell into a cupped recess on the outside of the machine. The skeleton vanished, witch, cat and bat ceased to move and the show was over. I snatched the card and was about to read it, when Mr Jimmy said: 'No, keep that till you get home and read it when you're alone. It's unlucky to show it to other people. Now, Francis, remember, not a word about our knowing one another. I shall be somewhere round here every day for the next few days between half-past eleven and half-past twelve, just in case you're able to come down and see me. I shall be disappointed if you can't, but I shall know it isn't your fault. I have a room in one of those houses over there'—he pointed to a cluster of tumble-down build-ings on the rising ground above the farther side of the harbour—'so it's no hardship for me to hang about for you. As a matter of fact, I nearly always come here in the morning. I've nothing much else to do. Are you quite sure you want to see me again?'

'Oh, I do, I do very much indeed.'

'Then you will.'

He tickled the palm of my hand as we said goodbye.

MAY THE FIRST—TAURUS THE BULL

You have a lovable character and are capable of strong affections. Dis-tinctions await you. Your greatest fault is a lack of will-power to resist temptations. Beware of companions who may lead you into bad ways. The forces of good and evil surrounding you are evenly balanced. But have no fear. If you do your best, good will prevail in the end.

(3)

That night, Aunts Letty and Diana went out to dinner with Lady Lucy and the Countess, whom they were taking to some amateur theatricals given in aid of a local charity. Lavinia, who now fancied herself as an actress, was to appear in one or two of the numbers. Aunt Sophy stayed at home to keep my grandfather company and I was allowed to join them for dinner, which we had half an hour earlier than usual. My grandfather didn't sit up long over his port, and I was still in the library when Aunt Sophy came back after saying goodnight to him in his room.

There was something a little strange in her manner. Instead of scolding me for being up so late, she said: 'Francis, have you ever seen a planchette?' I told her I hadn't and she went on: 'Well, Uncle Egerton has lent me one for a few days. You know, though you'd never think it, he's a *believer*, unlike the rest of the family. Shall we have a séance?' Without giving me any further explanation, she opened the secretaire-drawer of the bookcase and brought out a brown-paper parcel. She undid it reverently and disclosed a wooden object, heart-shaped and on little wheels. A pencil ran through the middle and the point, which was on the under-side, had been adjusted to the level of the wheels and acted as a kind of pivot. Then, after laying some sheets of foolscap on a table, she turned out the electric light and all the oil-lamps in the room except one in the far corner and said: 'Now you sit here and I'll sit opposite you. When the time comes, you must touch the edge of the planchette very lightly with the tips of your thumbs and little fingers—like this. Don't push at all. If the spirit is favourable, the planchette will move of its own accord and write down answers to our questions. Close your eyes for a moment and make your mind a blank, so as to shut out all worldly influences.'

I did my best and heard Aunt Sophy muttering a prayer. A mysterious feeling came over me and when she said: 'Now, open your eyes,' I almost expected to see a white-sheeted apparition bending over us. However, there was nothing but the glimmer of the red-shaded lamp, which left our table in deep shadow. 'Now', she said, 'touch the planchette with your finger-tips as I showed you—no, both your thumbs must be touching one another—stretch your little fingers as far as you can and keep very still. I will ask the first question.'

'*Are we in communication with a spirit?*'

The planchette seemed to quiver and to send a vibration up my arms. Then it began to waddle over the paper, moving an inch or two to the left and then to the right. Then it gathered speed, assuming a rotary motion. Then it slowed down again and came to rest.

'Take your hands away, Francis, and we'll see if we can make out what it has written.' Instead of switching on the electric light, she lit a candle and brought it to the table, and we saw that the planchette had written YES. The letters were shaky and intertwined like a monogram, but quite clear. She blew out the candle and said in a whisper: 'You see—*it* is here! Now do as you did before—no, more gently, you're pushing—and I will ask another question.'

'*What is your name?*'

The planchette went through the same performance as before, though its gyrations were more elaborate. When it came to rest and Aunt Sophy had relit the candle, she said: 'Now, Francis, you see if you can read what it has written.' I made out four letters fairly easily. They were LAST, but there was something before them and something after them which I couldn't decipher. Aunt Sophy studied the scrawl for a while, then said triumphantly: 'The first letter is A and the last two are OR. ALASTOR. I am sure I have heard of a spirit called Alastor, though I have never been in communication with him before.' She blew out the candle, and asked, as soon as we were in position: '*What does Alastor mean?*'

The answer was surprisingly easy to read.

SPIRIT OF SOLITUDE.

Aunt Sophy nodded at me sagaciously, and said: 'That's beautiful—that's very beautiful. It shows the spirit is good. But we'll make quite sure.'

'*Are the forces in this room good or evil?*'

GOOD AND EVIL.

The AND was very clear, as if it was meant to be underlined.

We looked at one another nervously. Then I said impulsively: 'Oh, Aunt Sophy, do let *me* ask a question.' She demurred a little, then gave way, enjoining me to ask reverently.

'*Will Francis Froxwell ever be a baronet?*'

It seemed as if the planchette would never stop.

IF HE—there were two more words, but try as I would I couldn't make them out. Aunt Sophy said: 'It's H something, then ATI, then something more, then CE. That might be a P. PATI, then—I know, HAS PATIENCE. IF HE HAS PATIENCE. I'll ask if that's right.'

'*Were the last two words "has patience"?*'

The answer came so quickly and was so short that I trembled in case it might be NO. But it was YES.

'Oh, Auntie Sophy, Auntie Sophy,' I cried, with shrill excitement, 'it's true, you see, it's true! I'm really going to be a baronet! Do let me go on. I've thought of another question I want to ask so much.'

Hardly waiting for her consent, I blew out the candle, and asked as solemnly as I could: '*Will Uncle Demetrius ever marry Lady Lucy?*'

This answer too was a matter of half a second.

NO.

Aunt Sophy looked at me aghast and said: 'Francis, I'm sure you were guiding the planchette. I could feel it.' I answered: 'I wasn't, I swear it on my honour.' (I nearly said: 'On my honour as a baronet.')

She stood up and said: 'I find it hard to believe you. Anyway, that will be enough questions for tonight. One must never weary the spirits. It's much more of a task for them to communicate with us, than it is for us to receive their messages.' When she turned on the light, she was trembling a little and her face was a blotchy red. She put the planchette hurriedly back in its box. I couldn't bear the thought of going to bed there and then and, partly as an excuse for staying up and partly with a real desire for enlightenment, I asked: 'Aunt Sophy, do you believe in good and evil forces?'

'Indeed I do—and the Bible, if you read it with understanding, tells us to believe in them. The world is full of good and evil forces. They are more real than the things you can touch and see—more

real than food or drink or the books in that bookcase.' If Uncle
Demetrius had been there, he might well have asked, 'Are they
more real than the Book of Life in that drawer?' But even if I
had thought of such a quip, I was in no mood to make it. I sat
enthralled, while Aunt Sophy let me into the secret of some of
her more esoteric beliefs. She told me that every human being had
two angels—a white angel and a black angel, an angel of light and
an angel of darkness—who waged a continual warfare for his soul.
The angel of darkness offered us lovely gifts and it was hard to
resist his blandishments. He could give us health, beauty, success,
a mysterious magnetism which enabled us to dominate other
people, and magical powers. Of course, all magic was not evil.
Magic, like the angels, was of two kinds, white and black. The
practice of white magic demanded self-sacrifice and self-control
and could only be acquired by long and strenuous endeavour. Black
magic was much easier to learn, though one learnt it at one's peril.
She ended by saying: 'Francis, never forget that you are always
surrounded by spiritual presences, who can see your most secret
and most shameful actions and read your most intimate thoughts.
They will be with you tonight, when you go to bed, and perhaps in
time you will come to realise how near they are.'

When I was on the verge of falling asleep, I seemed to see two
figures gazing fiercely at one another across my bed. One of them
had the features of Uncle Demetrius, and the other, my black
angel, had taken the form of my new friend Mr Jimmy.

(4)

As it happened, I could have slipped down to the harbour again
the very next morning, but my longing to see Mr Jimmy now
appeared to me in the guise of a temptation which at all costs I
must try to resist. So I took a walk in the opposite direction, all
along the dull stretch of the upper cliff, till I reached my grandfather's land which the Corporation wanted to buy. As before,
I found the sight of it uninspiring. Perhaps one's whole life was
bound to be uninspiring, if one resisted the seductions of evil!

I had to admit that in my heart of hearts I was more eager to see Mr Jimmy again than Uncle Demetrius who was coming to spend the Saturday to Monday at Number Six. I couldn't help feeling that my outing with him at half-term had been a failure, as if he had deliberately let me down by not bringing me good news of my baronetcy. I kept telling myself I was as devoted to him as I had ever been, and that, set in the scales against him, Mr Jimmy had the weight of a straw. But in spite of all my attempts at self-discipline, I still wished it were Mr Jimmy with whom I was to spend the Saturday morning. I had spent a pointless and tedious Friday, surely that was enough? When, just before going to bed, I dropped my watch and broke the glass, I felt fate had played me a very shabby trick at the end of a day of heroic self-denial.

Uncle Demetrius arrived about half-past eleven. He had a bad cold, which had reddened the end of his nose, and I had never seen him look less attractive. He and Aunt Diana and I went for a short stroll on the front, till he suddenly said he was going back to Number Six for an hour's reading in the smoking-room, where a fire had been lit for his benefit. So I spent the rest of the morning with Aunt Diana. We looked at the tulip-beds in Royal Parade Gardens, she called at the library about a book, I studied the window of the toyshop in Thanet Street. The signal gantry, price eight and six, was still there, but it now meant nothing to me at all and I wondered how I could ever have coveted it.

At luncheon, Uncle Demetrius seemed a little brighter, and as soon as the meal was over he said to me: 'Francis, would you like to come out for a walk? Perhaps the sea-breeze will kill my horrid germ. Shall we go to the harbour? We could look in at Paradise on the way and see what new attractions they're rigging up for the summer.'

If I could have found an excuse to take our walk elsewhere, I should have made it. But after all it wasn't the morning, and I had no reason to suppose Mr Jimmy would be anywhere near the harbour. So I said: 'Yes, it would be nice to pay a visit to Paradise.'

We didn't talk much to one another as we went down the long slope of Harbour Road, and I found my uncle's company less stim-ulating than usual. Perhaps it was his cold, or perhaps his thoughts were elsewhere. For that matter, my thoughts too were elsewhere. Then, as we turned into Sailors' Parade, a row of small trippery shops leading to the main gate of Paradise, I suddenly saw Mr Jimmy. Our eyes met for a second, then he looked away into the window of a shop that sold fishing-tackle. At that very moment my uncle decided to cross the road, so that we must inevitably pass quite close to Mr Jimmy, unless he turned abruptly in his tracks. I coloured self-consciously, hoping my uncle wouldn't notice it, and began to talk wildly about Paradise. But by that time he had caught sight of my friend and was giving him a puzzled, unfriendly stare, which must have been reflected in the glass of the shop-window; for, as we passed, Mr Jimmy turned his head round, inclined it and said, in a quiet, obsequious voice, 'Good afternoon.' Uncle Demetrius flicked a finger brusquely against the brim of his bowler-hat, murmured, 'Afternoon' and quickened his stride, so that I almost had to run to keep up with him.

As soon as his pace became normal, I couldn't help asking: 'Do you know that gentleman, Uncle Demetrius?' He said, 'No, I can't really say I know that gentleman, though I have met him once—perhaps it was twice. He isn't a person I should choose to know.'

'Why? Is he very poor?'

'He is, but that's his own fault. However, it isn't because he's poor that I don't want to know him. He's a blackguard. Perhaps that isn't his own fault, altogether. Can any of us help being what we are? I rather doubt it. Still, though I might bring myself to be sorry for him, I should never choose to have him as one of my friends, and I certainly shouldn't care for you to know him.'

'I thought he had a nice face.'

'Let's talk of something else.'

I had never heard my uncle speak so waspishly. I think he was ashamed of it; for he added: 'Now here we are at the gates of Paradise. I don't much fancy the Mingle-Mangle, do you? Anyway, it isn't ready yet. Would you like to try your skill at the coconuts? . . . The Glide of Death, then? No, they're still repainting it. The holiday season at Whitgate seems to start later every year. The trippers are getting so soft these days, they can't face our spring winds. Now here's something simple and safe. The witch will tell your fortune for a penny. Here you are, put it in. The first of May's your birthday, isn't it?'

The machine looked exactly like the one near the entrance to the pier, except that the paintwork was fresher. I longed to say I had had my fortune told only two days before, but feared it might lead to awkward questions, and put the coin in most reluctantly. The clockwork was in better shape than it had been in the other machine. The witch nodded her head and stirred more vigorously, the cat's tail described a bigger arc when it waved, the bat's flight was smoother and more of the skeleton was visible. I snatched the card as soon as it fell into the little cup.

MAY THE FIRST—TAURUS THE BULL

You have a lovable character and are capable of strong affections. Distinctions await you. . . .

Yes, it was just the same. I hardly bothered to read the rest of it, so intent was I on getting the card into my pocket. But my uncle said: 'Aren't you going to show it to me?' I hesitated and murmured something about its being unlucky to show one's fortune to anyone. He said testily: 'Whoever told you that nonsense? Surely you know the whole thing is a joke. Let me see it, please.'

There was a firmness in his voice that made me give in. He laughed as he handed the card back to me, and said: 'Well, there's nothing very alarming about that. Distinctions await you. Does that mean you are going to be made an archbishop in your old age? I hope I shall live to see your Grace's enthronement.' I was rather shocked by his flippancy and his indifference to the good and evil forces surrounding me, and it wasn't long before I was impelled to refer to them. 'Do I believe in them?' he said musingly. 'In a way, yes, but not in a personal form. I mean I regard them simply as abstractions, like the laws of mathematics or gravitation. I don't see them as white seraphs wearing halos fighting against black devils with red-hot pokers. I think I used the word *abstractions* just now. Do you know what it means?'

I had to admit I didn't, and did my best to attend while he

explained it, but as soon as I could, I brought out my next question.

'Aunt Sophy says everybody has two angels, a white one and a black one who fight for his soul. Do you believe that?'

'Frankly, no. When did Aunt Sophy fill your head with all this?'

'Last night. Uncle Egerton has lent her a planchette and we asked it all sorts of questions. It really did write. It said there were good and evil forces in the room, and . . .'

'What else did it say?'

I couldn't possibly tell Uncle Demetrius what it had said in reply to my two questions—the one relating to my baronetcy and the other relating to his marriage with Lady Lucy. So I answered evasively: 'Oh, a great many things. It said its name was Alastor and told us that it meant a Spirit of Solitude.'

'Did it tell you who wrote the poem?'

'What poem, Uncle Demetrius?'

'Have you ever heard of Shelley?'

'No, I don't think so.'

'Well, there was a famous poet called Shelley, who died nearly ninety years ago—eighty-eight years ago, to be exact. He wrote a poem which he called *Alastor or The Spirit of Solitude*.'

'Was it about a real spirit?'

'No, it was just a piece of fancy. I've no doubt Aunt Sophy read the poem at school. She may even have had to learn parts of it by heart, and so may you, some day.' Seeing that I didn't follow his reasoning, he went on: 'You know, Francis, whatever else I may or may not believe in, I certainly don't believe in the planchette. I don't accuse Sophy of consciously shoving the thing, though I wouldn't put it altogether past her, but . . .'

'But, Uncle Demetrius, she said she didn't know what Alastor meant. If she didn't, however could she have got it right?'

'But she *did* know, or had known once, which makes all the difference. She wasn't really getting more out of the thing than she put in it herself. I'm afraid that's rather beyond you—it's beyond me, too, in a way, as I've never gone in for the study of the subconscious—but I would bet a hundred pounds to one penny that if Aunt Sophy had never seen the title of that poem, the spirit wouldn't have said its name was Alastor and that it meant the Spirit of Solitude. It might just as well have called itself Casabianca and said it meant a Boy on a Burning Deck. I'm sorry she's been stuffing you with this rubbish of hers. She should have known better. It's odd that of all the members of our family, the two greatest materialists, Sophy and Egerton, should have taken to what they call "the occult". I don't go so far as to say there's nothing in it. There are even times when I'm inclined to side with Sophy against Augustus, who declares he believes all the dogmas of the Church. For example, I agree with Sophy that if one accepts the immortality of the soul after death, one must also accept the fact that it was immortal before birth and may have been many times incarnate. I find it an incredible thought that I should suddenly have sprung into existence out of nothing in 1876 and shall live on this earth, say till 1946, when I shall be seventy, and then, if I've given myself too good a time, shall suffer the torments of Hell for ever and ever. Personally, I doubt if there's any kind of existence at either end of one's bodily life, but if you demand it at one end, you must have it at t'other. But I shouldn't be saying this kind of thing to you and anyhow it's really beside the point. All I want to do is to warn you not to take Aunt Sophy's vapourings too seriously. Good forces, evil forces, white angels, black angels and spirit messages scribbled by the planchette—it really won't do. Well, I suppose we ought to be making for home.'

This cold douche of scepticism brought me both uneasiness and comfort. My hopes of a baronetcy seemed a good deal more slender without Aunt Sophy and her planchette to bolster them up. At one moment in our conversation I had been tempted to break the promise I had made to her and ask Uncle Demetrius point-blank if he thought there was any likelihood at all of my grandfather's being given a title. But I couldn't bring myself to face a complete disillusionment. What, go back to school—now only ten days ahead—without that sweet vision of the telegraph-boy cycling up the drive with the good news that would bring me a life-time of ease and celebrity? No, any uncertainty was better than that. On the other hand, it was a great relief to feel that Aunt Sophy's evil forces were only abstractions—I was proud of the new word—and

that I needn't really bother about them very much. At bed-time
that night, I was determined to make the most of my last chance
of seeing Mr Jimmy, which would be on the Monday, when Uncle
Demetrius had gone back to London.

(5)

On the Sunday, of course, I had to go to church with my three
aunts, and after that we were expecting the Countess and Lady
Lucy to join us for luncheon.

While Aunt Letty buttoned her gloves in the hall, she said: 'I do
hope the sermon isn't over-long. Eglinton seems to need more and
more supervision and I must be back in good time to see that all is
as it should be in the dining-room.' Aunt Sophy whispered to her:
'About the wines? There is no need for our father to offer his best.
Our visitors hardly touch it.' Aunt Diana laughed and said: 'Don't
you think he ought to offer champagne, in case there's a toast that
can only be drunk in that wine?' Aunt Letty replied severely: 'No,
Diana, I do not think so.'

They were all dressed in their best for church-parade on the
Upper Promenade, that majestic display of feather-boas, lorgnettes,
parasols, smart prayer-books, little bags of gold mesh and the slow
swish of long skirts. I was in my best, too, and wore an Eton suit
and a hateful, almost metallic contrivance called a dicky—not a
motor-car seat, but a stiffly starched shirt-front which sometimes
got out of control and burst out of the waistcoat. And I had a
horrible ready-made bow tie which kept turning on end. No adult,
of course, would think of wearing such a thing, unless he were a
manservant, a waiter or a cad, but as few schoolboys could tie a
bow, the tabu was relaxed in their favour. I also wore a top-hat, of
which I was proud.

It was a lovely day, the cold breeze had dropped and the sea
sparkled in the sunlight. None the less, though the church was less
than a quarter of a mile away, we drove there in one of Norris's
carriages. It was an occasion on which even the most penurious of
the Froxwells would damn the expense. One of my smaller phobias

was having to sit with my back to the horses, but I got through the short drive without feeling sick to the point of vomiting and, when we reached the church, jumped down like a footman and helped my three aunts to alight. The verger welcomed us with a respectful smile as we walked up the aisle. When we came to our pew, which had a card, 'Peter Froxwell Esqre, J.P.', fixed to the wooden front, Aunt Letty, who was the vanguard of our procession, stepped smartly aside, as if she were executing a military manœuvre, and Aunt Diana, moving into the breach, flounced to the farther end. I followed her and Aunt Sophy followed me and then Aunt Letty, spreading out her skirts as she sat down, made it clear that the Froxwell pew had its full complement.

For a moment, we shuffled with varying degrees of success on to our knees. Then the clergy and the choir came into view and we stood up. The choristers looked very smart in red cassocks beneath their surplices. Uncle Demetrius had once said: 'If I must go to church, I'd rather it were twopence-coloured than penny-plain', and indeed this church, though doctrinally broad, was far more ritualistic than the one to which Aunt Mary took me in St Albans. We prayed, sat and stood by turns. I noticed that Aunt Sophy had a peculiar prayer-book. It was larger than the usual size and bound in pale blue limp leather and had pictures in it. I managed to see the title of one of them while she was deep in her devotions— 'The Archangel Raphael bearing the Sacred Lotus to the Principalities.' The Sacred Lotus—that was new to me. Our pew was on the south side of the aisle and the sun struck suddenly on a stained glass window depicting the martyrdom of St Sebastian. The coloured glass reminded me of the window in the library at Number Six, but was even prettier. A boy in a pew almost opposite to ours caught my eye and winked. He was good-looking in the style of my cousin Frobisher, but more robust and with a much more sensual expression. About fifteen, one would say, in his second year at a public school, good at games no doubt. He might be a bully, but if he happened to like you, he could be very nice to you indeed. Oh, of course, he must be one of the Fulton boys, of whom I had heard vague talk. Aunt Diana said the Fultons were charming people. They lived in the next terrace to ours, smart, go-ahead, well-to-do, a little fast perhaps, though it didn't do to believe everything one heard. I wondered if I could ever rise to the level of the Fulton boys. Of course, if I became a baronet . . . for a few seconds I abandoned myself to that dream, then, finding the Fulton boy's eye still upon me, I gave a timid little wink in reply. I'm not at all sure Aunt Letty didn't notice it, for she frowned in my direction. We sat down again, and Aunt Diana looked at her watch, then wound it up. The sunlight shifted to the back of my head and I felt quite hot. We knelt, stood up and sat down. Aunt Sophy folded her arms in meditation, as the Vicar ascended the pulpit.

He took his text, which is one of which I have since grown very fond, from the fourth verse of the thirteenth chapter of St Luke— '*Those eighteen upon whom the tower of Siloam fell, and slew them, think ye that they were sinners above all men that dwelt in Jerusalem?*'—and delivered a strong rebuke to those who held that sudden calamities are necessarily the visitations of God's wrath. I wished my two Hemming aunts had been there to hear him. Only the previous holiday Aunt Violet had said of a man who had been killed in an accident: 'Well, he deserted his wife eight years ago!', and Aunt Mary too was addicted to such petit-bourgeois moralising. The Froxwells were far more enlightened in this respect, though even they were apt to regard sudden poverty as a merited punishment for a dissolute life. Anyway, it comforted me to think that, if dreadful things happened to you, it didn't mean you had done anything wicked. Then, thinking wishfully, I somehow twisted this doctrine round to a still pleasanter converse—namely that, if you did something wicked, it didn't follow that anything dreadful would happen to you. Yes, most certainly I would spend Monday morning with Mr Jimmy if I could.

We stood up. All round me there were creakings of whalebone and those intimate gurglings which Aunt Diana irreverently called 'church-noises'. The last hymn began. Sidesmen came up with red velvet collecting-bags. I put in my threepenny bit and wondered how much Aunt Sophy had put in. We knelt for the Blessing and prayed. The organ began very softly then gained courage. We stood up. There was a loud church-noise from Aunt Letty. Aunt

Diana may have heard it, for there was a smile on her lips. She was rather fond of lavatory jokes and was the only relative to whom Cedric and I had disclosed the existence of the Loo-list. She told us she had once seen a pan inscribed 'Gone with the Wind'. I now think this was an invention on her part.

The clergy and the choir made their exit. Four fifths of the congregation buttoned their gloves. Then came the scramble of getting into the aisle without pushing or seeming to be in too much of a hurry. In a thickening procession we passed out of the shadows into the open air, where for a moment the sunlight almost blinded us. Two hundred parasols were raised and opened, shading smiles and bows of recognition, some effusive, some marked by a cautious reserve. All tongues were suddenly loosened: 'An excellent sermon, and so eloquent!'—'Did you think so? I felt it touched on rather dangerous ground. I mean, if we are always to rule out retribution . . .'—'Mrs Summers-Fordyce wasn't here again. This makes the third time running.'—'But didn't you know, she has left us for St Catherine's. My dear, they have *incense!*'—'How very plain poor Dora Belfrage is looking!'—'Oh, this glorious spring-like weather. I do hope your dear father can get out and enjoy it. I hear your brother Demetrius spends most of his time in London now. . . . Ah, yes, no doubt he is working very hard.'

As soon as we had done our duty by Whitgate society, Aunt Letty announced that we must go straight home, or our visitors would be there before us.

Uncle Demetrius had excused himself for not coming with us to church by saying that he was going to call for the Countess and Lady Lucy and bring them to Number Six in a carriage. They went to a church near their lodgings. We were therefore much surprised when we got home to find him and Lady Lucy in the library with no sign of the Countess. It was soon explained that Lady Lucy, who had gone to the early service, had met Uncle Demetrius while she was on her way to Number Six to leave word that her mother was too unwell that morning to join the luncheon-party. (My grandfather would have no telephone in the house. Why should he? There was always a servant available to take an urgent message, and the doctor lived only three minutes away.) 'It's simply one of

Mamma's bad headaches, but she felt she couldn't eat any lunch-eon today. We thought we ought to let you know beforehand, but there was nobody we could send round. I had just got to the top of Harbour Road when I met your brother. He walked back with me to our rooms and waited while I had a word with Mamma, who asks me to tell you how dreadfully disappointed she is to miss this treat—and then we came back here. What wonderful weather! We are indeed glad to have settled at Whitgate.'

Aunt Letty withdrew as soon as she could, to rearrange the table, while the rest of us sat in the library. Should we take another turn on the front? No, Aunt Diana was sure Lady Lucy had had enough walking for one morning. How about crossing over to the gardens and sitting there? Aunt Sophy declared that there was a chill in the air despite the bright sun. May was a treacherous month. Lady Lucy assured us that she was more than happy to be in the library. My uncle had been showing her some of the books—such interesting ones, too. What a fine collection we had! Aunt Diana seemed to read a hint in this, for she said: 'If you'll excuse us, I think Francis and I ought to take another short stroll before luncheon. We intended to go out again as soon as we had come back with my eldest sister. Come, Francis.'

On our way out we saw Aunt Letty in the dining-room, giving instructions to Eglinton and the parlourmaid. Aunt Diana beck-oned to her sister and whispered: 'Demetrius is showing Lucy the books. Get Sophy away from them somehow. She's no sense at all.'

At last the purpose of our *sortie* dawned upon me, and when we were on the promenade again, I asked: 'Do you think he will pro-pose to her before luncheon?' Aunt Diana replied: 'I rather doubt it, but the least we can do is to leave them together as much as we can.' We walked up and down in suspense. As so often, my own feelings were mixed. It would be nice to have an earl's daughter as an aunt and Aunt Sophy had assured me that the marriage would be a step towards my baronetcy. On the other hand, I knew that once Uncle Demetrius was married, I should lose that peculiar, romantic friendship with which he alone of all human beings had enriched my life. Who else was there who could give it to me? Mr Jimmy, perhaps? When we reached the front-door, my thoughts

were busier with Mr Jimmy than with what might have happened
in the library during our absence.

I went upstairs to wash my hands and brush my hair and as I
was just going down again Uncle Demetrius came out of his bedroom. I said: 'But where's Lady Lucy?' He made a little face at me
and replied: 'Well, I hope you don't think I've got her in here!' He
had evidently got over the worst of his cold and was much livelier
than he had been the day before. He went on: 'I think she's tidy-
ing herself in the front spare-bedroom. But why all this interest?'
I didn't know what to reply, and he added: 'I wonder what those
silly women have been saying to you. Come along, I suppose we're
meant to assemble in the drawing-room. It's so long since we've
had strangers to luncheon here, I've forgotten the procedure.'
Strangers! No, clearly he hadn't proposed . . . and it was most
unlikely he ever would.

But this was only known to my uncle and me, another secret
between us like our drive in the green motor-car that belonged
to the nameless and perhaps unnamable lady. The others, most
definitely, were not in the know. Even Lady Lucy, who must
have been aware that she hadn't received a proposal of marriage
that morning, was pink with the joy of hopes that might yet be
fulfilled. My three aunts were gay and bright-eyed as birds that spy
a rich diet of worms. My grandfather, whose chair was wheeled
to the head of the table, while we stood round, radiated a twinkling good-humour, and when he said Grace—'For what we are
about to receive, may the Lord make us truly thankful'—his deep
voice boomed with delighted expectation. He made Lady Lucy
a graceful little speech as soon as we had sat down, regretting
the absence of 'your dear mother, but we all hope that is only a
pleasure deferred', and apologising for the fact that Lady Lucy was
not sitting next to him, 'but my deafness makes me such a poor
conversationalist that I prefer to inflict my company on my daughters, who . . . aha! . . . have to bear with it as best they can. I must
leave it . . . aha! . . . to my son Demetrius to do the honours for
me.'

Aunt Letty's place was on my grandfather's right, mine was
next, then came Aunt Diana's. Uncle Demetrius sat at the foot of

the table with his back to the window. Lady Lucy was on his right and shared that side of the table with Aunt Sophy. I was sorry not to be sitting next to Uncle Demetrius or, failing him, Lady Lucy, who always gave me a very friendly smile, though she didn't seem to know what to say to me. I felt I could say a good many things to her, and didn't find her at all intimidating. Aunt Letty's task was to supervise the conduct of the meal—a chicken-broth, a gigantic, rather tough sirloin of beef, served with Yorkshire pudding, roast potatoes and spring greens, choice of apple tart or castle puddings with a lumpy white sauce, cheese and biscuits and an unripe pine-apple by way of dessert—and to nod or shake her head in response to an occasional observation made by my grandfather. Aunt Sophy and I were rather out of things and from time to time we talked to one another across the table. Aunt Diana, Uncle Demetrius and Lady Lucy formed a lively group and on the whole I was content to listen to what they were saying.

Aunt Diana remarked: 'When we were children, our father sometimes used the old Grace his father used. I wonder if you know it, Lucy? It went like this:

> Some have meat but cannot eat,
> Some can eat but have no meat,
> We have meat and WE CAN EAT!
> The Lord be praised!'

Lady Lucy said: 'Yes, I have heard it in a Scottish version', and quoted it in so broad an accent that I couldn't understand. I remembered my English master saying the previous term: ' "Scottish" is the Scotch for Scotch. It isn't a word people should use, if they're trying to talk English,' and I longed to show off my knowledge. But Aunt Sophy had told me Brora was somewhere in Scotland, so Lady Lucy was probably Scotch herself, and might resent it. Uncle Demetrius said, rather loudly: 'I'm afraid it isn't always easy to be thankful for Mrs Eglinton's cooking.' Aunt Diana whispered 'Sh!', but Eglinton was at the far end of the table. He had shaved that day with more than usual closeness and his jowl was bright blue, except for a razor-gash that still oozed a little blood. Lady

Lucy leant across to me and asked me, in a voice full of interest, on which day I was to go back to school. Uncle Demetrius interposed: 'You know, that's a most unpleasant question. It's like asking someone on which day he's going to have his appendix out.' Lady Lucy said: 'Oh, I am dreadfully sorry. I didn't realise . . . I mean, some boys rather look forward to going back, don't they?' 'Hardly, I think, when they're as young as Francis.' She turned to me again. 'Will you show that you've forgiven me by sending me a postcard to let me know how you're getting on? You know our address, 9, Royal Terrace?' I was enchanted to think that I might soon be corresponding with the daughter of an earl, and gave my promise readily, almost resolved to have her for an aunt, however little Uncle Demetrius might wish to marry her. Then Aunt Diana threw in a remark about the King's visit to Whitgate. I listened intently, but the subject led to nothing and was soon dropped. The conversation next shifted to poetry. This gave me the opportunity of asking Lady Lucy if she knew *Tithonus*. She said she had once had to learn it by heart, which was another bond between us. Aunt Sophy said her favourite poet was Ella Wheeler Wilcox and Uncle Demetrius rallied her on her taste. Eglinton handed round the port and my grandfather boomed: 'Francis, my boy, take a quarter of a glass.' Then he added for Lady Lucy's benefit: 'I hold that by encouraging the young to drink in moderation one saves them from excesses in later life. I have always found . . . aha! . . . that the greatest drunkards come from teetotal homes. Now a toast—to our lady visitor, with the hope that next time we have the pleasure of seeing her here, her mother will be able to honour us as well!' Lady Lucy looked confused and said: 'Oh dear, that is too kind. I feel I . . . I ought to reply . . . but *can* he . . . ?' Aunt Diana came to the rescue by saying: 'Just raise your glass to him and bow and smile. He doesn't expect us to try to make him hear by shouting at him; at least, not at mealtimes, thank goodness!' Lady Lucy smiled vigorously at my grandfather, laid a hand lightly on her bosom and then blew him a kiss.

The excitement may have been too much for my grandfather, who had tea in his room instead of with us in the library. I was sitting alone there with Uncle Demetrius, half an hour after the meal, when Aunt Letty came in, looking much less calm than usual, and said: 'Demetrius, our father would like to see you . . . *now*.' She went out, he shrugged his shoulders and followed her, leaving the door ajar. I felt the tension, too. It was as if a school-friend of mine had been suddenly summoned to the headmaster's study. Twenty minutes later, I heard the door of my grandfather's room being opened, and before it shut again, the words 'behaviour of a cad' echoed down the hall. Then Uncle Demetrius strode past the door of the library on his way to the cloakroom. I went into the hall and hung about till he came out with his hat and coat. His face was white and angry. When he saw me, he said abruptly: 'I'm going out. Tell Aunt Letty I'm not sure if I shall be in for dinner.' I must have looked at him like a dog asking to be taken for a walk; for he added: 'No, I want to be alone and think something out.'

My grandfather had dinner in his room that night and I had mine with my aunts in the dining-room. The smiles of the morning had vanished and thunder-clouds brooded on all three faces. We ate almost in silence. When it was time for me to go to bed, Uncle Demetrius still hadn't come in.

(6)

To my relief he was with us at breakfast next morning. As if to make amends for his gruffness of the evening before, he asked me if I would like to drive with him to the station and see him off. I agreed gladly. He seemed on the whole in a fairly good humour, which was more than could be said for my three aunts, who showed in their various ways that he was making them anxious. Aunt Diana said plaintively: 'I don't suppose either of you want me to come with you?' and Uncle Demetrius replied 'No', and laughed. Aunt Diana tried to smile, but the other two looked very solemn.

We had hardly driven a hundred yards in the cab, when Uncle Demetrius said: 'You've probably guessed I had a frightful row with our father yesterday.' He spoke in the careless tone he had used when he mentioned the row between Demetrius the silversmith and St Paul. I asked him nervously what it was about. He said: 'Oh, I don't think I can tell you that. He was trying to force me into an important decision which I don't feel like taking—at any rate, yet awhile. He can be really terrifying when he's angry. No wonder none of us has ever made a mark in the world, brought up as we were on the slopes of such a volcano. He can be generous over big things, however stingy he may be over little ones, but only provided he gets his own way. "Maximilian, you seem to have literary tastes; you shall become a publisher. We ought to have a lawyer in the family; Egerton, that should suit you. Augustus, you're easy-going and not very bright; the church for you. As for you, Seymour, with your fondness for women and wine . . ." Uncle Seymour was a bit of a problem, because our father didn't like the idea of trade and Seymour was obviously unsuited for any profession except the army. He had a go at that, but failed in the exam. I think he did it on purpose. My temperament was rather like your father's, except that coming at the younger end of the family I didn't take things so seriously and lacked his moral earnestness. The only one of the aunts who's at all like me is Diana. I wish she could have got away from home and married someone she liked. Aunt Sophy was once nearly engaged to a kind of faith-healer, but the man was an utter fraud and it was probably just as well that our father found out in time to put a stop to it. Oh, I'm forgetting poor Beresford. He was vaguely scientific and our father settled he should become a doctor. His health would never have stood it. As for Aunt Letty . . .'

He was talking for the sake of talking, perhaps to relieve his own feelings or to stop me from asking awkward questions. I wished he would tell me more about himself and longed to mention Lady Lucy to see how he would react. But I was so sure that the trouble between my grandfather and him had been his unwillingness to propose to her that I felt such a remark would be too pointed.

As we approached the station, he gave my knee a light slap and said: 'In anything really big, make up your own mind. Hear other people's advice and give it its due, but always decide for yourself. Well, you know I shall be at King's Cross tomorrow week to pilot you across London to Victoria. I've suggested to Aunt Mary that you should arrive about twelve, so that we can have luncheon together. What will you do now? I suggest you should take a walk by the harbour. I think it's far the pleasantest part of the town.'

I thought my sense of direction was good enough to guide me to the harbour through the maze of mean little streets, some of them cobbled, that twisted downwards through such slums as there were at Whitgate. To keep my own moral problems at bay, I played a game called 'Ghosts' which I had invented for myself. When the alleys closed in and darkened, an evil spirit was just on my heels, but I knew he could never overtake me as long as I kept a patch of sunshine in view. The day was almost too bright for the game and I began it with a bored bravado, but it gradually took such a hold on my imagination that I felt really frightened. I had strayed into a small court-yard enclosed by tall houses that shut out the sky. There was no sign of life in any of them—perhaps they had been condemned and were awaiting demolition—but I thought I heard strange squelching steps approaching me from behind, whichever way I turned. I became suddenly convinced that in this place at least the forces of evil really did exist and that the only way I could escape from them was by abandoning my visit to the harbour and going straight home. I rushed wildly into the alley by which I had come, then took a turning, which, though it led uphill, seemed only to be another cul-de-sac. I was filled with panic and, when I turned round to flee downhill again, an old woman stood in my way, ragged and dirty, with tousled hair and a ferocious face that grinned at me disclosing toothless gums. 'Are you lost, little boy?' The words sounded like a threat. All the bogeys of childhood, gipsy kidnappers, stepmothers, ogresses, witches lurking in caves and my most recent terror, the forces of evil, were incarnate in her. I was too scared to speak and, lowering my head as if to butt her out of my way, I made a dash to the left. She stretched out a long, skinny arm, caught mine and said: 'Come, come, these aren't pretty manners, my pretty young man. How about giving your old auntie a kiss?' She held me tight and slowly bent her face down till it was only six inches from mine. I lost the last remnant of my self-control and screamed as loudly as

I could: 'Help, help! Save me, save me!' and struggled so violently that I broke loose from her grip; though when I was free, I was too dazed to run away from her and put my hands to my face and sobbed hysterically, while she stood watching with a ghoulish leer. Then suddenly I heard real footsteps behind me. This gave me courage to shout for help again. The woman moved two or three paces back and a man came into the alley through a narrow opening between the houses. He said authoritatively: 'Now, Bessie, what have you been doing to that boy?' Then he recognised me and added: 'Why, Francis, it's you. What's the trouble?' The woman said: 'I only arst 'im if 'e was lost,' and I said, at the same time: 'She wouldn't let me go. She wanted me to give her a kiss.' Mr Jimmy turned on her fiercely. 'You filthy old woman! For good-ness sake go away and have a bath. No, you'll get no present out of me today.' As he spoke, all the woman's supernatural attributes vanished. She seemed to become very much smaller and her voice changed too. ''Tain't often we see a young gentleman like 'im in these parts. You can't blame a mother's 'eart for yearnin' for 'im. Eight children I 'ad, and all of 'em dead . . . all dead.' She snivelled and I began to feel ashamed of myself.

Mr Jimmy took me firmly by the arm and guided me through the chink between the houses into a little street, just broad enough for a single line of traffic. He said: 'It seems my fate to rescue you from unpleasant people. That old woman is mad and very smelly, but she's quite harmless. Sometimes, when I've got some money, I give her threepence to buy a tot of gin.'

I murmured: 'It's magic, real magic, you being here. Did you know it was me?'

'No, I didn't. I heard someone calling for help and just popped through the twitten, as they call it, to see what was happening. This is a short cut from where I live to the harbour. As a matter of fact, I was on my way there at that moment, in case you should happen to turn up. Are you pressed for time? It's only a quarter to twelve.'

'No, I've got till one, and this'll be our last day. Do let's go and sit on the pier . . . if you'd like to, that is.'

'I should like to, but first you'd better come and wash your face in my room. I live round the next corner. If people saw us together, as you are, I don't know what they'd think I'd been doing to you.'

We took a turning that led slightly uphill, and soon came to a row of shabby cottages. We stopped at Number Eight and he opened the door, which led straight into the kitchen, where a fat, middle-aged woman was washing some clothes in the copper. Mr Jimmy said: 'I don't want to interrupt you, Mrs Fowler, but my young friend met Mad Bessie in Nelson Backs and he wants to wash away her memory.' Mrs Fowler took in at once what must have happened and replied pleasantly: 'I'm not surprised. This isn't the first time she's scared a boy out of his wits, though she means no harm. Still, I'm not at all sure as I don't agree with those as say she ought to be locked up. Shall I heat some water, or will the cold do?' 'Oh, the cold, of course. We'll use the jug in my room. This way, Francis.' He opened a door on the right and gently pushed me through it into a room which, apart from a bed and a wash-stand, was furnished like a parlour. He poured some water into a basin, gave me a towel from a hook on the wall and pointed to the soap. 'There. Take off your coat and have a good swill. Then brush your hair. My brushes are on this shelf. Can you reach them? Good!'

Rather to my surprise he had left the door wide open, so that Mrs Fowler, had she been so minded, could have watched me at my toilet. Instead of standing over me, he went to the doorway and chatted to her from there. I wondered if he thought it undignified to be alone with a boy in his bedroom. Or was he simply giving me time to pull myself together? I was overwhelmed with gratitude to him, not only for saving me from Mad Bessie's clutches, but for the tactful way in which he had described my terror-stricken screams as a call for help.

As we walked to the harbour, he said: 'Now you've seen where I live—Number Eight, North Place. Remember the address, just in case . . . I don't know in case of what, but it may somehow happen that you'll want me some day. I pay the Fowlers six shillings a week for that room. It's comfortable and, as you saw, it gets quite a bit of sun. They're nice people. The husband is a fish-porter. They've no children, which perhaps is as well. Shall we stroll round the harbour or go straight to the pier?'

I was feeling tired and confessed it, telling him that I had seen my uncle off at the station and had been walking ever since. When we reached the pier entrance, I said: 'Won't you let me pay? I've a lot of money this morning—three shillings.' He answered: 'No, I'll only let you do that when I'm really hard up. Besides, I'm rich, too, this morning. I won twenty-five shillings yesterday on a horse.' 'Twenty-five shillings! Will you teach me how to bet?' 'No, certainly not; at least, not till you're a great many years older.'

We sat down on two chairs at the far end of the pier, which cost him another twopence. The weather was even warmer and sunnier than it had been on the previous day, and I was serenely happy. I longed to be able to stay at Whitgate for ever and meet Mr Jimmy every day on the pier, and still more to have a room near him in North Place. If his only cost him six shillings a week, my three shillings should get me one for three days and a half! I still remembered that Uncle Demetrius had called him a black-guard, and that, if I was correct in taking him to be the D.M.'s half-brother, Aunt Diana had told me he was blackmailing his sister and living on her money. Indeed, it had been these two thoughts, and my identification of him with my Black Angel, which I had been trying to banish from my mind when I so rashly started to play 'Ghosts'. But in his presence none of this seemed to matter. Had he not twice been at hand to rescue me in a moment of peril? What had my White Angel been doing then? The forces of evil had become strangely confused with the forces of good.

I said, suddenly: 'You know, I saw you on Saturday.'

'Yes, I saw you. You were quite right not to show that you knew me.'

'But Uncle Demetrius seemed to know you.'

'Yes, I've met him twice at my sister's.'

'Your sister's?'

'I should say my half-sister's. I think I told you I'm living on her money. I've no scruples in taking it, as she more or less let my mother starve to death at a time when I could do nothing to help.'

'Why couldn't you help?'

'Because . . . no, that's something I can't tell you.'

I thought for a moment, then asked: 'What is your half-sister's name?'

'Her present name is Mrs Desmond-Moffat. She started life, of course, as Linda Waring. My mother was my father's second wife and she and Linda never got on together, though Linda was under three when my father remarried. It was Linda's fault. As soon as she could, she left home and became a governess in a baronet's family.'

'A baronet's?'

'Yes, but only one of those money-baronets. Linda was quite good enough for them in her way. Unfortunately she tried to vamp the son and heir—he was eighteen—and they gave her the sack. She came home for three weeks—my father had died meanwhile—and had a row with my mother and left. Only Linda knows what exactly she did after that, but she reappeared as Mrs Judson, the pretty, young wife of a well-to-do publican. A lot of gay sparks used to go to the bar, and among them a silly young man who'd come into the family fortune much sooner than was good for him—if it's ever good to come into family fortunes—and he was soon so besotted by Linda that he persuaded her to run off with him. I don't suppose she took very much persuading. Judson divorced her. Don't ask me what divorce means. Just wait till you do the reign of Henry the Eighth and see what your master has to tell you about it. However, unlike poor Queen Catherine of Aragon, my sister had a new husband waiting for her—that fool Desmond-Moffat. He gave up all his dull, respectable acquaintances and filled Moffat Grange at week-ends with his London friends, mostly actors and rather shady businessmen, who like him had been involved in divorces. Of course, the County set didn't recognise them, but that wasn't much loss. Then, without any warning, he had a kind of attack. Instead of sending for the doctor, my sister sent for the brandy bottle and he died. At least, that's more or less what came out at the inquest. She inherited everything he had to leave, his money—not much perhaps when judged by the standard of your family, but far more than she'd ever handled—and the estate, which is fairly heavily mortgaged. It went to her head. She was always mad on men. Desmond-Moffat had been a pretty poor specimen—but now—'Tis Pity!'

I echoed, "*'Tis Pity?*'

'That's the title—or part of the title—of a play by a poet called Ford. If you want another quotation, here's one that I might apply to myself:

> '*Lo, with a little rod*
> *I did but touch the honey of romance*
> *And must I lose a soul's inheritance?*'

Oscar Wilde, a later and perhaps a greater poet. I hope you've understood very little of all this?'

I hadn't understood much, but the words '*Tis Pity* and *little rod* stuck in my mind and when I was older I read not only Oscar Wilde's poems but Ford's '*Tis Pity she's a Whore.*

I said priggishly: 'No wonder you don't like your half-sister very much. I wish you'd tell me something about yourself.'

'Linda was the bad girl of the family and I was the good boy—at least to begin with. My father was a bookmaker. He made money and lost it by turns. His first wife, Linda's mother, was a London barmaid. His second, my mother, was quite different. Her father taught at a Board-school. She took after him and in some ways I took after her. When my father had money, I went to a good school. When he lost it, I educated myself by getting scholarships. I went to a university, one of the newer ones, and became a school-master. As I told you last time we met, I had a row at the school and had to leave. They wouldn't give me a reference . . . do you know what that means?'

Even at that age, I knew that the fear of not getting a reference was what made servants work fourteen hours a day. I said: 'Yes.'

'So I've nothing to live on now except Linda. After all, she's spending about two thousand a year entertaining and buying clothes and motor-cars, so I don't see why she should grudge the odd hundred she spends on me. I'm happier on it than she is on what she has. Now she says she's feeling the pinch and is going to put Moffat Grange up for sale. I don't blame her for that. What I do blame her for is . . .'

'What?'

'Being such a . . . but I've told you far too much about my wretched family. Let's talk about you instead.'

'This is the last day of my holidays here.'

'Yes, you told me so. Tomorrow you're going to your aunt at St Albans. Won't you like that?'

'I'm very fond of Auntie Mary, she's my mother's eldest sister. But Auntie Violet will be there with her two babies and her husband. He has my room when I'm not staying there. He'll be sleeping out, but coming in for meals . . .'

'And you don't like him?'

'Oh, he's all right. But he's not like Uncle Demetrius. He's not . . . he's not . . .'

'Do you mean he's not a gentleman?'

'Yes, I suppose I do. But if it wasn't for him, the business—I mean Hemming and Company—my mother's name was Hemming— would have gone bankbroke . . . is that the word?'

'Bankrupt. Is there no Hemming in the business?'

'Only Uncle Giles. He's much worse than Uncle William. He hates me because I'm a Froxwell. They don't like him, you know.'

'I understand.'

We sat back in our chairs. A caressing breeze blew softly over the German Ocean, as the geography books then called the North Sea. The sunlight streaming across the silky water made my eyes moist and the feel of teardrops on my cheekbones for some reason made me want to cry in earnest. I took out a handkerchief and wiped my eyes and murmured: 'I don't want to go away from here. It's all so beautiful.'

He said: 'You know, you might be grown-up to talk like that. That's a compliment. Well, I'm afraid it's very nearly twenty to one.'

'Oh dear, and we haven't done any Stocks and Shares!'

'What, on the last day of the holidays?'

'I don't mind work. It's these awful games I hate.'

'Hockey, cricket and football?'

'Yes, I'm so frightened of them.' There seemed to be nothing I couldn't confess to him, no secret shame, no form of unworthiness.

'Like all things, they'll only bother you for a time. Now we must go. If you're late, they'll ask you all kinds of awkward questions. Will you be here in the summer holidays?'

'Yes, but my cousins Frobisher and Cedric may be with me. They've been in quarantine for whooping-cough these holidays. But if I *can* get away . . .'

'Well, you know where I live. That's something. There's the old witch waiting to tell your fortune. Oh, but we did that last Thursday.'

'Yes, and on Saturday Uncle Demetrius made me try the other machine in Paradise. It said the same thing.'

'What was it? No, I said you must tell that to nobody.'

'Uncle Demetrius took the card and read it. He laughed at it.'

'Yes, he would. Goodbye, goodbye, Francis. It's been nice seeing you.'

He took my hand, squeezed it for a second, then sauntered northward along the road that skirted the harbour, while I made my way slowly uphill to Albert Terrace.

(7)

I was delighted to see Aunt Mary again, but apart from that I didn't really enjoy the last week of my holidays. Palmyra now struck me as a mean little house and, though the food was much better than our usual fare in Albert Terrace, there was a slapdash informality about our meals—with Aunt Mary darting like a servant in and out of the kitchen the whole time—which I thought common. I resented the presence of Aunt Violet and the twins as much as she and Uncle William must have resented mine. He never called me Mr La-di-da, like Uncle Giles, or twitted me on the fit of my silver spoon; sometimes he was embarrassingly servile— 'No, no, my boy, that's *your* chair. We're intruders here'—but we couldn't be comfortable with one another. When I described the luncheon-party with Lady Lucy or repeated one of Aunt Diana's somewhat acid jokes, he looked down his nose. He was fond of saying: 'Well, it takes all sorts to make a world. Of course, *we* in St

Albans . . .' then breaking off, as if he didn't like to tell me point-blank how vastly superior the morals and manners of St Albans were to those of Whitgate. I longed to tell him—and still more, Uncle Giles, who spoilt my birthday by paying us a short, rather shame-faced visit—that in all likelihood I should soon become a baronet and that they both might make a start on calling me Sir. I was also tempted naughtily to remind them that they were already in a sense my pensioners, since, if I had chosen to take a different line with Uncle Demetrius and Uncle Egerton, there might now be no Palmyra for them to come to.

I found myself almost as home-sick for Whitgate as I had been for Palmyra when I spent my first night at my grandfather's in the Christmas holidays. I missed the big rooms, the cases full of leather-bound books, the solemn sounding of gongs at regular hours, Eglinton's stately walk, the two staircases with the maids scurrying from one to the other, the massive furniture, the drawer where I knew the Book of Life was kept, so full of promise for me, my grandfather's impressive pomposity, Aunt Letty's clear, balanced phrases, Aunt Sophy's bursts of mysterious intimacy and Aunt Diana's sophisticated charm. Still more did I miss Uncle Demetrius and, though I would only admit this to myself in my frankest moments, I missed Mr Jimmy most of all. His two dramatic appearances as my deliverer were the most memorable events in my life, just as my two conversations with him on the pier were the most romantic. I shuddered to think how many grim weeks must pass before I had even the hope of seeing him again.

I am afraid Aunt Mary realised my discontent; for, when she was packing up some of my things the night before I was to go back to school, she said: 'I do hope, dear, you haven't been too upset at the house being so full. I know I haven't had time to be with you and take you out as much as I should have liked. But there's so much work to be done, especially now I haven't got Deborah.' (She had parted with one of her two maids so as to economise.) I said nothing and she went on: 'I know it isn't quite the same for you. But we hope it will only be for a time. I think Uncle Giles is really sorry for what he did. He takes Uncle William's advice on everything now and I'm sure he'd like to be friends with us all again. After all, he *is* my brother, and your uncle. You haven't been wishing you were in Whitgate, have you?'

'Well, in some ways, Auntie Mary.'

'Oh, Francis, don't say that! That really hurts me.'

I felt extremely uncomfortable and said: 'I don't mean I don't want to be with you, but I don't like St Albans as much as Whitgate. Couldn't you sell Palmyra, Auntie Mary, so that we could have a home there together?'

'Oh, Francis, don't ask that of me! Don't! I should be wretched.'

'But why?'

'Well, I shouldn't see Auntie Violet or the twins, and then . . . all those Froxwells. They have a way of making me feel so small, as if I was a silly little nursemaid and not really fit to mix with any of them. The Hemmings would have been just as good as they are, if we'd had their advantages.'

'Do you mean even Uncle Giles?'

'Yes, I do. You know, Francis, you might try to be a little nicer to him. He finds your stand-offish manner very upsetting and he's much more sensitive than you might think.'

I rudely put my hands in my pockets and jingled my money. Then I saw that Aunt Mary was in tears. My ungracious mood left me at once, and I began to cry, too, partly because I had made Aunt Mary so sad and partly because I was so soon to leave her and go to school. When she kissed me goodnight, we were firm friends again.

(8)

I cried a little when she put me in the train the next morning and, having a compartment to myself, gave way to intermittent tears throughout the journey. I felt very forlorn. All the discomforts, fears and humiliations of the previous term came back to me with sudden vividness, and for some reason I could no longer summon up the vision of my baronetcy to give me comfort. I was leaving everything and everyone I loved for thirteen weeks of torment.

Uncle Demetrius saw the trace of tears on my face and asked me, when we were settled in the cab on our way to Victoria, where we were to leave my luggage. 'What's the matter, Francis? Are you so worried by the thought of school? Tell me your trouble. You know, you needn't hide anything from me.'

I had never known him so kind and sympathetic. None the less, I didn't feel I could speak to him as freely as I could to Mr Jimmy and hesitated.

'Do they bully you?'

'No.'

'Are you sure?'

'Well, a little perhaps. Before the geography class begins . . .'

'Yes?'

I told him that there was a boy called Potter in my geography class who egged on the others to make me stand up so that they could flick paper pellets at my face with little elastic catapults.

'But why stand up?'

'Oh, they all say I've got to. They say I'm target-practice for the term and if I don't . . .'

'Well, what then?'

'Oh, I don't know what they'd do.'

'Probably nothing.' He paused and said reflectively: 'The first night I spent at a boarding-school—mind you, things were very much rougher in those days—all the new boys were made to strip to their combinations and stand on a table. Then the others threw boots at us. It wasn't nice and it's difficult to know why these things have to be endured. Luckily one of the new boys—not I, I should never have had the courage—caught a boot and threw it back very hard. It had some sort of an iron support along the sole and hit the chief bully on the cheek and cut it open. He didn't bleed to death, unfortunately, but the ghastly business stopped, and next term nobody thought of starting it again.'

He didn't suggest that I should throw anything at Potter, perhaps guessing that, if I tried, my aim would be so bad that I should hit the least offensive person in the room. But he had managed to raise my spirits a little. After all, paper pellets were very mild missiles compared with iron-shod boots.

He changed the subject. 'I had thought of taking you to have luncheon at my club, which is just off Pall Mall. That's not very far from Victoria. But you're of an age when one prefers meringues and *monts blancs* to roast lamb, and I doubt if we could cater for your sweet tooth. Besides, you might be plagued by cheery, red-faced old men coming up and asking what hopes you had of getting your colours at cricket. They might even tell you that your schooldays are the best days of your life, which of course is a lie. So I think we'll try Rumpelmayers in St James's Street.'

I made a big meal and decided that I liked Rumpelmayers even better than Buszards, which seemed by comparison a provincial establishment, suggesting St Albans rather than the West End. My uncle was looking particularly smart that day, with his top-hat, morning-coat, striped trousers, spats, clean grey suède gloves and gold-mounted cane. I had heard vague talk of 'men about town' and supposed that, in his way, my uncle was one of them. I greatly wished I could be one of them, too. Of course, if I became a baronet . . . . As I finished my third pineapple fizz and my uncle sipped his black coffee, I gave myself up to grandiose daydreams.

He looked at his watch and said: 'Your horrid train leaves at half-past two. We've still got nearly three quarters of an hour to fill in. There's quite a good stamp-shop in Victoria Street. Let's walk there and shake our meal down. I suppose, by the way, you still collect stamps?'

'Oh yes, Uncle Demetrius. I've got seven hundred and ninety one, all different, and three of them cost sixpence each.'

'I can see you're thinking on the right lines. Far better have a dozen rarities than a whole album full of rubbish. I hope you pencil in the price, as I suggested?'

'Yes, every time, if the stamp costs a penny or more.'

'I must tell our father that. He'll think you a most creditable Froxwell. Have you got to the stage of having favourite countries yet?'

'Well, I really like British North Borneo best, but a boy at Cedric's school says his father says, who's a very keen collector . . .' I passed on the warning about buying stamps cancelled to order and my uncle seemed greatly impressed. He said: 'I see the salesman will have to look to his laurels this afternoon.'

When we were a short distance from the shop, my uncle gave me five shillings and said: 'Spend this, but no more. You mustn't make inroads on the term's pocket-money.' I promised to do no such thing, took his hand and almost dragged him to the shop-window, where there was a tempting display of packets and sets arranged in beautiful patterns. It was a much bigger and grander stamp-shop than any I had been in before and, when the salesman asked: 'What can I show you, sir?', I hardly knew what to answer. Then suddenly I had a bold idea and said, as calmly as I could: 'I should like to see some stamps of the Cape of Good Hope.'

The salesman raised his eyebrows slightly, took a volume down from the shelf and after giving my uncle a quick look, as if to assure himself that he would be compensated for any damage done by my schoolboy fingers, he turned slowly to the first page and, still keeping a wary eye on me, said with quiet pride: 'We happen to have a very fine stock of this country.'

The first stamp I saw was priced at eighteen shillings, and the next, which looked just like it, at twenty-five. I could hardly believe it and gasped: 'Those prices are *shillings*?' I was about to add: 'Not pennies?', but the salesman anticipated me by saying: 'Oh yes, shillings; not pounds unless specially marked.' My uncle thought it time to intervene: 'I'm afraid these are hardly suited to the schoolboy purse. Have you nothing more modestly priced?'

'Oh yes, sir. If we look at the end of the volume we shall find some priced even as low as one penny. Here we are.'

As soon as I saw them, I protested indignantly: 'But I like the three-cornered ones. These are very plain.'

'They have a beauty for those who can appreciate it, but if you've set your heart on a triangular, I must warn you that the cheapest one, the fourpenny blue, is two and three pence.' He turned back towards the beginning of the book. 'There you are, sir.'

My uncle bent down, looked over my shoulder and said: 'I don't know very much about these things, but to me most of them seem badly cut about. Half the lettering has disappeared from the left side of that one, and as for this . . .' The salesman replied: 'I quite agree with you, sir. That's why the price of those stamps is two and three pence. Had they been in superb condition, it would have been seven and six, or even more.'

My uncle turned to me and explained: 'You see, Francis, it isn't only the rarity of a stamp that gives it its value. Quality also counts. You will find that applies to other things besides stamps. But I'm afraid you are wasting this gentleman's time. What about those French Colonial issues I see over there? They have the merit of being beautiful and the prices are within your means.'

Dahomey, Congo Français, Guyane, Guinée Française, Côte Française des Somalis—the bright pictorials revealed a new world to me. In future when I exhibited my collection, I would say: 'You see, I don't only go in for the *British* Empire; I go in for the *French* Empire, too.' I chose stamp after stamp and my five shillings seemed inexhaustible.

At length, my uncle looked at his watch significantly and said to the salesman, who had become a little restive: 'I'm afraid you're not used to these big purchases.' At the time I took the remark quite seriously and felt I was a notable philatelist.

We reached the station a quarter of an hour before the train was due to start. My uncle suggested we should get my luggage out of the cloak-room and put it at once into the luggage-van, so that we could escape from the boys and parents who would soon be clustering round it. I was only too glad to fall in with his idea; for I had already seen quite a number of horrid little caps (blue quartered with amber) like my own, which I was keeping in my pocket till the very last minute. I have found that at every large reunion the people one sees first are those whom one would have preferred never to see again. Yes, Potter was over there, with two women as badly dressed as my Froxwell aunts, though they hadn't the Froxwell dignity. And there was Betteridge, the spectacled second prefect, with a tall, thin, spectacled man who must be his father. They were talking to Mrs Dykes, the headmaster's wife, who, with her eyes darting this way and that, seemed like a proud hen clucking to her gathering brood. She had probably come up early for a morning's shopping. I pointed her out to my uncle and he said: 'Oh dear, do you think we shall be safe from her by the bookstall? Let's make for it at once.' As we were walking towards it, I noticed that he kept looking at the station clock, and comparing it with his watch.

Then suddenly an apparition bore down on him, tapped him smartly on the shoulder and cried: 'Demetrius!' He looked round; I looked up. She was a scented cloud of smoky pink lace over grey tussore silk, crowned by the biggest Merry Widow hat I had ever seen, a huge cartwheel of grey and rose. It was the lady who had given us the ride in her car. My uncle seemed completely taken aback. He almost gasped: 'You, Linda! We . . . it was fixed for twenty to three!' She produced a roulade of artificial laughter, tossing back her head like a prima donna snatching notes from the air. 'No, Demetrius. I'm quate sure you said twenty past two. You might at least say, "Better early than never!" And this is my young friend who took such an interest in my motor? Your name is Francis, isn't it?' I said defiantly: 'Yes.' She smiled elaborately and asked, 'Don't you know mine?' I said: 'No', and she turned imperiously to my uncle and demanded: 'Demetrius, don't you think it's time you introduced me properly to your nephew?' He pulled a little face and then said good-humouredly: 'Allow me to present my nephew, Francis Froxwell—Mrs Desmond-Moffat.' Still smiling, she answered: 'That's better. I hope, by the way, I'm not interruptin' a passionate farewell? Shall I retire to the ladies' cloakroom?' I longed to say: 'Yes, for goodness sake do!', but my uncle touched her gloved fingers—her grey gloves ran right up to the elbow—and murmured something and at that moment a little group of boys and parents, headed by Mrs Dykes, encircled us.

'Ah, Francis, I thought I saw you by the luggage-van. Is this your uncle?' Before I could answer, she turned to him with an ingratiating smile and said: 'I am Mrs Dykes, the headmaster's wife. I was so sorry not to meet you last term, when you called on my husband.' Then she swung round towards the D.M. and added archly: 'And this lady is an aunt, perhaps?' My uncle raised his hat, bowed gallantly and said: 'No, I'm afraid this lady is not an aunt . . .' To my amazement the D.M. completed his sentence with the words: 'Not an aunt, but a godmother!'

I protested loudly: 'You're not . . .' and then became speech-
less at her effrontery, while even my uncle looked shocked. Quite
undeterred, she produced another roulade and went on: 'At least,
I'm a *fairy* godmother!' There was a general laugh. It seemed to me
that everyone in the station was gazing at her, the men with bold
admiration and the women with a much more critical appraisal.
Whatever they might by instinct divine about her, and however
'County' they might be in their own right, she made them all look
dowdily provincial. It was indeed as if the Merry Widow herself
had stepped down from the stage and had condescended to mingle
miraculously with a mothers' meeting in the pit.

Had I been less involved in what was happening, and had I
been fifteen or twenty years older, I should have enjoyed the scene
enormously. Some women are said to derive a peculiar pleasure
when they see males in gladiatorial combat, and some men, of
whom I regret to say I am one, are equally titillated when they
witness the more subtle, but no less barbaric, social tussles that
so often occur between one woman and another. As it was, I was
much relieved to hear Mrs Dykes, who herself was by now not a
little embarrassed, saying: 'Dear me, we have only four minutes!
Has anyone seen Mr Jury?' (He was the second master and our
official conductor back to school.) Betteridge answered officiously:
'Yes, Mrs Dykes, he was talking to Raikes's parents outside our
carriage. Raikes Minor's nose was bleeding and they had to take
him to the waiting-room.' The parents made sympathetic noises,
while the D.M. looked a little petulant, as if annoyed to think that
the bleeding of a schoolboy's nose could distract attention from
her loveliness.

My uncle, who had kept his self-possession fairly well, though
a frown belied the smile which he forced to his lips, said: 'Well,
Mrs Dykes, perhaps I can hand my charge over to you now? His
luggage is in the van. We Froxwells are not fond of effusive fare-
wells. Goodbye, Francis, and good luck!' We shook hands like
strangers and for manners' sake I turned towards the D.M. though
I was terrified she might want to kiss me (Better a thousand times
a kiss from Mad Bessie in Nelson Backs than from that painted
Jezebel!) But she stretched out a long languid arm, giving me the

tips of her fingers, and said: 'Goodbye, Francis. Perhaps in the summer we'll go for another motor-ride together.' In that moment of tension, though I remembered 'D.M.' and D'mee-Morndenne, too, 'Desmond-Moffat' had gone completely out of my head—and I muttered feebly: 'Goodbye, Mrs ... er ...' Her head swooped down to mine like a snake and she hissed in my ear: 'If you like, you may call me Aunt Linda!' Mrs Dykes, having uttered a comprehensive goodbye, was already waddling along the platform, and I turned round abruptly and followed her.

Two minutes later I was with seven other boys in one of the compartments reserved for the school. The engine whistled, the train pulled itself together and the platform with its waving hands and handkerchiefs began to slide past the window. The summer term had begun.

V. THE SUMMER TERM

(1)

4th May, 1910.   Mapp's Club,
                                                    St James's, S.W.

My dear Francis,

I'm sorry our leave-taking was so bustled yesterday, but perhaps
it was as well. Such moments are always trying. I hope you are
beginning to settle down and find yourself among companions
you are able to like. Always remember that most people, especially
the little tin-pot heroes of the hour, are as a rule quite unimpor-
tant.

Now I want you to give me a promise. We have already one or
two secrets between us and I should like what happened yesterday
to be another. I had promised to take Mrs Desmond-Moffat to see
the tennis at Roehampton. Unfortunately, there was a misunderstanding about the time and she appeared twenty minutes too
soon. For reasons I prefer not to give you, I don't want you to
mention this meeting to anyone at all, either by letter or by word
when you are with us once more. I feel I can trust you in this,
because I think you are fond of me.

As soon as you have read this letter, tear it into very small pieces
and destroy them. *Don't* keep it in your pocket. You might lose
it, or worse, the matron might find it there overnight and read it.
Matrons always read letters they find in schoolboys' pockets. This
trick of theirs nearly led to a boy being expelled, when I was at
school. So be warned!

Send me a line to let me know you've got this, but don't refer to
what I have said. I rely on you, Francis.

                          Your affectionate Uncle, Demetrius.

I read my uncle's letter so many times that, when I came to destroy it, I knew it by heart. I was grieved to think that our outing in London together was for him only the prelude to another outing of such a different kind. It seemed to me that there had been a sort of treachery in his planning, and the thought of it soon took my mind back to the disappointing visit he had paid me the previous half-term. So far as I was concerned, its purpose had been to acquaint me with Aunt Mary's trouble. But remembering the green car I had seen in the Grand Hotel drive, I was now convinced that I had been quite right in thinking that it was the D.M.'s. No doubt they had driven down in it to Eastbourne, and he was to rejoin his lady-friend as soon as he could get rid of me at the school-gates.

O false white angel! When I wrote my reply, I found it hard to keep my bitterness out of it.

5th May, 1910.   Winton House School,
                                      Eastbourne, Sussex.

My dear Uncle Demetrius,

Thank you very much for your letter. I have done what you said and give you my promise. Thank you very much for the lovely lunch and the stamps. I have been moved up in Latin and French and Maths and somebody I told you about has been moved up in geography but I am not, so I don't have him in my class and it's quite nice now. I wish we played tennis here, not cricket. I must stop now, as we have to change for 'nets'.

                          Your loving Nephew, Francis.

(2)

The next news that came to me from the outside world was of the sudden death of King Edward the Seventh on the sixth of May. All the boys were told to wear black ties. The masters wore black armlets as well and their wives and other ladies attached to the school vied with one another in the depth of their mourning. One or two of the boys were already talking of the coronation of

George the Fifth and the holiday which the event might bring—at least a whole day, and with luck even a week—but we were all greatly moved by what had happened and for about forty-eight hours behaved as if we were in church. I am quite sure, however, that nobody felt the shock as keenly as I did.

8th May, 1910.   Winton House School,
                                                  Eastbourne, Sussex.
My dear Aunt Sophy,

Of course you have heard the very dreadful news about the King. Do you think there is *any* hope that the *new* one will come to Whitgate in September to open the promenade? Or is it all off? Do tell me. You know what I mean. This is a *very dreadful* disappointment to *me*! I hope you are well.

Your loving Nephew, Francis.

10 May 1910.   6, Albert Terrace,
                                                  Whitgate, Kent.
My dear Francis,

I am not surprised you are much distressed, as indeed we all are, by the late King's death, though I was more prepared for it than most people. I went to see Uncle Egerton early last week and found him alone. We had a séance together and the P........ predicted what has happened. It really did write the words, 'Long live the King', which is what they cry when a new king comes to the throne. No, I am afraid there is no chance at all that he will come to Whitgate in September. But they are talking now of making some gardens, to be called the King Edward VII Memorial Gardens, all along the new promenade, which means that they will need *all* our father's land in that part. Remember that a coronation is a great time for the giving of honours. So you must be patient till next summer, as indeed the P........ warned you. I hope you have not forgotten its message.

I thought Uncle Egerton was very much better, when I saw him. The rest of us are as usual. I hope you are happy and working hard.

Your affectionate Aunt, Sophy.

(3)

11th May, 1910.   Palmyra,
                                              Throngley Avenue,
                                              Oatingford Park,
                                              Nr. St Albans.

Darling Francis,

Since I wrote to you last, we have had a terrible time. (No, I don't mean the death of the poor King, though of course it did come as a great shock.) Sweet little Rose had violent stomach-pains and the doctor thought it might be appendicitis and said she must go to a nursing-home. Auntie Violet was almost distracted, as you can imagine. Uncle Giles has been very kind about it all and offered to lend Uncle William fifty pounds to pay for the operation, if it had got to be, but luckily it turned out to be an ordinary stomach-upset, though a very bad one, and Auntie Violet is going to bring Rose home tomorrow. I do hope you are happy. A week of the term is already gone. Perhaps I shall be able to come and see you at mid-term.

Yes, I have heard Rumpelmayers is a wonderful place. I have never been there. I suppose it is very expensive. You must try not to let your head get too full of grand ideas. If you do, you will only store up disappointments for yourself. There is so much more in life than going to smart restaurants and mixing with titled people.

We are all so very thankful about Rose and pray she will never have another attack like that.

                              Your loving Auntie Mary.

May 11th, 1910.   6, Albert Terrace,
                                           Whitgate, Kent.

My dear Francis,

I had a letter from Uncle Demetrius yesterday, saying he saw you off safely to school and that you showed, as he put it, a fair equanimity during the ordeal. Since you left us, this house has seemed elderly and colourless. I think of you when I pass the toyshop with the signal-gantry in the window. But I gather stamps have put model railways out of your mind.

We have seen Lady Lucy three times since she came to luncheon when you were with us, and her mother twice. Uncle Demetrius has been busy in London, but we are expecting him on Saturday for two nights. Both Frobisher and Cedric are back at school, hard at work, I hope, though I think that unlikely in Cedric's case. Your cousin Lavinia, who is now in her last term before she goes to a finishing-school in Paris, has been given the part of Lady Sneerwell in Sheridan's play *The School for Scandal*, which they are performing at the end of term. They were all terrified (especially Lavinia, who thinks herself a second Ellen Terry) that they might have to abandon the idea owing to the King's death. However, it has been decided that this is unnecessary.

I am glad to say our father is keeping well, as we all are, except poor Uncle Egerton, who tires easily. I send you twelve penny stamps and hope you will spare one of them to send me a line.

Your affectionate Aunt, Diana.

The same post brought me a third letter, which pleased me more than either of the other two.

11th May, 1910.   9, Royal Terrace,
                                                  Whitgate, Kent.
Dear Francis,

Just a line to say I hope you haven't forgotten your promise to tell me how you are getting on. I hope you are happy and are making a great many runs and will win all the prizes. I am sure you will. Your aunts are all well. They took my mother and me for a lovely drive yesterday to South Whitgate Sands. We passed some of your grandfather's land, where they say they are going to build a new promenade. We are still having lovely weather here. I expect you are, too.

Your sincere friend, Lucy MacQuiggin.

When the hour for writing letters came round on Sunday, my answer to Lady Lucy took precedence over all the rest of my correspondence. I had bought a postcard with a picture of the school buildings on the back—it was a large and hideous late-Victorian house with excrescences added—and wrote in my neatest hand:

'Dear Lady Lucy, this is our school. Thank you very much for your letter. I hope you are well. I hope the Countess is, too. Your sincere friend, Francis Froxwell.'

Morton Major, the third prefect—the only boy in the school for whom I had developed a faint *schwärmerei*—was on duty that week, to see that all the letters were legibly addressed and properly stamped. Some of the less responsible boys had a way of leaving their envelopes unstamped or putting the stamp facetiously in the middle, a practice which Mr Dykes rightly frowned upon. Morton took my card and, under cover of scrutinising it, read my message, as, I must admit, I had hoped he would. That afternoon as we were preparing to go for our walk up Beachy Head, he came up to me with an elaborate casualness that didn't deceive me and said: 'Oh, I say, Froxwell, my mater was asking me, was that lady who saw you off at Victoria Lady Lucy MacQuiggin?' This of course was a bit of a lie. His mother had probably said: 'I wonder who that smart, over-dressed lady is with the tall gentleman and the very small boy. I'm sure she's a well-known actress, but I can't place her'. I replied simply, 'No, *that* wasn't Lady Lucy.' 'Oh?' He seemed to ask for more and I gave it him. 'She's very much richer than Lady Lucy is. She has a motor-car and drives it herself. But I know Lady Lucy much better than her and I like her much better, too. She and her mother are great friends with my aunts.' He said: 'Oh, I see,' gave me a pleasant smile and went to his place in the procession.

(4)

22nd May, 1910.   The Vicarage,
                                                              Broadforsters,
                                                        Nr. Whitgate, Kent.
Dear Francis,
    Thank you for that post-card of your school. I hear you sent one

to Lady Lucy, too. I must say it doesn't look much, but then ours doesn't, either—not like Marlborough where I'm to go next term if I can pass the entrance-exam. I'm working hard for it, but I'm keen to get into our first eleven too. If I do well in the match next Saturday I may stand a chance. This will be your first cricket-term. I don't expect you are much good at it or like it much.

It was bad luck I was in quarranteen for whoaping-cough all the Easter hols, and of course it didn't keep me from going back to school to the minute—or Frobby either. It's a pity about the King, isn't it? No fireworks on the peer, but we'll make up for it next year and probably have a week off for the coronation.

Oh, about Lady Lucy. I had tea at Albert Terrace last Sunday and Lavinia was there. She had been to lunch there too, though I wasn't invited till tea, and Lady Lucy was at lunch but not at tea. Well, Lavinia went up to the drawing-room about three to say something to Aunt Letty, but she wasn't there but Lady Lucy *was* and she was blubbing to herself on the sofa. I expect she thought Uncle Demetrius would be there and pop the question, but he sent a telegram on the Saturday saying he couldn't leave London. I told Mummy and Daddy and Daddy said, 'Lavinia is a silly stage-struck gossip' and went to his study but Mummy looked very worried. Millicent says she heard Daddy say to Mummy that the doctor says Uncle Egerton is really very ill. I bet that's something Lavinia doesn't know!

I don't know if I want this term to be over or not. Being one of the senior boys and hoping to get into the first eleven I'm quite enjoying it and of course it will be a bit of a jump in the dark going to Marlborough, specially not having been to a boarding-school like you. Daddy said in his last sermon 'The soul is never allowed to sit down for very long', which I think is a very clever and true saying. No doubt you are wishing that *your* term was over.

Your affec. Coz. Ceddy.

How right Cedric was! It is true that in some ways this term was an improvement on the last. My fingers were no longer covered with chilblains, the morning cold-shower was less of a penance, there were now three boys in the school who were my juniors and thanks to Potter's promotion I had ceased to be the target for paper missiles in my geography class. Indeed I now found Potter almost likeable. But two new bugbears had reared their hideous heads. One was our weekly visit to a swimming-bath in the town, and the other—far worse, since in some form or other it spoilt every single day of the week except Sunday—was cricket. In the childish version of the game which I played before, we always used a soft or semi-soft ball and I had no conception of the horrible hardness of the real thing.

As early as the second day of term, the games-master brought in two boxes of new balls and suggested that we might each like to buy one. There were two prices, six-and-six, and four-and-six, and we were told that payment could be made by a deduction from the term's pocket-money. The older boys, and also some of the younger ones who fancied themselves at the game, bought six-and-sixpenny ones. I could hardly bear the thought of spending any money at all on such a revolting object, but, as not a single boy had declined the offer, I felt bound to say I'd have a four-and-sixpenny one. The master tossed it to me and, instead of catching it, I let it drop on my toe. This caused no little amusement and my hatred of the shiny red sphere increased. Even when it was not in use, it bulged my pocket and chafed my thigh. It was like being compelled to carry about an instrument of torture to be used on oneself.

My feeling for cricket soon became so pathological that the mere sight of any of its trappings—balls, bails, wickets, bats, pads, batting-gloves, even scoring-books—made me almost hysterical. My performance at the game was so abjectly bad that I soon ceased to be a subject for ridicule. Perhaps this was because I was too frightened to funk. When the ball approached me, a kind of fatalism impelled me to put some part of my body in its way. I soon had bruises all over my legs and some on my arms; my palms and fingers were blistered. I regarded 'nets', fielding-practice and the matches we played on the two weekly half-holidays with equal horror. Nothing mattered except to get through those awful hours. I would joyfully have learnt long columns of the principal parts of Latin verbs or extracted square-roots from numbers of ten digits, if by so doing I could have been excused the daily ordeal.

On Thursday the twenty-sixth of May—a date which I shall always remember, since its remoter consequences were to give a big twist to my whole life—about ten of the younger boys including me were ordered to turn out for fielding-practice when afternoon school was over. This meant that we had to stand in a circle round one of the seniors who hit the ball towards us in rotation, with the intention that we should either catch it or stop it somehow or other. The spectacled second prefect, Betteridge, was in charge that day. To do him justice, he made full allowances for my known feebleness at the game and, when my turn came, he sent me so gentle and easy a catch that a normal child of three could have taken it. I missed it, of course, but stopped the ball with my chest and threw it back in almost the right direction. One round was over, and I sighed with relief, praying that I should get off as lightly next time. The boy on my right, whose turn came after mine, was a player of promise, though a trifle swanky about it. Betteridge said: 'Now, Symonds, you're much too near. Go farther into the deep and I'll give you one that'll really take some fielding.' However, Betteridge, who wasn't himself a very grand cricketer, miscalculated his shot and sliced the ball straight at me. He shouted 'Duck!'—that is the last thing I really remember about the whole episode—but I must have been in such a blind panic that instead of doing as I was told I thrust my head forward as if I were heading a football. It struck me full on the forehead. When I came round, I was in the school sanatorium.

I think the school doctor thought I was shamming. Perhaps in a sense I was, though not deliberately. He diagnosed a case of mild concussion—luckily Betteridge hadn't managed to hit the ball nearly as hard as he had intended—and prescribed a week's rest. The bruise on my forehead took a normal course and I had a few unpleasant headaches, but they were trifling compared with a feeling of utter helplessness and despair which turned my waking life into a nightmare. I had nightmares, too, when I slept, and would wake up screaming.

Uncle Demetrius and Aunt Mary came to see me, but I was as apathetic with them as if they were strangers. At their instance I had some visits from a neurologist, who talked a good deal about 'nerves'. In those days the psychology of shock was in an elementary stage. A fortnight after my accident, though the bruise had vanished and my headaches had almost ceased to trouble me, I was still quite unfit to go back to school, and it was decided that I should spend the rest of the term convalescing at Whitgate.

My school-books were packed, in case I cared to make use of them, but the neurologist had decreed that I mustn't be pressed. It would be a good thing, he said, if I could find some gentle hobby which would take me into the fresh air. How about collecting butterflies or wild flowers, or sketching? I told him languidly that I would try sketching.

VI. CONVALESCENCE AND CURE

(1)

I TRAVELLED up to London with the Matron, who was going there for a few hours' shopping, and from London to Whitgate with Aunt Diana who had come up with the same purpose. Aunt Mary, who was to have met me *en route*, had written to say that she couldn't leave St Albans, as my baby cousin Rose was ill again.

I dreaded the meeting with my grandfather—though I seemed to have lost my capacity for pleasure, I was still only too able to feel afraid—but his welcome couldn't have been kinder. Instead of telling me that no normal boy would have had my accident, and threatening me with a beating from Eglinton if I didn't try to pull myself together, he merely said: 'They tell me you're a good worker, my boy. This rest will do you no harm. Make the most of it and of our fine Whitgate air. The climate of Eastbourne . . . aha! . . . is liverish and relaxing compared with ours. We are all glad to see you.' Even Aunt Letty unbent so far as to ask me if I fancied anything special to eat.

After three or four days I began to feel more myself and school seemed infinitely far away. In any case, I had been promised that I need never play cricket again. The distant prospect of football was less frightening. For one thing, the game was very much shorter than cricket, and for another—as Uncle Augustus surprisingly observed—with a little skill one can very often get through a whole match without any contact whatsoever with the ball. 'You simply notice which way it's likely to come and make for the opposite direction as fast as you can. You can always say you made an error of judgement.' He had been the least athletic of my Froxwell uncles.

I had hardly been at Albert Terrace a week, when Uncle Egerton, disregarding his doctor's advice, went to the golf-links, did the sixth hole in two, collapsed and died in that moment of triumph on the green. The shock roused me a little from my numbness and I asked if I could go to the funeral, but it was held that my spirits were not yet robust enough to be harrowed in this way.

I had no sense of personal loss—Uncle Egerton had been my least favourite uncle on the Froxwell side—nor I think had Aunt Diana or Uncle Demetrius. The latter came down from London for the funeral and I had a short walk with him before he went back. His mood was gloomy rather than sad. He said: 'Sometimes I think our father will outlive us all. It's rather dreadful to think he has already survived half his sons—your father, Beresford and now poor Egerton. By the way, Egerton's firm will still look after your father's trust, unless your Aunt Mary has any objection, which isn't likely. A new trustee will have to be appointed, of course. You could have Ledward, who was Uncle Egerton's partner. Or would you prefer some member of the family—say Aunt Diana?'

I asked: 'Couldn't you become my trustee, Uncle Demetrius? I'm sure Auntie Mary would prefer you to Mr Ledward, or Aunt Diana. And I should like it, you know.' He replied: 'There's no fun in being a trustee. You get all the kicks and none of the ha'pence. Still, I suppose, from your point of view, I'm the obvious person. I must warn you that at present I'm not in very high favour with our father, who will have to be consulted. He would choose Augustus or any of the aunts rather than me. Still, if you think Aunt Mary will back you up, he might just manage to put up with me. . . . There's my cab. I'll soon be coming down to see you again.'

Aunt Sophy made the biggest parade of grief and perhaps really was the most afflicted of the family. However, she was not without consolations. She declared that she was in constant communication with Uncle Egerton 'beyond the veil' and even boasted that he appeared to her in person at odd moments and in odd places. She spoke with such conviction that I might have been thoroughly scared, had it not been for Aunt Diana, whose scepticism sometimes provoked her to open ribaldry. One day she went so far as to say 'I hope Uncle Egerton has reminded Aunt Sophy that there isn't any toilet-paper in the bathroom. You know, he told her yesterday that it was time she had her shoes repaired.'

Aunt Letty was full of the plight of Uncle Egerton's widow, Aunt Lorna, and the three children whose income was bound to shrink. Could they afford to go on living in their large house in Bardon Road? Surely the promised year at a finishing-school in Paris was out of the question now for Lavinia? It would be very wrong of them to expect any special help from 'our father', though, of course, it was only right that Aunt Lorna's father, who had quite a fat Book of Life, should come to their rescue, since Lorna was his only child.

I myself felt no small curiosity as to what had happened to Uncle Egerton's page in our Book of Life, and one afternoon when the coast was clear I took it out of the drawer in the library to see if, by any happy chance, the securities earmarked for him had been distributed among the rest of us, as Uncle Beresford's had been. But the only change I noticed was that at the top of the page 'Egerton Froxwell' had been altered to 'The Late Egerton Froxwell's Trustees'. It hadn't dawned on me that Uncle Egerton's three children had in every way as much claim to their father's share as I had to my father's.

I had now recovered sufficiently to take an intermittent interest in my baronetcy, especially after Aunt Sophy had stimulated me by saying that Uncle Egerton's spirit had assured her that the family would receive a great distinction the following year. Cedric came to tea a day or two later and, though I still felt bound to keep the pledge of secrecy I had given Aunt Sophy, I thought it no breach of faith to state a case to him in general terms. I asked: 'Supposing Granddaddy should get a title of some sort that he could hand down, do you know who would get it after him?' He replied at once: 'My father would now Uncle Egerton's dead. Then Frobby; then I should get it.' Taking care not to reveal my greater knowledge, I said: 'But what about Frobby's children?' 'Frobby? Oh, if he's going to become a missionary, he'll be eaten long before he has any. Besides, in any case, he's the kind of person, like you, who won't have children.' 'How do you know?' 'Oh, you can generally tell.' Then he added: 'Of course, doctors always know.' I asked: 'Do

you think Uncle Demetrius will have any children if he marries?'
He considered the matter and answered: 'I should say, no.'

That evening, when I was alone with Aunt Diana, I said: 'Aunt
Diana, is it really true that a doctor can tell if you're going to have
any children?' She exclaimed: 'What a very extraordinary question! Yes, I suppose in a way he can.' I asked: 'How *does* he tell,
Aunt Diana?' She repressed a smile and said gravely: 'I'm not quite
sure, but I imagine he'd ask you to put out your . . . tongue!'

(2)

By the last week in June I should have been quite well enough to
go back to school, except that my nights were still full of alarms.
However courageous and carefree I felt by day, when I went to
bed my spirits sank at once. In spite of the summer weather, my
bedroom seemed as chilling and unfriendly as it had seemed on my
first night in Albert Terrace. I began to imagine that it was haunted,
not only by those evil forces of which Aunt Sophy talked from
time to time, but by the ghosts of human beings. I had somehow
gathered that Uncle Beresford had died in my room and, when one
evening I pumped Aunt Letty on the subject, her evasiveness con-
firmed my worst fears. I was now sure that the moment I blew out
my candle, a spectre would stand by the foot of my bed and stare
at me with sulphurous eyes. I lay on my side watching the precious
flame till there was only half an inch of candle left. I knew that at
all costs I must hoard the meagre remains in case of emergency,
but it took all my courage to plunge the grim room into darkness.

I shut my eyes as tightly as I could, but this only increased the
alertness of my ears, which began to hear strange rustlings and
faint moans approaching me through the open window. During
the hour which followed, I would have given anything for the
rough-and-tumble companionship of my dormitory at school.

My sleep that night was a long series of dreams, full of vague
frustrations. There was something I had lost and had to find, but
I kept finding things I wasn't looking for—a human finger in Aunt
Letty's workbox, three shoes, all of them fitting a left foot and

hanging on hooks in the cloak-room among the coats, the Book of Life in a waste-paper basket (When I opened it, I found a picture postcard of my school pasted over every page.) My hands were bleeding, but I couldn't find a towel or handkerchief with which to wipe away the blood. I had been bitten by the vampire-bat which lived in the penny-in-the-slot machine by the pier. The witch, who was a cannibal, had eaten Frobisher and was stirring the cauldron in readiness for me. Suddenly, Mr Jimmy was by my side; he was coal-black like a nigger and his whole body was covered with black hair. He looked very sad and asked: 'Why have you been keeping away from me for so long? I rescued you twice. Don't you know I can rescue you a third time? Don't you trust me now?' I said: 'Yes, but do you belong to the forces of evil?' He answered, 'The white angels have been telling lies about me. They are often jealous hypocrites. The black angels are just as good as they are. Come with me.' He took my hand and we both rose slowly into the air and glided up through the smoke of the witch's cauldron into the sunlit sky at the end of the pier. I had a sensation of inde-scribable ecstasy, such as even in dreams I had never had before. I asked: 'Are you taking me to Heaven?' He said: 'No. Heaven is Hell seen through Alice's looking glass. I shall take you to a place you've never heard of.' Then for ten years we moved backwards and forwards among the clouds.

The clock on the church in Ramsden Square struck six and I awoke. My bedroom curtains had a silver edge which narrowed and broadened as they stirred in the breeze. They suggested to me the sails of a pleasure-boat moving languidly through calm waters. I felt well and strong.

Aunt Diana and I were the first in the dining-room. She said: 'You look very bright this morning, Francis. It's a pleasure to see you as you used to be. Have you had a nice letter from somebody?' She looked at an envelope I was holding in my hand and probably saw that it was from Uncle Demetrius. I replied: 'Well, no, it isn't very nice really . . . but it wasn't the letter that . . .' Just then Aunt Letty came into the room with Aunt Sophy. I put the envelope hurriedly into my pocket and Aunt Diana gave me a quick nod of understanding as I went to greet them.

When we were alone again after breakfast, she said: 'I don't want to pry into your secrets, but was that letter from Uncle Demetrius? It's nearly a fortnight now since any of us have had a line from him. He hasn't been ill, has he?'

'No, he doesn't say so. I don't think he would mind if I showed you his letter. Here it is.'

30th June, 1910.   Mapp's Club,
                                              St James's, S.W.

My dear Francis,

This is about the trusteeship of your estate. I have heard both from Aunt Mary and our father. Aunt Mary, at my sugges-tion, wrote to him saying she would be glad to have me as her co-trustee. Our father replied to her that he thought Mr Ledward —you remember, he was Uncle Egerton's partner and is now head of the firm—a much more suitable person. His letter to me was short but not at all sweet. He said that, until I gave evidence of greater stability and showed more awareness of my duties to the family, he preferred that I should not be associated with any trust to which he had contributed. So that's that. For obvious reasons I can't advise you to go against his wishes. Besides, he may be quite right. I should probably lose all the Trust accounts—even your Book of Life. I have nothing against Ledward, except that he's an insufferable bore.

I shall try to come down and spend a day with you in about a week's time. But I shan't spend the night in Albert Terrace.

                               Your affectionate Black Sheep,
                                         Demetrius Froxwell.

Aunt Diana gave the letter back to me sadly, and said: 'Oh dear, oh dear, are things as bad as all that? You were quite right, Francis, not to show the letter to anyone but me. Oh, it's a thousand, thou-sand pities . . .'

I asked: 'What is?'

'That he ever met this . . . I oughtn't to talk to you about it at all, but somehow I feel you know quite a lot already. Do you remember, you asked the other day when Lady Lucy was coming to luncheon again, and Aunt Letty put you off rather huffily? You see, Lady Lucy is very much in love with Uncle Demetrius. He's a fine man and some day he'll be well off. And after all, though the Froxwells don't claim to be County, they do claim to belong to the *haute bourgeoisie*. You don't understand what that means? Well, it means they are people of substance and education, and have been for three or four generations, which is a good deal more than can be said for some of the County, even though they think themselves the salt of the earth. I believe I've told you all this before, but I *haven't* told you . . . and perhaps I shouldn't . . .'

She looked at me as if she sought encouragement. I said: 'You mean, he's fallen in love with someone else?'

She nodded sadly. 'Yes. He's simply besotted with an adventuress. She's in London now. That's why *he* stays in London. He hasn't quite the pluck to propose to her, because he knows that if he did, our father would strike his name out of the Book of Life at once, and he doesn't want to be poor, any more than the rest of us do. But meanwhile . . . I keep forgetting you're only ten years old and there are things I shouldn't even hint to you . . .'

She paused again, and I asked boldly: 'Is the D.M. in love with Uncle Demetrius?'

Aunt Diana blushed deeply and said: 'I've got into much deeper waters than I meant to. But I may as well go on, since you've guessed so much. The D.M. likes handsome men. And, Heaven knows, Uncle Demetrius is handsome enough for her. Besides, if she became a Froxwell, she'd have a position that her scrubby husband—I mean, her second one, Desmond-Moffat—could never give her in spite of all his County connections. But the position of *our* family would be most dismally changed. Oh, silly, silly, silly Demetrius! Of all my brothers—after your father, Francis—he's the one I love best.'

There were tears in her eyes and she wiped them away carelessly, as if my seeing them didn't matter now, any more that it mattered how much I knew or understood. But there was one point I had to get quite clear, even at the risk of betraying Aunt Sophy. I asked: 'Do you mean there'd be no chance of Granddaddy ever being made a baronet if Uncle Demetrius married the D.M.?'

She answered: 'Oh, I wasn't thinking of baronetcies, though most certainly there'd be no possible chance of that. Imagine introducing her to our friends, "Our sister-in-law, the ex-barmaid!" Besides, she'd soon kill Uncle Demetrius when the next man came along, as she killed Desmond-Moffat. There's nothing I wouldn't do to bring him back to sanity. To throw himself away, with all his gifts and his charm and his expectations—it can't be real love, it's too nonsensical.'

We looked at one another. For a few moments she seemed on the verge of breaking down, then she pulled herself together and said with a smile: 'Francis, I've been making a fool of myself this morning. Please try to forget every single thing I've said, or, if you can't, at least don't speak about it to anybody. You're the kind of person in whom people will always be tempted to confide. Poor things—never let them down. You never know how desperate they may be feeling. Well, it's another glorious morning. What are you going to do?'

'I shall go and sit on the pier and do some sketching.'

'Yes, that'll do you good, though somehow now you don't look as if you needed doing good to. You're so full of life again; it's like a miracle. I promised Aunt Lorna I'd go and help her to sort out Uncle Egerton's clothes. He had one or two suits that might do for Frobisher. Aunt Letty was for selling all his wardrobe, but Aunt Lorna doesn't fancy the idea. Have a nice time.'

For a moment I thought she was going to give me a kiss—no Froxwell aunt had ever kissed me in the morning—but she didn't and walked out of the library with a sprightliness that I am sure she didn't feel.

(3)

I went up to my bedroom for my sketch-book, box of crayons and two school-books, and then crept downstairs, praying that neither Aunt Letty nor Aunt Sophy would intercept me. When I reached the front door, I ran almost the whole length of Albert Terrace before slowing down to my ordinary pace. At the beginning of Harbour Road I hesitated, then turned to the left along a road parallel to Thanet Street, and thence, at its lower end, into the maze of streets behind the harbour. That morning I had no need to play at 'Ghosts' to keep guilty thoughts at bay, and if I had met Mad Bessie in Nelson Backs, I should have the courage to say: 'Go away, you nasty old woman!'

I found North Place without much difficulty and knocked on the door of Number Eight. To my great relief, Mrs Fowler opened it. I asked: 'Is Mr Jimmy still living here?' She said, 'Mr Jimmy? Oh, you mean Mr Waring, and you're the young gentleman he brought here about three months ago to have a wash. I remember, of course. Yes, he's in his room. That door, there.'

She led me through the kitchen and banged on the door. 'A young visitor to see you, Mr Waring.' His voice from inside said: 'Oh, just a minute', but she had already opened the door, revealing Mr Jimmy who was sitting on his bed stripped to the waist, swarthy, but less black than he had appeared in my dream. She exclaimed: 'Oh, I beg your pardon, I'm sure! This young gentleman was asking for you.'

He came forward, holding his trousers up with one hand, and said: 'Francis, of all miracles, it's you. I dreamt about you last night. But why aren't you at school?'

There were so many questions to be asked and answered that I can't remember their order. He told me that he'd been painting the shed in the back yard and his shirt-sleeve had slid down into the paint-pot. He was trying to get the stain out with turpentine. The paint had got on to his trousers, too. 'Go outside for five minutes and make sweet conversation with Mrs Fowler and I'll be with you.' She asked me to sit down two or three times and did her best to make me talk to her, but I wandered restlessly round the kitchen with one eye firmly fixed on Mr Jimmy's door. When he came out he was wearing a clean cricket-shirt and a pair of light grey flannel trousers.

As we walked down to the harbour, he asked me again why I wasn't at school. I told him about my accident at cricket, though I found it hard to describe my subsequent illness. He said: 'Do you mean to say you've been here a whole month, without trying to get in touch with me?' I told him I hadn't felt well enough and then mentioned my dream of the previous night, in which he seemed interested. I asked him what he had dreamt about me, but he said all he could remember of it was that I was drowning and calling for help. 'Did you save me?' I asked, but he said he couldn't be sure, as he woke too soon. When we reached the turnstile, I said: 'I've been given sixpence a week specially to spend on the pier, but somehow I never felt I could go there till today. I want to pay for both of us; please let me. It might bring us good luck.' He replied: 'If you put it that way, I can't refuse.'

We sauntered slowly up and down the pier and then settled in two chairs facing north. He noticed the books I had been carrying and asked what they were. I said: 'Oh, one's a French grammar, one's a Latin grammar—I've got as far as the rhymes about the prepositions—and that's my sketch-book. I told one of my aunts I was going to do some sketching by the harbour and I shall have to do something, in case she asks to see it, but it won't take me long. When I come down here another time, I'll do the sketches beforehand to save time.'

He asked me if I wanted to be an artist and I answered: 'No, not really.' Then he said: 'Anyway it's a splendid excuse for your coming here as often as you want to. I suppose you'll be staying in Whitgate till the middle of September. But what about all those cousins of yours? Won't they be here as soon as the summer holidays begin?' I told him that Uncle Augustus was to have a fishing holiday in Scotland during the first three weeks of August, and would be taking Frobisher and Cedric with him as soon as their schools broke up. They were the only cousins who might have interfered with my movements. Uncle Seymour was bringing his two children over from France, but they were too young for me to play with. As for Uncle Egerton's daughters—well, after all they were girls and I shouldn't be expected to go about with them. I added truthfully: 'Not that Lavinia or Esmeralda would want me. They think themselves young ladies and Lavinia wants to be presented at court when she comes out. But of course, that won't be till she has been to her finishing-school in Paris, *if* there's enough money to send her there. Did you hear about my Uncle Egerton dying?'

'Yes, it made quite a stir, even down here by the harbour.'

I continued: 'He was my guardian, you know . . . no, not my guardian, I mean my trustee. Aunt Mary's my guardian and my other trustee as well. I've got to have another trustee now, instead of Uncle Egerton. I hoped Uncle Demetrius could be it, but Granddaddy thinks Mr Ledward, who was Uncle Egerton's partner, would be better. Do you know Mr Ledward?'

'Yes, I do, . . . slightly.'

His face had hardened and there was a grimness in his voice.

I asked: 'Do you like him?'

'No. I should have thought your Uncle Demetrius was much more suitable. He's the only one of your uncles, isn't he, who's ever really bothered about you and it's obvious that he's really fond of you. Are you fond of him?'

'Yes, I'm more fond of him than . . .'—I was going to say, 'than anyone in the world', but there was a curious challenge in Mr Jimmy's eyes which made me leave the sentence unfinished. Besides, I now knew very well that I was no longer as devoted to my White Angel as I was to my Black one.

After a pause, he said: 'Don't you think you ought to get your sketching done, instead of leaving it to the very last minute?'

'Oh, I can't settle down to it just now. Tell me, is it true your sister's putting Moffat Grange up for sale?'

'More than that, she's sold it. The new people take over on September quarter-day. I'm supposed to be keeping an eye on the place till then and doing some of the dirty work for her—I mean getting the things she wants to keep packed and arranging to sell the rest of the stuff and so on. She's raised my wages to five pounds a week, for the time being. So you see, I'm very rich. I could have afforded to pay for the pier today.'

I suddenly had a completely new idea and asked him: 'If the D.M.—I mean your sister—died, who would get her Book of Life?'

'Her what?'

'Her Book of Life. Isn't that what people call the book where their stocks and shares are all written down?'

'Oh, I remember. You brought out that phrase the first time we met. So the Froxwells' idea of a Book of Life is what most

people call an investment-book. Well, it's not a bad name for it. I
haven't really thought about what you've just asked me . . . well,
I have, just a little from time to time, but I try not to. I suppose, if
she died without leaving a Will, what she has would come to me.
But of course, if she leaves a Will, her money may go to anyone,
your Uncle Demetrius, perhaps, or even that bounder—Captain
Goodrow, I think he calls himself—who taught her to drive her
car. By the way, I suppose you know she isn't really rich? I told you
that, didn't I?'

'But when she's sold Moffat Grange, she'll have all the money.'

'That won't be much, when the mortgages are paid off.'

I didn't know what mortgages were, except that Lady Lucy's
brother had a great many and wished he hadn't, but I resisted the
temptation to ask about them and stuck to my point.

'Do you think she *has* made a Will?'

'No, frankly I don't.'

'So, at any rate, you'd get something if she died?'

He shook his head and said: 'My dear Francis, I'm quite convinced that kind of windfall will never come my way.'

'Granddaddy lets *us* all know what we shall get when he dies, if
we do as he wants.'

'If you do as he wants . . . do you think you'll always do that?'

'I don't really see why I shouldn't.'

'But suppose . . . no. I'm going to the other side of the pier to
watch those men fishing. You can get your sketch done.'

He left me and I wasted a couple of pages, listlessly drawing
some boats grounded on a patch of mud near the harbour wall. At
any rate they'd do for Aunt Diana. Mr Jimmy rejoined me twenty
minutes later and asked: 'Won't you show me?'

'I'd rather not, they're so bad.'

'Very well.' There was a long pause, then he said: 'Do you know
why your grandfather won't have your Uncle Demetrius as your
trustee?'

'Yes, I think I do.'

He nodded, then giving me a searching look he said: 'I believe
you already know my sister.'

'Yes. She took me and Uncle Demetrius for a ride in her motor-car at the end of last summer holidays, and I saw her again at the beginning of this term in Victoria Station, when Uncle Demetrius was seeing me back to school. She told him he'd made a mistake about the time she was to meet him.'

Mr Jimmy laughed and said: 'What a liar she is! She turned up early on purpose to show herself off in your uncle's company. She shrinks at nothing when she's in one of her moods. How would you feel if your uncle married her?'

I said fiercely: 'I should hate him to. I should lose him altogether if he did. As it is, I feel I've almost lost him since he got so . . . so . . .'

'So much involved with her?'

'Yes. It wouldn't matter if he married . . . oh, somebody else who wants to marry him . . . in fact it would be a good thing for us all . . . but your sister . . .'

I broke off in dismay, as I suddenly realised that I was being outrageously rude about a member of his family. He laughed and said: 'What a worldly-wise young man they're turning you into! Don't worry about me. As you know, I'm neither fond of my half-sister nor proud of her. If I make use of her, it's only what she deserves. Let's end the conversation on a pleasanter note before we say goodbye to one another for the morning. Do you still want me to give you a lesson in Stocks and Shares?'

'Well, I've done them in the arithmetic book by myself, and somehow I've got most of the answers right, but I don't think I really understand what they are, except that you put them down in your Book of Life and live on what they bring in. What puzzles me is when it says you buy a ten pound share say for nine pounds and it pays six per cent—but you really get more than that—then you sell it at twelve pounds and put the money in a four per cent share which costs five pounds and you get still more income.'

'Isn't it wonderful how in these sums one's income always increases and never goes down?'

I said eagerly: 'Oh, but there is one sum—I'll show it you when I bring the book tomorrow—I didn't quite know what it meant—which says a widow's investments depreciate, or something like that . . .'

'Depreciate? That means become less in value.'

'Yes, that was it. And to maintain her standard of living she has to sell some of her capital and buy an ann . . . something, and how much has she left?'

'Annuity, I expect. Well, it's half-past twelve, and I think we'd better put off the lesson till tomorrow. I'll walk with you to where the respectable part of the town begins, in case you meet Mad Bessie on the way.'

'Oh, I'm no longer afraid of her now. You've cured me of that. You've cured me of everything.'

(4)

Another practice frequently resorted to was the making of a small image in clay or wax of the person whose sickness or death it was desired to bring about, and maltreating it, by sticking pins into it, by mutilating its members or even breaking it in half. Those who had no skill in modelling gave their crude efforts a personal identity by writing the victim's name on a small piece of paper and incorporating it in whatever material was used. The authorities differ as to what incantations should accompany the act, but Volastus avers that if the intention in the modeller's mind is sufficiently clear, no special ritual is needed to cast the spell. (Volastus, De dominatione incuborum, X.) On the other hand, Paracelsus maintains . . .

Aunt Sophy came in.

'Why, Francis, are you reading my magazine? It isn't at all suitable for you—at least, parts of it aren't. Give it to me. Aunt Letty doesn't like seeing it about the house and Aunt Diana pokes silly fun at it. Are you going out again?'

I mumbled evasively and picked up my French grammar. Fortunately she was so intent on getting the magazine up to her bedroom that she went there at once.

A few minutes later I hurried down Thanet Street to the toyshop just before it shut for the night. My signal-gantry was still in the window, but my passion for it was now utterly dead. I noticed a few scratches on the enamel. It had evidently had some careless handling. Soon, probably, it would be reduced in price and marked 'Slightly shop-soiled'.

I went inside and asked for some Plasticine. What colour did I want? I said: 'Flesh-colour.' The old lady wasn't sure they had it in flesh. No, the pale pink was the nearest. Would that do? I said it would, paid and walked guiltily out of the shop. As I was crossing the road, deep in my thoughts, I was startled by the sudden roar of a motor-car and a road-hoggish blowing of the horn. The car swerved and swept past me. I had just time to notice that the body-work was deep green with brass fittings and that it contained a man and a woman. The woman was driving. She was heavily veiled but I recognised her at once as the D.M. and I was almost sure that the man, though I saw him less clearly, was Captain Goodrow who had driven me and Uncle Demetrius on the last day of last year's summer holidays. Neither of them looked round and I had no idea if either of them had recognised me. Instead of shaking my fist, I shook my packet of Plasticine at them as they vanished.

When I got back, I filled in the time before my supper by writing to Uncle Demetrius. My excuse for writing was to tell him how sorry I was that he couldn't be my trustee. I managed to keep this up for a dozen lines. But the real sting of the letter lay in its tail:

'I had just come out of a shop in Thanet Street and was crossing the road when a motor nearly knocked me down. I am sure it was Mrs Desmond-Moffat driving and I think the gentleman with her was the one who drove us before. They were going very fast and I don't think they knew who I was.

                    Your affectionate Nephew, Francis.'

I said goodnight to my three aunts, went to my bedroom and unwrapped the Plasticine. It was a very bright pink, but not too bright, perhaps, for a woman who put rouge on her face—a prac-tice which to my aunts on both sides of the family, except Aunt Diana, suggested abominable depravity.

I modelled what was meant to be a human figure; it had two legs with little blobs for feet, a trunk, two arms with little blobs for hands and a neck below a disproportionately big blob representing a head, with a flattish projection round the top of it symbolising a Merry Widow hat. I gave the face features: two hollows for the eyes, a long pinched nose and a broad, grinning slit for a mouth. I forgot the ears. Then, being unable to find any tissue paper, I took a scrap of toilet-paper from the bathroom and wrote on it in very small letters, 'Mrs Desmond-Moffat'. I rolled the paper up into a ball, made an incision in the trunk of the image, inserted the paper and smoothed over the surface. Then, holding the image between my thumb and index-finger, I gazed at it with an exultant hatred and chanted three times in a relentless monotone: 'Mrs Desmond-Moffat, you are in my power!'

I put the image on the pedestal-cupboard beside my bed, and while I undressed considered to what indignities I would subject it. I would prick it every night three times with a pin, I would singe it a little in the flame of my candle, I would squeeze the throat, I would pinch off bits of pink flesh. Then I knelt down and began to say my prayers, but they might have been an easy multiplication-table for all the attention I was giving them, till I came to the words, 'Forgive us our trespasses as we forgive them that trespass against us.' Suddenly the grossness of my guilt came home to me. I rose from my knees in horror and sat on my bed looking aghast at the image, realising more vividly every moment that I had been planning to commit a gloating, cold-blooded murder. Surely a devil had entered into me—a real devil, not just one of those vague evil forces that Aunt Sophy was so fond of talking about. My conscience had awakened only just in time. In another two minutes I should have lost my soul.

When I felt a little calmer I got into bed and tried to think things out, examining my motives in the hope that they might excuse me. Why was I so eager for Mrs Desmond-Moffat to die? Because I hated her for being a wicked woman? No, there was much more to it than just that. Because if she died, her money might go to Mr Jimmy? Yes, partly—and that part of my wish at least was unselfish, or would have been, if I hadn't liked Mr Jimmy so much. But again, that wasn't by any means the whole story. Was it because I wanted to save Uncle Demetrius from making a marriage that could only bring him unhappiness? Again only in part. My deepest concern, the whole time, had been with the good name of the family, which, if tarnished, would beyond all doubt destroy any hope I had of becoming a baronet. That, among all my motives, was paramount. I, Francis Froxwell, aged ten, was prepared to commit murder for the sake of a title. 'If they do these things in the green tree, what will they do in the dry?' It had been the text of the sermon on the previous Sunday, and the memory of it brought me a vision of myself in old age—a hellish monster, beyond the pale of redemption.

Well, I hadn't yet killed. My good angel—what colour was he?—had saved me in the nick of time. As I thought of white and black angels, I wondered what Uncle Demetrius would think of me if he knew what I had been about. He would, of course, have been hurt and very angry, but at the same time he would have been full of contempt for the gullibility with which I had lapped up another sample of Aunt Sophy's mumbo-jumbo. The thought of his scepticism blunted the edge of my repentance a little.

I blew out the candle and turned over to go to sleep, but a new fear troubled me. Suppose I stretched out my arm in the night and broke the image in half by knocking it off the pedestal-cupboard? Well, if I did, it would be an accident, without any of that evil intent such as Volastus seemed to think must be present if the spell was to work. On the other hand, Paracelsus—what did Paracelsus think? What a pity Aunt Sophy had snatched the magazine from me just as I was reaching his views. However, I didn't dare to take any risks and groped very gingerly for the match-box, praying that my finger-nails would make no dent in the image while I did so. When I had lit the candle without mishap, I got out of bed, fetched a clean handkerchief and, holding the image as tenderly as if it had been the egg of a very rare bird, wrapped it up and put it in one of the small drawers in the base of the looking-glass on the chest of drawers.

I was so relieved to have stowed the image away that I soon fell asleep and had quite a fair night. But almost as soon as I awoke the next morning, my worries returned. Suppose one of the servants knocked over the looking-glass or lifted it so that the drawer fell out, or even merely opened the drawer to line it with fresh paper? Clearly I should have to find a better hiding-place. I padded round the room in my bedroom-slippers searching for crannies. I had read a story of treasure hidden underneath a floor-board, but none of mine seemed to be loose. I thought of the canopy over my bed, which I could just reach by standing on the pedestal-cupboard, but the thought of sleeping with the image only a few feet above me was intolerable. I was almost in despair and began to feel that I should have to carry the image about with me, as the Ancient Mariner carried the albatross, when I had the idea of exploring the fireplace. I knew only too well that in such a Spartan household no fire would ever be lit there except in the case of a serious illness. The grate was not laid, but lined with slightly soiled white paper, with another piece of paper folded like a fan to hide the opening of the chimney. I removed the fan and found, behind the firebrick, a small, sooty niche between the grate and the flue. It wasn't an ideal hiding-place but it was better than the drawer below the looking-glass, and I transferred the image with great care, trusting that the D.M. wouldn't find her new quarters too humiliating.

I went down to breakfast with very much less gusto than I had shown the day before. There was a moaning letter for me from Aunt Mary—little Rose's tummy was giving trouble again; Uncle Giles had been most kind and given Aunt Violet ten pounds so that she could consult another specialist; the maid at Palmyra had been offered higher wages elsewhere and was leaving at the end of the month. She had been complaining lately of overwork, though Aunt Violet had been most considerate and helped as much as she could. 'So she ought to', I thought irritably, 'sponging on Auntie Mary—yes, and on me too! *I* never asked her and her wretched babies, not to mention Uncle William, who has *my* room, to settle at Palmyra, while as for Uncle Giles . . .' For one wicked moment I wished someone would make images of the whole sickening lot of them—excluding, of course, Auntie Mary—and then annihilate them as quickly as possible.

Aunt Letty saw my frowns and said: 'You're very silent this morning, Francis. You seem almost sulky. Those are not good manners, whatever you may be feeling. And you haven't finished your marmalade. It is wasteful to take a bigger helping than you require. When we were your age, we had marmalade only on Sundays.' I murmured: 'I'm sorry, Aunt Letty', but I didn't mean it and I didn't show her Aunt Mary's letter which I knew she was longing to see. Meanwhile, the devil was whispering: 'You know, if you wanted, you could make an image of Aunt Letty, too!'

It was a grey and close, dispiriting day and, though I was on my way to meet Mr Jimmy, I felt little exhilaration. I was still plagued by the thought of the image lying in my bedroom grate. At that very minute, the servants might be turning out my room. What had possessed me to read Aunt Sophy's dreadful magazine? I felt that henceforward my life could never be the same again. If a mishap befell the D.M. I should always believe I was responsible for it. And what would happen when I went back to school? That awful day, though happily still far distant, would come round in due course, unless I fell ill or died. But what could I do with the image during term-time? I shouldn't dare to leave it behind, but, if I took it with me, it would run terrible risks.

It wasn't long before Mr Jimmy noticed my preoccupation. I had met him, as arranged, at the end of the pier but, though I made my greeting as warm as I could, I found it hard to talk to him naturally and he suggested that I might like to have my first lesson in Stocks and Shares. I agreed, but listened to him so inattentively, that he said suddenly: 'Francis, tell me the truth. Has it been a bore for you to come and see me today?' I blushed as I answered: 'Oh no, I've been so much looking forward to it.' 'Well, then, what's the matter? You're quite different from what you were yesterday. Are you worried about something?'

I hung my head in silence, till he said: 'Come along, Francis. There's nothing you need be afraid of telling me.' Then he dragged the story out of me bit by bit, except that I couldn't bring myself to tell him whom the image was supposed to represent. I was in tears when I came to the end, tears partly of shame and partly of relief at having found someone to share my secret. But instead of making any immediate effort to comfort me, he said, rather firmly: 'I'm very glad you changed your mind in time. Not, of course, that anything you might do to the image could possibly

affect another person; that belief is utter nonsense, whatever your
Aunt Sophy may say. There's no need for you to worry about that.
The only thing you might worry about is that you came so near to
giving way to a nasty impulse.' Then he squeezed my hand and his
voice became less severe, as he went on: 'But that's quite enough
of a sermon, especially from me. After all, the main point is that
you didn't give way, so you've nothing on your conscience. As for
the image, as you call it, you'd better bring it to me next time we
meet and I'll get rid of it for you.'

I brought it the following morning. It was raining hard when I
left the house and Aunt Letty shouted at me through the dining-
room window to come in. But I pretended not to hear and hurried
down the road before she could send Eglinton to bring me back.
As I approached the pier, I began to fear that the rain might be too
much for Mr Jimmy. Despite all his reassurances, the possession of
the image still weighed on me and I resolved that, rather than be
burdened by it for another twenty-four hours, I would seek him out
at his lodgings if he failed to turn up. But he kept his promise. He
was wearing a fisherman's oil-skin cape and when he waved to me
the rain-drops splashed from his arm. We went on the pier—there
were very few people about, owing to the bad weather—and sat in
a shelter. I unbuttoned my overcoat and took from my pocket the
small chocolate-box in which I had packed the image and said, as
I gave it to him: 'There's one thing I didn't tell you yesterday, but
I ought to. It's the name of the person who . . .' He stretched out
his hand to take the box from me and replied: 'I've guessed that. It
struck me at first that it might be one of your relations who had
upset you but, when I thought over what we had talked about the
day before yesterday, I felt quite sure it was my wretched half-sister
whom you wanted out of the way. Well, perhaps I do, too, but not
to the point of wanting to murder her. . . . So this is the lovely Mrs
Desmond-Moffat! I've a good mind to put her on the mantelpiece
in the drawing-room at Moffat Grange, when I go there next.' I
took him seriously and cried: 'Oh no, please promise me, please,
you won't do that!' He said: 'That was only a joke. No, I think
we'd better throw the lady into the sea.' There was a grimness

in his voice which reawakened my fears and I asked nervously:
'Are you really quite sure that doesn't mean she'll be drowned?'
He said: 'You silly boy!', laid the image in the palm of his hand
and picked at the stomach with his fingernail till he dislodged the
little ball of paper, which he unrolled and straightened so that he
could read what I had written. He smiled, then said: 'I hope she
doesn't develop violent pains in her tummy this afternoon, or
you'll begin to believe all that rubbish again. Now come with me.'
I followed him to the railings and watched as he snapped the image
in half and tossed the two bits carelessly down into the water. At
that moment a small steamer coming into the harbour gave a loud
hoot. I jumped and my face must have gone white; for he said: 'I
suppose you think that was her death-agony? No, my dear Francis,
we shan't get rid of her as easily as that. Now for the paper.' He
tore it into small pieces and threw them, too, over the side of the
pier.

As we walked back to the shelter, the rain began to stop and a
blurred rainbow appeared by the harbour mouth. He took off his
cape, spread it out to dry, then, sitting down beside me, he put his
arm round my shoulders and gently tickled my armpit. 'There,'
he said, 'that's all over. This has been our first real secret. Let us
hope we have many more, but may they be pleasanter. Won't you
get a frightful scolding for coming out on a day like this? Your coat
is wringing-wet and . . . yes . . . the bottoms of your trousers are
wet, too. I wonder if we could dry them at North Place . . .' As he
was feeling them, a heavy step sounded just outside the shelter.
He withdrew his arm quickly and edged away from me and went
on in a rather different voice: 'No, I'm afraid that's impossible. It
would take too long. For one thing, the fire won't be lit and . . .'
A fisherman passed along the glass partition. He was fiddling with
his rod and didn't look at us. For some reason I felt glad he didn't.
Then I began to stammer out my pent-up thanks, telling Mr Jimmy
that he was the greatest friend I had or ever would have, and was
soon so carried away by my gratitude and devotion that I started to
sob. He spoke rather sharply: 'Really, Francis, I think we'd better
talk of something quite different. How about twenty minutes of
stocks and shares? You haven't forgotten to bring your arithmetic-

book? Good. Well, let's have a look at the question about the unfortunate widow who had to invest in an annuity. (How I pray we shall both be spared the horrors of genteel poverty in our old age!) Ah, here we are . . .' The lesson began. I tried hard to follow his explanations, but showed myself so muddled that in the end he said: 'We'll go on with this when we're a little calmer. In any case, it's probably wrong of me to keep you sitting about in these damp clothes.'

(5)

I did better at stocks and shares the next day and a day or two later Mr Jimmy declared that I had mastered the subject and we tackled something else.

My meetings with him had now become a part of my daily routine, and if, as happened only very seldom, I found some other engagement forced upon me, my day was spoilt. Being with him gave me a strange feeling of excitement. Our silences were never embarrassing and his conversation never failed to hold my attention. There were times, indeed, when it did much more than this; for it had a way of leading up to something or other, suggestive of a door which in due season he would unlock for me, though he was careful to put the key in his pocket just when, as it were, I was about to grasp the handle.

I couldn't have said what lay beyond the door, but I developed a kind of instinct which told me at once when we were on the road which led towards it and did all I could to keep him from turning aside. One day, for example, I reminded him of the bit of Latin I had read in Aunt Sophy's occult magazine, which I could now think of without any qualms. I said: 'You never told me what *De dominatione incuborum* means.' He replied: 'I don't know. It all depends whether *incuborum*—what case is that, by the way?' I said it sounded like the genitive plural of a second declension noun, and he went on: 'Quite right. Well, it all depends on whether the genitive is subjective or objective.' He explained the difference between the two. 'Did the *incubi* dominate, or were they domi-

nated? One can't tell, without knowing what the treatise is about.'
Then I asked: 'But what does *incubus* mean, Mr Jimmy?' 'Strictly
speaking, a nightmare—something lying on your stomach, like
food you can't digest. But I think the rather bogus writers of later
times intended it to mean an evil spirit.'

'An evil spirit lying on the top of you?'

'Yes, the opposite of a *succubus*—or, more usually, in the femi-
nine, *succuba*—an evil spirit lying underneath you.'

'Which is the worst kind, Mr Jimmy?'

He looked at me searchingly, then said with a strange smile:
'Well, I suppose that depends upon one's tastes!'

We had reached the door, but he didn't open it.

Another time, my approach was more deliberate. I mentioned,
out of the blue, that Cedric declared one could often tell if people
would have any children, and how he had said that Uncle Demetrius probably wouldn't have any, nor Frobisher (who in any case
was to be eaten by cannibals while still quite young) and that I
certainly wouldn't.

Mr Jimmy said: 'Your cousin must be a most remarkable boy.'

'Oh, he isn't really. He only picks things up. He likes listening
to grown up people talking—so do I—but he often gets it wrong.
He said anyway a doctor could always tell. Do you think they
can?'

'No, I'm not sure that I do.'

I went on boldly: 'I asked Aunt Diana how a doctor would do
it . . . I mean, tell if you were going to have any children.'

'And what did she say?'

'She said he would probably ask you to put out your tongue.
But that's nonsense, isn't it?'

'Yes, I think that is nonsense.'

'Then how would they do it, or try to do it, Mr Jimmy?'

He didn't answer and I caught him by the sleeve and repeated
my question. He shook his head and said: 'I should like to explain
it all to you, but it wouldn't do, coming from me, of all people, to
you . . . at your age. In five or six years time, if we still know one
another—and I hope we shall—I may feel able to tell you . . . but
till then . . . no.'

Again, the door remained locked, but I was now quite convinced that it led to a world of enchantment beyond all imagining.

Never again, in our talks, did we approach so closely to 'the facts of life', though sometimes, as if he couldn't resist the temptation, he would throw out a word like 'puberty' which he knew I shouldn't understand, and then give me a guarded and partial enlightenment: 'That's the time when, in boys, the voice changes, and other things too . . .' watching me carefully to make sure I hadn't fully absorbed his meaning, nor yet altogether missed it. He did once say to me: 'If ever you get into any kind of peculiar trouble—something quite different from any trouble you've had so far—something you're too ashamed of or shy about to tell anyone else—do remember that you can always tell it to me and I shall understand it and forgive you. Be quite sure of this, there's nothing you can possibly do that I haven't done. Some day you may find that thought very comforting.'

As he had intended, I had a slight glimmering of what he might have in mind.

In an odd way these conversations of ours reminded me of the way Uncle Demetrius sometimes talked to me. He too, when in the mood, would, as it were, skate for my benefit over thin ice and give me for an instant just a touch of the same peculiar titillation. Perhaps that was one of the reasons why his companionship had meant so much to me. But his increasing fondness for the D.M. had made such a change in the balance of my feelings that I now dreaded to hear that he had decided to pay a visit to Whitgate, which might deprive me of Mr Jimmy for a whole week or perhaps even longer. Indeed, this and similar fears were never far from my thoughts. Without them, those weeks of high summer would have been a period of unclouded happiness. I put on weight, my complexion became a brown-pink instead of a greyish-white, my cheeks filled out, my morbid inhibitions began to leave me one by one. Who knows what kind of a man I might have become, if that sweet holiday could have lasted for ever?

VII. ANGELS IN TROUBLE

(I)

ONE afternoon, soon after the August Bank-holiday, I was sitting on the narrow strip of lawn that separated the promenade from the private road belonging to our terrace, when Eglinton came down the steps of Number Six and made straight for my chair. I was still more than a little afraid of him and began to wonder if I could have done anything to annoy him. He said: 'Master Francis'—his voice was far from genial—'the Master wishes to see you at once.' I followed him back to the house and waited uneasily while he knocked on the door of my grandfather's room.

A roar from inside ordered me to go in. Eglinton opened the door and shut it behind me. My grandfather, who had been unwell for the past few days, was in bed, but he looked even more formidable than he did when he was in his wheeled chair. He was sitting propped up by three pillows, with a muffler round his neck and a dingy brown shawl over his shoulders. He wore a skull-cap over his white hair, which suggested to me the black cap such as I had heard judges wore when they were about to sentence a prisoner to death. He said grimly: 'Stand there, where I can see you, boy!' and pointed to a patch of sunlight which fell obliquely through the slatted blind on to a spot only a few feet from the bed. When I was in position, he went on: 'I have to tell you that you were seen this morning . . . aha! . . . in the company of a most undesirable character, a man named Waring. Is that so?' I had to nod. However loudly I shouted, I could never have explained to him that, though I admitted to knowing Mr Jimmy, I did not admit that he was undesirable. Besides, I was much too frightened to defend him.

'Is this the first time you have talked with this man?'

I shook my head.

'Aha! How often have you talked with him?'

I tried to count—the day he saved me from the little bully by the name-plate machine—the day he saved me from Mad Bessie—the day I sought him out at his lodgings—the day I told him about the D.M.'s image—the day he destroyed the image for me—the day he took me for a row in a boat—the day we talked about *De dominatione incuborum*—the day he told me the story of Macbeth—each day had its special label in my mind, but the difficulty was to recollect them simultaneously. My grandfather, impatient with my long silence, which he may have taken for evasiveness, shouted suddenly: 'I asked you how often you have talked with this fellow?'

'About twenty-five times.' I strained my voice to its uttermost, but I couldn't make him hear. He said: 'Hold up your fingers and count on them!'

I held up my right hand five times, feeling on each occasion the stroke of an imaginary cane across the palm.

'Do you mean five times in all, or twenty-five?'

'Twenty-five . . . about twenty-five.'

He just managed to hear me. 'Twenty-five times, you say?' I nodded. 'Go to that desk. You will find some scribbling-paper on the left . . . aha! . . . behind the calendar. Write out an account of how this acquaintanceship began, and how it came to continue. Don't cry, boy. I haven't scolded you . . . yet!'

I went miserably to an ugly roll-top desk and sat down on a horse-hair settee in front of it. At first, my fingers quivered so much that I couldn't write, but at length I got a shaky grip of my pencil and produced the following:

'He rescued me from a boy who said he would knock me down when I was playing with one of the slot-machines near the pier. Next time he came up when a dreadfull old woman wanted to kiss me and he drove her away. He said he would teach me Stocks and Shares and he has and I know them now. He has heard me all my Latin grammar and some French, too, and he showed me how to use a fishing-line.'

I was wondering what else I should add, when my grandfather boomed suddenly from the bed: 'Don't be all day! I am not expecting . . . aha! . . . a treatise. Bring me what you have written.'

He read my confession aloud, interpolating: 'There is only one
"l" in *"dreadful".'* Then, after a minute's silence, he said deliberately: 'I see from what you tell me that the neighbourhood of the
pier is not suited to a boy of your age. In future you will take all
your walks elsewhere, unless one of your uncles or aunts accom-
panies you. However, I am glad to find that you have not been
spending your time too unprofitably. Had you come to know
anyone else in this way, I might . . . aha! . . . subject to proper
inquiries have permitted the acquaintanceship to continue. Unfortunately, or perhaps I should say fortunately, Mr Ledward, who,
as you know, is now your trustee in place of your Uncle Egerton,
was himself in court, acting on behalf of an interested party,
when this man Waring only just escaped a stiff sentence. This very
morning, when Mr Ledward was setting out with his family for
a short cruise in one of the pleasure-steamers, he saw you sitting
with Waring on the pier. Most properly, as soon as he returned to
his home, he wrote me a letter to that effect and had it delivered
here by hand. I do not propose to tell you the nature of the offence
for which your late mentor—a mentor is one who gives advice and
instruction—your late mentor . . . aha! . . . came so near to going
to gaol. At your age, you would have no notion of its nature. So
far, I think there has been nothing for which I need blame you.
But understand this very clearly indeed . . . aha! I forbid you ever
to seek out this man again or to hold any kind of communication
with him. If he tries to communicate with you or to molest you
in any way whatsoever, I order you to let me know immediately.
You understand?'

I could do nothing but nod my head wretchedly.

(2)

A merciful numbness carried me through that evening. My
three aunts knew that I was in some kind of disgrace and didn't
rally me on my lack of appetite or my inability to speak to them.
So far as any feelings were left to me, I longed to be alone in my
bedroom. But when I got there, I sat shivering on the edge of

my bed, despite the warmth of the evening, till the church clock struck ten. I hadn't lit the candle and realised suddenly that the room was completely dark. What did it matter? What did anything matter? I undressed in the dark and fumbled for my pyjamas under the pillow, where they should have been. But they weren't there. (I learnt afterwards that the maid who should have brought up the clean linen had been summarily sacked that morning for being impertinent to Aunt Letty.) Rather than see if I had a spare pair in a drawer, I went naked to bed. The feel of the sheets round my body thrilled me as if I had stripped myself for a shroud.

I suppose I slept. I had a great many dreams, but they left no message behind them. I awoke soon after five, feeling so sick that I went to the bathroom and tried to vomit, but nothing came up except a little white froth. Still, I felt physically rather better. When I got downstairs, there was a letter for me from Aunt Mary. 'Dear little Rose' had been dreadfully ill again and the specialist said that they might have to operate. This deepened my gloom, though I felt no affection for Aunt Violet's babies.

After breakfast, at which my appetite just managed to pass muster with my aunts, Aunt Diana took me aside and said kindly: 'Francis, you must really try to shake off your low spirits. Our father has only acted for the best and isn't in any way displeased with *you*. I promised to go and see Aunt Lorna this morning. Would you like to come with me?'

I replied sullenly: 'No, thank you, Aunt Diana. I . . .' While I was wondering if I dared tell her that if I couldn't have Mr Jimmy's company I preferred to have none, she asked suspiciously what my plans were. I told her I wanted to go and sketch the caves at South Whitgate Sands. 'You promise you won't go anywhere near the harbour?' I promised. She shrugged her shoulders and said: 'Very well.'

I am sure that when I left the house two or three pairs of eyes were watching to see if I turned my steps northwards or southwards.

But I kept my word. I was far too frightened of my grandfather to disobey him so flatly, and I hurried southward along the dull stretch of Uppercliff Avenue as fast as I could, as if intent on putting myself beyond the reach of temptation. When I reached Broughton Road, which led down to South Undercliff promenade, I had to sit on a seat for five minutes to get my breath back. I looked at the sea but it had no charm for me, nor had the trim little gardens bordering the road and the modern red-brick or roughcast villas which, to my grandfather's disgust and the detriment of his older properties, were now so much sought after. One might as well, I thought, live at Palmyra, hemmed in by the suburban spruceness of Oatingford Park, as live in South Whitgate. Both seemed equally distant from any possibility of romantic adventure.

I walked down the hill and hadn't gone very far along the lower road, when a wave beat against the stone of the promenade and drenched me with spray. From the top of the cliff, the sea hadn't looked so rough. I kept to the landward side of the promenade and thought how many times I had watched the waves with Mr Jimmy in one of the shelters on the pier, and the knowledge that I was never to do so again broke through the hard, protective crust of apathy which had congealed over my wretchedness and I gave way to a torrent of desperate tears which splashed on my shoes as if another wave had caught me. At that very moment Mr Jimmy would be waiting for me by the harbour. It is true I had failed him two or three times before, through no fault of mine, and once he had failed me—the D.M. having made some sudden demand upon him—but such disappointments had been only temporary. Everything now was changed. He would go to the pier the next day and the day after that and still I shouldn't be there. How soon would it be before he gave me up?

Then a new thought struck me. At our last meeting, which should have been a flawless memory, one inharmonious note had jarred our friendship. He had been talking about the D.M.'s late husband and had remarked—as indeed, he had done once or twice before—that Desmond-Moffat might not have been such a wastrel if he hadn't come into his money when far too young. He added: 'It isn't the first time unearned wealth has sent a man to the devil.' I hadn't very much cared for this observation. After all, my own innermost hopes centred round my grandfather's death and the passing of his baronetcy to me, and I couldn't help thinking that the sooner that happened the better. So, raising my eyebrows in an adult way, I said: 'Mr Jimmy, are you a Radical?' In those days, the word 'Radical', as used by the Froxwells and others such, denoted a Liberal with dangerous views, hardly less extreme than those held by self-confessed revolutionaries who called themselves 'Labour'. According to Aunt Letty, my own father had passed through a Radical phase soon after he went down from Cambridge. 'It greatly distressed our father and I'm not sure that Maximilian's name didn't disappear for a while from the Book of Life.' Fortunately it was only one of those fleeting aberrations to which clever young men are subject, and by the time the Boer War came, my father was quite orthodox in his attitude. I had been much relieved to find that Aunt Letty's story had such a happy ending and fully expected that Mr Jimmy would answer my question with an indignant 'No'. But he said: 'Yes, I suppose I am a Radical.' 'But you can't be,' I said. 'Think of all the lies they told about Chinese Labour in the mines.' He looked at me almost coldly and asked: 'What do you really know about these lies, as you call them?' I knew nothing, of course, but didn't like to admit it and sat gazing with a wooden face at the water. Then he put his arm round my neck and patted my shoulder and said: 'My dear boy, for goodness' sake don't let's quarrel over politics. I understand your point of view very well. We're still good friends, aren't we?' I replied: 'Of course we are,' and meant it.

But could he now be sure that I had meant it? Might he not think I found his Radicalism so offensive that I no longer wanted to be with him? At whatever cost I mustn't let him think that.

I had nearly reached the end of the lower promenade, where the little bay known as South Whitgate Sands began. There was a fair number of people on the beach and two of the six bathing-machines were in use, despite the chilly look of the rough sea. By the bottom of the steep road that curved down from the cliff, three motor-cars were parked on the shingle. None of them could vie with the D.M.'s in beauty, but a little crowd had gathered to admire them, and I should have joined it if I had been in better spirits. Behind the motors there was a small kiosk, where they sold matches, tobacco, sweets and picture-postcards. The latter hung down in streamers either side of the door and flapped in the wind. When I saw them, I had an idea. I couldn't send a post-card to Mr Jimmy, but I could write to him, if only I could get an envelope. I asked for one, but the woman told me they were only sold by the packet, which would cost me twopence. I had threepence on me. This didn't permit the purchase of writing-paper, since I should need my remaining penny for the stamp. However, I could tear a page out of my sketch-book.

I walked round to the farther side of the bay and a boulder jutting out from the cliff-side provided me with an uncomfortable seat.

'My dear Mr Jimmy, I have the most terrible news. We were seen yesterday by that Mr Ledward you said you knew a little. I told you he is one of my Trustees—I always hated him. Well, he told my grandfather. He sent for me and asked me a lot of questions about how we met and how well I knew you, and now I have been forbidden ever to see you again or even go down to the harbour by myself. I am wretched and don't know how I shall pass the days.

'I am writing this at South Whitgate Sands. Excuse it being on a page from my sketch-book, but I've no paper. Oh, my dear Mr Jimmy, please don't think I was angry because you said you were a Radical. I feel I can't bear not seeing you again. Perhaps when I'm older or Granddaddy dies I shall. I shall always want to. Please burn this letter. It would be most dreadful for me if it was found.
                    Your loving friend, Francis Froxwell.'

When I had addressed the envelope and sealed it, I had another of my outbursts of tears, and turned over on to my stomach and pressed my face against the scrubby grass that grew in patches on the cliff. Luckily that corner of the beach was deserted and nobody heard my sobs. I lay there till my sketch-book suddenly slipped from under my arm and dropped down on the shingle. This reminded me that I must have some sort of a shot at drawing the caves, in case I had to produce evidence that I really had been to South Whitgate Sands that morning. The three caves were twenty feet above the beach, in a bare and almost perpendicular part of the cliff. I remembered how, three or four years before, when I was still a child, Uncle Demetrius had told me romantic stories about them. One, he said, ran underground as far as Ramsgate, another to Dover and the third came out in the crypt of Canterbury Cathedral. At one time they were used by wreckers and smugglers. He promised me that when I grew up he would lower me by a rope from the top of the cliff so that I could explore them. At the time this had seemed a fine and heroic exploit, but I now knew quite enough about myself to be sure that I should never dare to undertake it. Besides, Uncle Egerton had destroyed the legend by telling us that the caves were merely excavations made in the middle of the last century to provide material for some local purpose or other, and that the biggest one hadn't a depth of more than thirty feet.

My sketch showed little more than the outline of the three entrances in the middle of a blank space but, as I drew, I began to weave my own fantasies round the caves. Mr Jimmy should make his home in one of them and I would slip out from Albert Terrace by night and meet him in it. I would help him to furnish it and make it comfortable. I had found a roll of old wall-paper in the drawer in the bottom of my wardrobe, with which we could brighten up the gloomy walls. We could search for phosphorescent shells among the pebbles and fix them in crevices to provide us with light. We could have feasts of gulls' eggs and cook them on a fire of driftwood collected from the beach.

My thoughts were flowing almost happily, when I noticed that most of the trippers had left the bay, while the few who remained were having a picnic meal. I looked at my watch. If I stayed any longer I should be late for luncheon.

I had to make a slight detour on my way back to get a stamp. I could hardly wait to gum it on to the envelope and drop my letter in the post-box, so that I could have no second thoughts about what I was doing; for I knew that for the first time in my life I was deliberately disobeying my grandfather.

I reached Albert Terrace just as Eglinton was sounding the gong. My grandfather, fortunately, was having luncheon in his bedroom, but I was so breathless and flustered that my three aunts looked at me with a mixture of suspicion and concern. Aunt Letty asked me sharply if I had washed my hands. I admitted I hadn't and was sent to the cloakroom to do so, while my plate of thin soup grew cold. Aunt Sophy said: 'It doesn't seem quite the day to spend much time on the beach', and Aunt Diana hoped I hadn't caught a chill. When the sweet course was served—prunes and rice—Aunt Sophy said artlessly: 'Caves must be very funny things to draw. When you're outside one you see nothing but a black hole and when you're inside you can't see anything at all. It seems to me you could draw them perfectly well without going near them.' In a desperate effort to turn the conversation away from myself, I said: 'I think I saw Lady Lucy and the Countess at South Whitgate Sands this morning.' My red herring was so effective that I felt no qualms at all at having told a lie. My three aunts said in excited unison: 'No, surely not!' 'Yes,' I continued, 'they were in a carriage with a gentleman . . .' 'A gentleman? How old was he, would you say?' 'Oh, I should say about as old as Uncle Demetrius. He wore a straw hat and a grey flannel suit and had a white rose in his button-hole. He sat with his back to the horses. I could see him better than I could the ladies. It was just by the end of the lower promenade.' This produced a broadside of questions. Had the ladies seen me? Was the gentleman . . . er . . . good-looking? Did Lady Lucy seem in high spirits? What was she wearing? What was the Countess wearing? I replied most convincingly that I couldn't say, adding by way of explanation: 'You see, I didn't like to go too close to them. In fact, I went down on to the beach so as to keep out of their way. Do you think I ought to have said "How-do-you-do", Aunt Letty?'

'No, Francis, I think that would have been too forward. You were quite right not to thrust yourself upon them, if it was they.'

Aunt Sophy said: 'But don't you think . . . I mean, Lucy has been so very kind to Francis, writing to him when he was at school and so on. After all, he's not supposed to know anything about . . .'

I asked: 'About what, Aunt Sophy?'

Aunt Diana gave me a grim look and spoke up for her foolish sister. 'About what you know quite well you're not supposed to know about! Francis, are you quite sure you really saw them?'

'No, Aunt Diana, I'm not sure at all. The older lady looked very like the Countess. She was hunched up and in black and the other lady was sitting a little sideways, as Lady Lucy does here, with one shoulder a bit lower than the other. It seems a long time since they've been here, Aunt Letty.'

Aunt Letty winced at my remark but ignored it and spoke to her sisters: 'I think it is most unlikely that they were there. You know how very unwell the Countess has been. Lucy said so in the little note she wrote to me about poor Egerton.'

Aunt Diana got up and as she passed my chair she touched my arm and said: 'Never mind, Francis. If it was a vision on your part, it's been a great success with all of us.'

Aunt Letty followed her out of the room and Aunt Sophy said: 'Now, Francis, come with me to the library so that you can show me your sketches.'

(3)

From that morning—till my life took another twist—I found it hard to know what to do with myself.

For some days I kept a close watch on the post, hoping to have a letter from Mr Jimmy. When none came, I decided that either he was afraid that my incoming mail was censored by the family, or he was so disgusted at my cowardice in not risking everything to come and see him that he didn't want to have any further truck with me. This thought made me miserable. Though my acute distress at the loss of his companionship began to abate, it left behind an emptiness which I didn't know how to fill.

Then Aunt Diana, my only ally in that difficult household, was suddenly taken from me. She had an invitation from the Geldenmosers to go with them to the North Sea and the Baltic for a month's cruise in their private yacht. There was a good deal of discussion as to whether or not she should accept. Aunt Sophy was all against it and said: 'It's clear you're only being invited as a stopgap. Besides, however rich the Geldenmosers may be, they don't belong to our world.' Aunt Letty agreed with this sentiment

but, probably because she always felt Aunt Diana's presence in
the house to be a slight threat to her own supremacy there, she
declared that she was content to abide by 'our father's decision',
well knowing that Aunt Diana had already talked him round. I
nearly cried when I saw her setting off with Lady Geldenmoser
in their superb motor-car with its zebra-stripes, for Tilbury, where
Sir Isaac and the rest of the party awaited them aboard the yacht.

Aunt Mary was to have spent the third and fourth weeks in
August at the Hydro. I hadn't seen her since she came to Eastbourne during my concussion, and she would have been a most
welcome change from Aunts Letty and Sophy, whom it seemed
nothing could ever dislodge from Six, Albert Terrace. But Rose's
condition was now so serious that Aunt Mary couldn't possibly
leave home. Only an operation could save the 'dear little thing'.
As for the cost of it, Uncle Giles, of course, had done all he could,
but that wasn't enough and Aunt Mary had been forced to borrow
some money on the security of Palmyra. 'Oh, Francis dear, I
simply hated doing it, but if I hadn't and anything should *happen*, I
should have felt like a murderess!' I began to feel more than usually
jealous of Baby Rose.

The Augustus Froxwells were still fishing in Scotland. I remembered how, during those precious weeks when I could enjoy Mr
Jimmy's society almost every day, I had dreaded the time when their
holiday would end. Now I wished it would. Cedric at least would
have been company for me, though I felt I should have to bridge a
big gulf to get back to those unsophisticated pleasures which six
months before had been such a bond between us—our collections
of this and that, the Loo-list and our irresponsible gossip.

It is true, I had five other cousins on the spot, but they might
almost have been strangers. Lavinia was now in low favour with
Aunt Letty, since in spite of her father's death she had refused to
give up her part in The School for Scandal. I myself heard her say:
'But, don't you see, Aunt Letty, the show must go on!' Aunt Letty's
jet ornaments quivered as she expostulated: 'But, child, your father
is hardly six weeks in his grave!' Lavinia tossed her head. She was
already one of the 'bright young things' of a later age. Another
grievance against her was that, although her mother's income

had been reduced by Uncle Egerton's death, she was still to go to
the finishing-school in Paris, largely at my grandfather's expense.
Even Aunt Sophy, who, owing to her special affection for Uncle
Egerton, was the most indulgent of my aunts towards his children,
remarked: 'I confess I cannot quite understand our father's generosity in this matter.'

To Lavinia, on the threshold of her brilliance, I was naturally of
no account at all. Nor was I much more to Esmeralda, who aped
her elder sister in everything and had always disliked me as much
as I disliked her. Oenone was such a poor thing that I could afford
to ignore her. Indeed, I once said, with an affectation of elderli-
ness: 'I never know whether you're you or Millicent', a piece of
rudeness which sent her in tears to her mother and brought me a
strong reproof from Aunt Sophy who overheard.

Uncle Seymour, his two children and their English nurse, were
as last summer staying at Prince's Hotel. The children were too
young to give me much by way of companionship, but Claude had
at least the merit of speaking French with a proper accent, and
this was some compensation to me for the time I was expected to
spend with them on the beach. He was even worse at ball-games
than I was, and we passed the hours building castles in the sand and
decorating them with shells, sea-weed and dead star-fish, while I
tried to learn from him whatever I could. Aunt Letty resented his
talking French to me and seemed to think that as an English boy
he should talk nothing but English while he was with us. 'Besides,'
she said to me, 'you won't find that the kind of French he talks
will be of the slightest use to you at school.' In this she was not
altogether wrong.

Meanwhile, Uncle Demetrius never came near us. I had three
picture-postcards from him—one from Brighton, one from Felix-
stowe and one from Ostend—and at last a letter from London.

17th August, 1910.   Mapp's Club,
                                                    St James's, S.W.
My dear Francis,

I'm selfish enough to say I hope you are missing me a little. I
have missed you, but I'm afraid it's unlikely that we shall meet as

long as you are at Whitgate. I don't fancy staying at Number Six, particularly while Aunt Diana is away, but if I stayed elsewhere in the town our father would be even more displeased with me than he is at present. It is a change for me to find myself the bad boy of the family instead of Uncle Seymour, whom I hope you are keeping in order. Aunt Sophy tells me that Uncle Augustus and his family will be back at Broadforsters on the 25th, so you will have some weeks of Cedric's company before the unmentionable date comes round. I am sorry to hear the news of your Aunt Mary. She is having more than her fair share of trouble. If she cannot get to Whitgate, you must certainly go and see her at St Albans for a day or two. That might give me the chance of meeting you *en route*. I don't like London in August, but there are many reasons for my being here. As you will have seen from my postcards, I have already taken three little holidays. I have hopes of another one in about ten days' time. Let me hear from you soon.

Your affectionate Uncle Demetrius.

(4)

On Saturday the nineteenth of August I got back from the beach just as the postman was in the act of putting two letters and a postcard into our letter-box. One of the letters was addressed to Uncle Demetrius, while the other and the postcard were for me. The postcard, which bore a Norwegian stamp and the Bergen postmark, said: 'Having a glorious time and the sea still kind. Hope you are well and happy. Love, Aunt Diana.'

The letter was typewritten, which excited me. I had only once had a typewritten letter before, and that was from Uncle Egerton when he wrote semi-officially to me at school, asking for my views as to the disposal of the income from my own little Book of Life. But this did not look like a solicitor's letter. The envelope was squarish instead of oblong and the typing was blurred and rather irregular, as if either the typist was an amateur or the machine was almost worn out. I took the letter straight up to my bedroom and read it there.

18th August, 1910.   8, North Place,
                                                       Whitgate.

My dear Francis,

I am sure you understand why I never answered your letter. It was good and brave of you to write to me. I was most distressed when I heard what had happened. I ought to have foreseen it, for your sake. Playing with fire has always been one of my weaknesses, but it's not a thing one should do at the expense of someone else.

I am taking the risk of writing to you now for three reasons. The first is to tell you that I'm leaving Whitgate on Monday and doubt if I shall ever come back. I rather think I have missed the last post tonight, so you may not get this till Saturday afternoon, but in case you do happen to get it in the morning, please don't make any attempt to come and see me to say goodbye. It would only make both of us unhappy, and might get you into very serious trouble.

I had a blazing row with my sister this afternoon. I gave her a piece of my mind about her behaviour, and she accused me of blackmailing her! I have always been aware that she made me my little allowance not because she was in any way fond of me, but because she knew I could tell some nasty stories about her, both while her second husband was alive and after he died. I have never threatened her in any way, though, as I think I told you, I had no scruples in taking what she gave me. Now she has sacked me from my little job of seeing to the closing of Moffat Grange—in any case, it wouldn't have lasted more than another few weeks—and cut me off without a penny. Luckily, I have had the offer of a post on the staff of a small, second-rate cramming establishment in London. Perhaps if I hadn't, I shouldn't have dared to speak to her as I did this afternoon. The pay is poor but, as you know, I can't pick and choose.

My second reason for writing to you will surprise you. It is to tell you that I have written to your Uncle Demetrius and shall be posting my letter to him when I post this one. I don't of course know his address, but I trust one of your good aunts will forward it to him at once. The matter is very urgent and if only he will take my letter seriously, it may save him from a lifetime of misery. I'm well aware he has a poor opinion of me and I won't pretend I'm taking this step for his sake. But I know how devoted to him you are and can guess how much you have been missing him these last weeks. If he will act on my warning, I think he will be restored to you again. I thought at first of writing anonymously, but decided against it. Anonymous letters are unpleasant things—I ought to know, having had some myself—and if one is wise, one takes no notice of them. I must hope that the disclosure of my identity won't lessen your uncle's belief in the truth of what I say. ('Disclosure of my identity!' There's a fine, journalistic phrase for you— the kind of thing we're so proud of writing at the age of eighteen and blush for at the age of twenty-eight!) If you want to know what all this means, ask your uncle, but not yet, unless you want to put the cat among the pigeons. Better wait till he's forgotten all about my letter to him and you have—

I was going to say "forgotten all about me", but I'm silly enough to hope you won't ever do that. And this brings me to my third and best reason for writing to you. I want to send you a stamp for your collection. I believe it is one which schoolboys regard as something of a treasure. I got it in Margate, as I couldn't find a specimen in Whitgate. I've no doubt that if you become a serious collector, you'll think it hardly worth a place in your album. But till then it may help you to remember

Your most affectionate friend,
Jimmy R. Waring.

The stamp, enclosed in a transparent envelope, was a fourpenny triangular Cape of Good Hope.

I read the letter through several times and then spent a quarter of an hour walking round the room so as to calm myself. When I went downstairs again, I noticed the letter to Uncle Demetrius still lying where I had put it, on a side-table in the hall. I picked it up and looked at the envelope and saw that the typing was just like that on my envelope. It was a fatter letter than mine and had an odd bulge in the middle. I was still holding it in my hand, longing to open it, when Aunt Sophy came down from the drawing-room.

I said: 'Aunt Sophy, here's a letter for Uncle Demetrius. Shall I re-address it and take it to the post?' She said: 'Let me see—it may be a circular. No, it has a penny stamp.' She held it up to the light, as if she too would like to know what was inside. Then she put it down regretfully and went on: 'Well, as it's Saturday evening, there's really no point in posting it till tomorrow. However, if you want something to do, take it by all means. You know we always send letters to his club,—Mapp's Club—a funny name, but it's a very smart club—St James's—J-a-m-e-s-apostrophe-s—London, S.W.' 'Oh yes, Aunt Sophy, I know.'

I had evidently shown too much eagerness, for she suddenly changed her mind and said: 'On second thoughts, no. It wouldn't look well that you should see to the readdressing of his letters. He might think Aunt Letty and I couldn't be bothered. I'll take it. I have one or two letters to write tonight and will put it out with them for Eglinton to post tomorrow morning.'

I was aghast and filled with the wildest fears. Aunt Sophy might steam the letter open and read it—in some of the school stories I had read, the villain made a habit of that sort of thing—or she might deliberately hold it up for a few days or she might lose it and never post it at all. Then most luckily, Aunt Letty, who came out of my grandfather's room, appeared for once in the guise of an ally.

'What is that, Sophy?'

Aunt Sophy explained the situation rather vaguely, but Aunt Letty said: 'I think Francis is right. As it came today, it ought to go today. It might be important.' She put her hand out imperi-ously and Aunt Sophy gave her the letter with a bad grace. 'Come, Francis, I'll readdress it in the library and then you shall slip along to the post with it.'

I ran most of the way and, as soon as I heard the envelope flop down inside the box, I was seized with a curious feeling of expec-tancy, which increased with each uneventful hour.

It was as if I were suddenly looking at life through glasses that magnified every detail of it enormously. Saturday evening seemed as long as three days and Sunday morning far longer.

Uncle Egerton's wife and her three daughters were coming to luncheon at Six, Albert Terrace, and instead of going to their usual church had joined us at ours. There was no room for all of us in the Froxwell pew, and I had to sit with Aunt Sophy and Oenone right at the back, among the less notable members of the congregation. I thought this quite wrong. After all, apart from my grandfather, was I not really the head of the Froxwell family? Poor fools, little did they know what schemes were afoot!

I had by now firmly persuaded myself that the letter I had posted the previous night would accomplish miracles. It would lead at once to a rupture between the D.M. and Uncle Demetrius and to his immediate marriage with Lady Lucy. From this to my grandfather's baronetcy was an easy transition, and still easier the transition from his baronetcy to mine. Then indeed I should find the whole world at my feet. My first act, after my ennoblement, would be to write to Mr Jimmy and offer him the post of my tutor; for, of course, I should never think of going to school again. I might go to Cambridge, but he would have to come with me there as my secretary. Aunt Mary should have all the money she wanted to pay for Rose's operation and to buy Aunt Violet and Uncle William a home of their own, preferably a long way away. Needless to say, when I acquired my baronetcy, I should also acquire my grandfather's Book of Life. The emotions of the young are volatile and I hardly know which of all these promised delights came first with me. I hope it was the restoration of Mr Jimmy. But it would also be lovely to have a motor-car, bigger and better and brighter than the D.M.'s, and as for my stamps . . . my excitement became so intense that I involuntarily gave the back of the pew in front a strong kick, which brought a loud 'Hush!' from a fat woman on my left and a severe look from Aunt Sophy on my right, while, beyond her, Oenone began to giggle. I composed my straying thoughts as well as I could, and the service seemed to go on interminably. Indeed, the only part of it that passed at all quickly was the sermon, to which as usual I paid a critical attention.

The preacher that morning was a visiting parson whom I disliked at first sight. He drew a long comparison between the Roman and the British Empires—the two greatest that the world has ever known. In its heyday, the Roman Empire seemed so firmly established that no one dreamt it could ever come to an end. Yet it did, leaving behind hardly a trace of all its glories. In our own time, the British Empire was the guardian of world-civilisation and *Pax Britannica* had superseded the perished *Pax Romana*. There were some pessimists who drew a false analogy between the two empires and maintained that, like the Roman, the British Empire, too, must inevitably decline. Ah, but these self-styled intellectuals had overlooked one most important fact. The Roman Empire was founded on paganism—a creed, if it could be called one, which filled every right-thinking man with disgust—whereas the British Empire was firmly based on sound Protestant principles and as long as it kept them uncorrupted would be predominant over all other nations upon earth. Surely, if ever there was a cause worth dying for, it was the preservation of the British Empire.

The hymn that followed, no doubt by the preacher's special request, was 'Fight the good Fight', which I detested more than any hymn I had ever heard.

It was over at last and we gathered outside the church for the grand parade, which seemed like a secular extension of the service. To my inflamed imagination it had never been such a splendid affair. That day it was the women's headgear that struck me most—fantastic bonnets resembling beehives and busbys, arch, whimsical toques, cartwheels festooned with flowers, feathers and fruit, their multicoloured caprices piquantly set off here and there by the black sleekness of an escorting top-hat. My family, of course, still wore deep mourning for Uncle Egerton, but that didn't prevent Lavinia and Esmeralda from strutting like manne-quins in the wake of my aunts, while by my side little Oenone strutted, too.

Every few yards the cavalcade would halt for bows, smiles, handshakes, inquiries and gossip, while I had to stand still, with the talk flowing over my head. '. . . I see you have tempted your sister-in-law to *our* church. It has such a wholesome atmosphere, don't you think? . . . I gather your brother—I mean Mr *Seymour* Frox-well, of course,—is staying here as a grass-widower. He hasn't, I hope, adopted his wife's religion? . . . Ah, that's good. On fine days like these, gentlemen are apt to play truant. . . . And your dear father still keeps fairly well? . . . And Miss Diana? . . . Really, with the Geldenmosers! She must be having a memorable adventure.'

Once or twice I myself became involved. Lady So-and-so hoped I had profited by Mr Beaton's magnificent sermon. 'One is never too young to learn how fine a thing it is to be a patriot.' I said daringly: 'I liked the Vicar's sermon about the Tower of Siloam much better than this one.' She looked at me blankly. 'The Tower of Siloam?' I said: 'Yes. It was very near the end of the Easter holidays. Don't you remember?' Lady So-and-so shook hands hurriedly and left us. Aunt Letty gave me a glance of more than usual disapproval, which found a smug echo on Aunt Sophy's flat face. Meanwhile Lavinia nudged me with her elbow and said in a resonant voice: 'Good for you, Francis! She's been giving herself absurd airs since her husband bought that tin-pot little knighthood.' Her mother said: 'Hush!' and Aunt Letty's frown became still more severe.

At another encounter there was a mention of Moffat Grange and I pricked up my ears. 'We hear some really nice people have bought it. He's a Brigadier-General—I don't recollect the name— and she was the daughter of a Rural Dean. They get possession early next month, I believe. I think it's such a very good thing— don't you?—a real *deliverance* for the neighbourhood. We never felt that woman would stay there long.' I glowed with the pride of a more intimate knowledge. Soon, very soon, all this sort of thing and these people would be of no importance in my life. I should no longer be trailed like a toy-dog up and down the promenade. Let them wait, I thought, and they would find they had something really worth talking about.

Uncle Seymour joined us for luncheon and for the first time for some days my grandfather took his place at the head of the table. We were eight in all, as Uncle Seymour's children had been left behind in charge of their nurse. The liveliest talk was between Uncle Seymour and Lavinia, who, with her Parisian finishing-school in mind, drew eagerly on his knowledge of France, which she had only visited for a few days. My grandfather, though he couldn't hear a word they said, enjoyed their animation and didn't seem in any way to share the views of Aunt Letty and Aunt Sophy, who indicated as plainly as they dared that they considered the finishing-school a sad waste of their father's money and that Lavinia's behaviour was indecorously light-hearted in view of her bereavement. Aunt Lorna, who was sitting on my left, was not by any means unaware of this and tried hard to restrain her daughter's exuberance. To me she said little or nothing, and I resented it. Well, if things turned out as I hoped they would turn out, there would be no finishing-school for Lavinia, nor for Esmeralda whose imagination had leapt forward two years to her own. If I had my way, they should both become nursery-governesses. Oenone, who was on my right, kept asking me questions about boys' schools and mine in particular, a subject of which I did not care to be reminded. One of her remarks was: 'I suppose, when you go to your public-school, you'll be Cedric's fag.' I replied angrily: 'I shall probably be in a much higher form.' At this, she leant across the table and asked loudly: 'Uncle Seymour, did you hear what Francis said? When he goes to Marlborough, he'll be in a much higher form than Cedric.' The whole conversation ceased and I blushed deeply. Aunt Letty shook her finger at me severely and said: 'Francis, that was a foolish and boastful thing to say. I hope school will teach you a little modesty.' Then fortunately she added: 'As for you, Oenone, you are talking far too much. It is most ill-mannered to interrupt the discussion of people older than yourself.' There was another silence which lasted till Uncle Seymour uttered an irresponsible 'Hear, hear!' and then resumed his badinage with Lavinia.

Like the service and the parade on the promenade, this luncheon, too, seemed unconscionably long. So did the afternoon and evening which followed it. I had hoped Aunt Sophy might take me out for a walk; for with her I could at least talk about my baronetcy—provided, of course, I called it my grandfather's—but Aunt Letty pounced first and I had to bear with her tedious praise of Uncle Augustus's children—Frobisher's fine moral character, Cedric's simple kindness and Millicent's daintiness—a requital, I suppose, for my comment on Cedric's lack of brains. In the end I managed to turn her thoughts to Lavinia and her two sisters, about whom Aunt Letty soon said a great deal in which I could agree with her. After this, unprompted by me, she made a few digs at Uncle Seymour's children, Claude and Nicolette, poor little things, who were the most harmless of all my cousins. 'I am convinced they are being brought up as Pagans—or perhaps I should say, Roman Catholics. Their mother is one and I'm told their priests never let them escape. Our father insisted they should have an Anglican nurse, but I doubt if she counts for much when they are in France. Uncle Seymour hardly seems to care about these things. He and Demetrius have little respect for religion. I hope you, Francis, will never let yourself be influenced by their examples. Aunt Diana, too, has a conscience that is dangerously easy. Do you suppose the Geldenmosers have a chaplain aboard their yacht?'

I suggested that they might go to church when ashore, but Aunt Letty said: 'No, not they. Of course, no one has ever seen the Geldenmosers going to the Synagogue, but I dare say they creep there when they are unobserved. If our father knew all! But since his day the world has become so changed and insecure. Someone called Lloyd-George made a speech the other day—it was in some horrid little mining-village in Wales—and he said. . . .'

She proceeded eloquently from horror to horror, while I thought, 'It's all very well for you to lay down the law like this, but in a day or two, perhaps in less time than that, you'll have a shaking!' Had I, like my father and Mr Jimmy, a Radical streak in my make-up after all?

As we turned in from the promenade to Albert Terrace, I saw a large green car with brass fitments standing by the corner of the road. I couldn't contain my excitement and said: 'Oh, that might be *her* motor! I must go and see!' Aunt Letty asked: 'Whose motor do you mean?', but as she spoke I was already running across the strip of grass that lay between the promenade and the road. No, it wasn't the D.M.'s. The bonnet was of quite a different shape and the speedometer was a puny affair, registering only up to fifty miles an hour. I rejoined Aunt Letty and said feebly: 'It isn't the one I've seen about here before.' 'Which one is that? You don't mean Sir Isaac's?' 'No, his has black and white stripes.' 'Then whose do you mean?' My aunt looked like an elderly school-mistress, choosing the words with which to reprimand me. Her primness goaded me, and at the risk of betraying Uncle Demetrius—though his secret, alas, was common property by now—I said: 'I was thinking of Mrs Desmond-Moffat's motor.' Aunt Letty quickened her pace and held my arm like a gaoler escorting his prisoner, and asked: 'How do you come to know what her motor is like?' I suddenly repented of my recklessness—it wasn't yet the time for such disclosures—and said: 'But everyone knows it. Aunt Lorna has often seen it. She pointed it out to Aunt Diana one day, when it was in Market Square, and Aunt Diana pointed it out to me when we were walking down Thanet Street.' I piled up the evidence, trusting that by the time Aunt Diana came within reach of Aunt Letty's cross-examination, all explanations would be superfluous. Aunt Letty said grimly: 'There seems to be a great deal that other people know and I don't. Before we have dinner you must wash your hair. I noticed at luncheon how very dirty it was.'

When I went to bed, I thought: 'This is my last night in this house before something really important happens.'

But it wasn't. There was the Monday to get through. I hung about the house all the morning, expecting a telegram or a messenger or perhaps even Uncle Demetrius in person. Nobody called, except the doctor, who was paying a routine visit to my grandfather. In the afternoon we went for a family picnic to South Whitgate Sands. I disliked the idea from the start. That bit of rock in the south-west corner was mine—it was where I had written my letter to Mr Jimmy and wept because I was never to see him again. And the caves, whose three uninviting entrances lay behind and above the very spot where our picnic basket was unpacked, belonged to Mr Jimmy and me and nobody else. Those vulgar August trippers —in whose number I included my aunts and my cousins—had no share in them. I spent as much time as I could with Claude and learnt that *Ta gueule* was the French for *Shut up!* Apart from this, it was a wasted afternoon.

I was by now in such a state of tension that I felt that, if nothing special happened on the Tuesday, I should go mad.

I was down long before breakfast, awaiting the post, and this

time I was not disappointed. There was a letter for me from Uncle
Demetrius.

Monday, 21st August, 1910.   Mapp's Club,
                                                St James's, S.W.

My dear Francis,
   I am paying a visit to Whitgate tomorrow—that is Tuesday, the
day you should receive this letter. I should very much like you to
meet me at the station at three o'clock. If other plans have been
made for you, get out of them if you can, without letting it be
known that you are expecting me. But if the worst comes to the
worst, produce this letter. After all, however low my standing may
be in Albert Terrace, I am your Uncle and your Godfather, and the
only person who has any right to prevent you from seeing me is
Aunt Mary in her capacity of your guardian. A fig for Aunt Letty
and another for Aunt Sophy, should they try to interfere.
                    Your affectionate Uncle and Godfather, Demetrius.

(5)

   He got out of the train looking like anything but a Londoner.
He wore a dark blue blazer with a coat of arms embroidered on
the breast-pocket, an almost transparent white silk shirt, a large,
floppy grey bow-tie, pale grey trousers, grey silk socks and brown
and white shoes. There was a picotee carnation in his button-hole.
He might have been going to a smart but Bohemian garden-party.
In his right hand he carried his gold-mounted walking-stick and in
the other a small brown leather bag.
   When he saw me, he waved his stick and said: 'Hello, it's good
to see you. Let's make a start by putting my bag in the cloakroom.' As I took the bag, all my old affection for him seemed to
come back to me. I asked him if he was going to stay the night in
Whitgate, adding that I had heard all the hotels were full. He said:
'I've very little idea what I'm going to do. It's hot enough to sleep
out on the beach. London was . . . like the Hell I've been living

in. What glorious air! That's one of the things our father really is
quite right about.'

When I look back now upon his conversation, I realise that it
was always apt to be inconsequent and full of abrupt transitions,
as if his mind were busy with several trains of thought at once.
Today this trait was more strongly marked than ever. He was like
a brilliant schoolboy, trying to do a dozen examination papers on
different subjects simultaneously. It was I who had to get some
sense out of his answers and to recall him to problems he'd tossed
aside.

We walked out of the station and I asked him where we were
going. 'Going?' he said, 'I hadn't thought of that. Somewhere cool
and breezy, where we can sit down. Not of course in the genteel
part of the town, where we might meet the family or their friends.
Shall we try the pier?'

I told him that I believed Uncle Seymour was taking his two
children for a steamer trip to Margate that afternoon. He said:
'Oh, I see. You mean, they might find us there?' I replied: 'Yes' and
nearly added: 'That was how I was caught with Mr Jimmy, only it
was that vile Mr Ledward who trapped us.' Uncle Demetrius said,
'One's got to take risks, and I think we'll take that one. We can
always make rude noises at them and say "Go away!", if they come
up with party-manners. I'm not in a mood today to be intimidated
by anyone.'

When we reached the main road, a stream of traffic held us
up for nearly five minutes. As I watched it, counting the motor-
cars, Uncle Demetrius said: 'You know, Francis, I'm not at all sure
that we're bringing you up on the right lines. The British nation
is turning itself into a nation of chauffeurs and will soon destroy
the class which ought to be employing them. I'm afraid that in
a few years all these elegant accomplishments with which we're
doing our best to fill your head—history, poetry, dead languages—
may be more of a hindrance to you than an asset. If you live long
enough, I doubt if you'll even be left your Book of Life. There'll
be no room for the cultivated eccentric in the mechanised world
of tomorrow. Nor will our Froxwell thrift and long-headedness
carry us through. We shall have wasted the best years of our

lives. Perhaps I'm thinking of myself more than of you. Shall we thread our way down through the little streets? I used to find them romantic when I was younger, especially as our father had some property right in the middle of them—rows of wretched hovels. If the tenants were cold, they used to tear the banisters from the stairs and use them for fuel. One couldn't get damages out of them. The only thing to do was to evict them, and that cost money. When our father told us about them, we could hardly believe such wickedness was possible. I'm afraid there are people today who would say the wickedness was on our father's part.'

We were now so near the turning that led to Mr Jimmy's lodging in North Place that I felt I might at any moment see him stride into the alley through which we were sauntering. If that had happened, I think I should have claimed acquaintance with him at once, for I was beginning to share my uncle's reckless mood. As it was, when I saw Mad Bessie, toothless and open-mouthed, asleep in a broken chair on a door-step, I pointed her out and volunteered that she had once tried to kiss me. My uncle seemed to take this as a matter of course and merely said: 'No wonder you don't set much store by female caresses, if that was your first and only experience.'

His next remark was: 'It's funny how large families always split into groups. Your father and Aunt Diana and I formed one. Aunt Letty and Augustus and poor little Beresford formed another, and Egerton and Sophy were always close friends. Seymour played a lone hand and kept his friendships outside the circle. On looking back, I think that, of all of us, he's come off best. Of course, he had some narrow squeaks. More than once it was touch and go whether he'd keep his page in the Book of Life. But he's got away with it so far, perhaps because he never lets his emotions get out of control. Do you think, Francis, that you could ever care for another person so desperately that you'd be willing to sacrifice all your prospects without any certainty that you'd ever really get what you wanted?'

I said hesitantly: 'I don't know. If I was sure that the other person loved me . . .'

He exclaimed: 'Is one ever sure?' and then went on, in a different voice, 'I think we shall have a thunderstorm tonight, the air's so close. If I'm sleeping on the beach, you'll have to come and bring me a mackintosh. Now we have reached Paradise. Would you like to go in?'

'Could we go later, when it's cooler?'

'How very sensible you are today! Very well, we'll make straight for the pier. I've no doubt the beach will be like a slice of yellow meat, eaten by swarms of flies and stinking horribly. Do you know that in Sweden there are special beaches where men and women can bathe together, naked? Do you fancy that idea?'

I didn't fancy it at all. Aunt Letty naked! I pictured all the women I knew and the thought of their nakedness was either embarrassing or laughable. What sort of a figure would the D.M. cut—I knew Uncle Demetrius was thinking of her—without her fine clothes? I felt she would exude a poisonous oil, the smell of which would make one sick.

The pier was so familiar to me that when we reached it I found myself saying: 'There's a little shelter by the gentlemen's lavatory, where we can see the boats and be out of the sun.' For all his wool-gathering, Uncle Demetrius seized on the remark. 'When were you last here?' I blushed and replied: 'It was weeks ago. I haven't been since . . . since . . .' He took my arm gently and said: 'Aunt Diana wrote to me and gave me an idea of what has happened. I'm not an ogre—least of all today.' I was silent and he continued: 'Am I to gather you haven't seen your friend since you had that trouble with our father?'

I murmured: 'No, not since then.'

'Have you written to him?'

'Once . . . to explain . . .'

'And has he written to you? No, these are nasty questions. I withdraw them, because I think I know the answers.'

'Once . . . only once.'

'That was the letter he wrote you last Friday?'

'Yes.'

'Do you know, I think this shelter smells a little. Let's move to the side and take two of those deck-chairs. What, a penny each? In my day, they were a halfpenny. Our father was a shareholder in the pier, till he realised it could never pay more than five per cent. He had a wonderful head for business and was always willing to admit a mistake and cut his losses. That's a thing few of us can do. How do we know that the loss won't become a profit? But he seemed to know. The number of bankruptcies of the companies in which he'd sold his interest would fill a page in the Gazette.'

For a while, my uncle rambled on in this dull way, while I, who had seen the iron glowing red-hot and hoped he would strike it, found its cooling unbearable. I interrupted him suddenly and asked: 'Uncle Demetrius, why have you come to Whitgate today?'

He looked at me and sighed, then said guardedly: 'Because I want to find out if your friend spoke the truth. Did he strike you as truthful?'

I answered eagerly: 'Oh yes, always. But how will you find out?'

'You must leave that to me. It's not impossible that I shan't find out anything and shall go on being plagued by these hideous doubts. But there's just a chance I shall be able to clear things up. I'm afraid I'm not giving you a very gay afternoon. Is it getting near time for tea? I seem to remember there used to be a café halfway up North Harbour Hill—not a very grand place, but they gave you scones and jam and clotted cream, which might appeal to you. Shall we go there now?'

'If you like, but it isn't four yet.'

He laughed and said: 'You might be the uncle, Francis, and I the nephew. By the way, did you leave word at Number Six that you'd be out for tea?'

'No, I didn't think of it. Besides, I couldn't be sure . . .'

'That I'd stand you tea? You might have known I should, but it doesn't matter. I feel I can't be alone this afternoon, and you must bear with me as well as you can. If I keep you too late, I'll send them a message somehow, to stop them setting up a hue and cry. Why can't our father have a telephone put into the house? His meanness over that is incredible. He may regret it some day. I wonder Eglinton doesn't insist on it. It would save him so many errands.'

I said: 'Oh, Eglinton isn't there today. He had a telegram this morning saying his sister in Dover was dying of a stroke and would he go at once. He left before luncheon—Gwen did the waiting—

and Aunt Letty said he needn't come back before tomorrow. Mrs Eglinton went with him, so there'll only be a cold supper tonight.'

'I wonder who will see our father to bed.'

'I think he's going to stay in bed all day. He didn't get up for luncheon. The doctor called about twelve.'

'I believe I said after Egerton's funeral that it looked as if our father was going to outlive the lot of us. He still may, but Aunt Diana told me in the last letter she wrote me before going abroad that the doctor wasn't very happy about him. You can have no idea, Francis, how terrified of him we were when we were young. I don't want to shock you, but I must admit I never loved him as children are expected to love their father. Do you love him, Francis?'

'What? Love granddaddy?'

'I see you find the notion unthinkable. If you told me you loved him, I should think you a hypocrite. My word, what a difference it would make to all of us . . . if it isn't too late . . . too late . . . if . . .'

He broke off and sat in his chair, apparently intent on studying the black smoke of a little crane on the far side of the harbour. Then, pulling himself together with an effort, he turned to me and said: 'Don't waste your life waiting for people to die, however great the temptation may be. Come along, it must be time for tea now.'

We left the pier and circled half round the harbour to a road that ran up the cliff on the north side. The café to which he took me was of a more popular type than those at which we sometimes shopped in Thanet Street. When we finished our tea—my uncle ate nothing, but I made up for that—I said boldly: 'You know, Uncle Demetrius, you don't always have to wait very long for people to die.'

'What makes you say that?'

'Well . . . Mr Desmond-Moffat . . . he came into his money very early, didn't he?'

He laughed grimly and said: 'Yes, that was the exception which proves the rule. He didn't wait long . . . and he didn't enjoy it long.'

'What did he die of?'

'It was not—as perhaps you've been told—an overdose of

arsenic. As a matter of fact, I believe he had an internal hæmor-
rhage. Did any of your informants suggest he was murdered by
his wife?'

'Aunt Diana said some people said so.'

'Oh, Diana was it? I thought it might have been someone else.
Now let's call for the bill. I think we're entitled to an hour or so in
Paradise.'

My uncle seemed determined to try every single sideshow at
the fair. I was shocked by the amount of money he was pouring
out in threepences. Some of the more boisterous amusements—
the swing-yer-round, the skelter-bottom and the sky-trapeze—
were almost too much for me. I began to regret having eaten such
a huge tea and urged him to be content with gentler pastimes. His
air of distinction and his smart, rather foppish clothes contrasted
oddly with the cheap tawdriness of the crowd and I noticed a good
many young women admiring him. One of them, who was on the
roundabout, dropped a spray of imitation roses just as she passed
us. My uncle picked it up and waited gallantly till the machine
ceased to turn and she dismounted and came up to claim her finery.
He raised his straw hat as he presented her with the flowers. She
said: 'Oh, that's ever so kind of you, I'm sure', and hung about, as
if she hoped that her charms might be strong enough to persuade
him to get rid of me and become her cavalier for the evening. But
he raised his hat again, smiled, took my arm and led me towards
the houp-là stand.

I said jealously: 'Did you know that lady, Uncle Demetrius?'

'Of course not.'

'I think she didn't really *drop* those roses at all. She threw them
down on purpose.'

'Of course she did.'

'Well, that isn't lady-like, is it?'

'You called her a lady. I didn't.'

I continued sulkily: 'I think she was a horrid and common
woman. I should have stamped on the roses instead of picking
them up.'

'Then you'd have heard such a torrent of foul language that

you'd have wanted to wash your ears. But apart from that angle, I can't say I altogether dislike it when a very pretty young woman shows she finds me attractive. It restores one's good opinion of oneself.'

I was tired of the subject, and physically tired as well. The noisy bustle of the fair-ground bewildered me and I longed to be sitting with my uncle in the palm-court of the Victoria, Whitgate's smartest hotel, sipping a soft drink while the orchestra played pretty music in the distance. Then perhaps my uncle would really open his heart to me and tell me his secrets. The afternoon had seemed to promise so much, but it was passing without getting us anywhere.

I remarked wistfully: 'We've only another half-hour together, Uncle Demetrius.'

He answered, too casually for my taste: 'Oh, we've much longer than that. I told you I'd send a message back to Number Six to say you were with me. We'll have supper together. Well, as you seem to have had enough of Paradise, I suggest you go on to the pier again and sit down, near where we sat before, and wait for me there while I make one or two little arrangements. I'll be with you again as soon as I can. I don't suppose I shall be more than twenty minutes at the outside. Do you mind?'

He gave me one of his most agreeable smiles and, though I hated the idea of his leaving me, I replied: 'Very well. But how long shall I wait . . . if . . . I mean, suppose . . .'

'Do you mean suppose my business takes much longer than I expect, or suppose I get lost or run over?'

I looked so worried that he smiled again and shook my arm gently. 'I'm only teasing you. I'll come back all right, but if, for some extraordinary reason, I'm not with you by seven, go straight home and tell them how you've spent the afternoon. Now, the sooner I start, the sooner we shall be together again.'

I made one more feeble attempt to alter his plans.

'You know Granddaddy said I was never to go on the pier without some member of the family being with me.'

'Well, you'll be there with me for all practical purposes. Here's the penny for your chair—keep the change.'

He gave me a shilling. When we reached the main exit of Paradise I paused, hoping to see which way he was going. But he took my shoulders and turned me towards the road that led to the pier, gave me a little shove behind, such as one might give a toy-boat when one launches it in a pond, and said: 'Be off with you!' I hadn't the brazenness to look round.

I was full of uneasy forebodings as I walked to the pier and, as if fate were set on justifying them, I had only gone a dozen yards beyond the turnstile, when I heard a babyish voice exclaiming, *'Tiens, mais c'est François!'*

It was Nicolette, just returned from the steamer-trip with her father and Claude. In my panic, I made the mistake of trying to slip past them, trusting that only Nicolette had caught sight of me and that the other two would take no notice when she told them. But Uncle Seymour caught me up only too easily and said: 'Hello, Francis, this is a surprise. What are you doing here? You know it's well after six. Are you expecting a friend?'

I stammered: 'No . . . yes . . . I mean . . .', then broke off miserably. Uncle Seymour laughed and said: 'Well, I'm the last person to interfere with anybody's fun, however peculiar or precocious it may be. I hope she's kind to you! Come along, Nicolette. Your cousin is disinclined for our company this evening.' As the three of them walked away, he turned his head round and added: 'Don't let anyone make a fool of you, young man. So long!'

My immediate feeling was one of great relief. I had feared he might drag me back by force to Albert Terrace. I wasn't at all sure how much he knew about my grandfather's embargo on the pier or what had led up to it, but even if he knew a good deal, he wasn't the type to sneak, unless by refraining he missed the chance of telling an amusing story. But my peace of mind was soon disturbed again. Claude or Nicolette, however discreet their father might be, would inevitably blurt out that they had met me alone on the pier. It was true that Uncle Demetrius had promised to send Aunt Letty a message letting her know that I was with him, but his mood had been so capricious and irresponsible throughout the afternoon that I dared not rely on him. Would they believe me if I told them the uncorroborated truth?

I sat down wearily, crushed by the weight of the double or even treble life I was trying to lead. If only Aunt Mary could replace my grandfather as the power which governed my destiny! If only Uncle Demetrius would break once for all with the D.M. and become what he had been the year before! I began to weave fantasies on the old lines—my uncle's marriage with Lady Lucy, who liked me and would always take my part, followed swiftly by my grandfather's baronetcy, which even more swiftly would be followed by mine. I should have more money than I could spend, I could see Mr Jimmy whenever I wanted to, I should never have to go to school again . . . and so on.

Then suddenly I had a fit of scepticism such as I had never had before. My daydreams were all far too good to be true. Things didn't happen like that, at least to me. I should never be much better off than I was, never have a title, never be free to choose my own friends until I should be so old that no one would want to make a friend of me.

For some minutes I sat listlessly watching the slow movement of the water as it swung the moored boats. The air was very warm and North Whitgate Head was almost hidden by a low-lying mist with a row of thundery clouds poised high above it. The pier was emptying fast at the call of high tea. Life was passing by me as it always would. My access of loneliness was so acute that big, heavy tears began to form in my eyes. I pressed my handkerchief on them with my two hands, bending my head forwards to hide my sobs. I felt there was no one in the world who could comfort me. Aunt Mary was too busy with her own affairs; besides, I had almost forfeited my claim upon her by becoming so much of a Froxwell. Mr Jimmy had been brutally taken away; and a new premonition told me that that very day I was to lose Uncle Demetrius for ever. I even began to think he wouldn't come back to the pier as he had promised and that I should have to sit there alone till seven o'clock and then make my way back to Albert Terrace to face the aftermath of my truancy as best I could.

While I was still lost in my mood of self-pity, I heard footsteps behind me and a moment afterwards felt a hand on my shoulder. I gave my eyes a quick rub and looked up. It wasn't Uncle Demetrius—whom, indeed, I now hardly expected ever to see again—but the man in charge of the chairs, coming up for my penny. When I gave it to him, he must have noticed my tear-stained cheeks, for he said: 'You don't look as if you're enjoying your holiday. Are you waiting for somebody, sonny?' I said: 'Yes, I've got to wait here till seven. If he doesn't come then, I'm to go home alone.' He answered: 'Well, you've got nothing to worry about. When I was your age, I hadn't a home to go to. And I've met others since then,—yes, on this very pier—as didn't know where they were going to spend the night. You must try to look on the bright side of things and count your blessings. Could you do with a cup of tea? I'm just going to make one for myself. There'll be nothing doing here for another half-hour.' I thanked him for the kind thought but told him that I'd already had a very big tea indeed. I must have expressed myself rather stiltedly; for all his sympathy dried up at once. He cleared his throat and spat over the railings into the sea, as if to show his disapproval of me, then turned round and said: 'Oh, you're a toff, are you? Waiting for the footman, I suppose, to call you to join the family in their carriage!' I longed for him to go away and didn't answer. Quite evidently, the man was a Radical, though not in the least like Mr Jimmy, who so far was my only Radical friend. But he hung about, either to goad me into speech or just to annoy me. All my class-consciousness rose to the surface and gave me a kind of comfort. I sat stiff and upright and tried to hum the air of 'Charlie is my Darling', which at the moment was my favourite tune. Then, when my new-found bravado was beginning to fail me, I heard more footsteps approaching—they were much quicker and lighter than the ticket-collector's—and Uncle Demetrius suddenly leant over my chair and tapped my arm.

'My poor Francis, forgive me.'

I jumped up with joy, while the ticket-collector made swiftly for some recess in the pier, designed for him and his like.

I said: 'Oh, Uncle Demetrius, it's you . . . it's really you!'

He smiled gaily. '"Journeys end in lovers' meetings." Cheer up. We'll have a lovely shrimp-supper at the Tree of Heaven. You didn't think I'd forgotten you?'

'I thought I might never be going to see you again.'

'But why? My dear boy, if you get into this kind of state over someone who, after all, is only your uncle, how will you get through the real emotional crises of life?'

As he spoke to me, I noticed a funny smell in his breath, which I afterwards realised was whisky.

While we walked off the pier, my first concern was to tell him about my meeting with Uncle Seymour and the two children. He said: 'What bad luck! But it's just what you thought would happen, isn't it? However, don't worry. I'll deal with it.'

The Tree of Heaven was really a public-house, but the owner had bought the adjoining cottage and made it into a little restaurant, which, for the benefit of young persons, was in theory non-alcoholic. There was a small garden in the back, where in fine weather one could eat in the open. It was now past the hour of the trippers' evening-meal and most of them had already left for Paradise or the pier. We sat down at a tin table in the shade of the *ailanthus glandulosus* which gave the pub its name and my uncle ordered two portions of shrimps, brown bread and butter, some biscuits and cheese and two bottles of lemonade, both of which were for me. Then he said: 'I've an urgent letter to write. I wonder if Mrs Beamish could oblige me with a sheet of note-paper and an envelope and a small boy who'd like to earn a shilling by taking a message to Albert Terrace at once?' The waitress said she would see what she could do, but looked rather doubtful, and my uncle added: 'Perhaps I'd better talk to Mrs Beamish myself. I can get myself a drink at the same time. All right, Francis, I shan't be more than two minutes.'

The moment he'd gone, I felt uneasy again. Why couldn't I have a friend who would never leave me? The waitress brought out our supper, but the sight of the shrimps, which normally would have aroused my greed, left me unmoved and, instead of looking at them, I looked at my watch and counted the minutes. As each one passed, my anxiety increased, but after the seventh my uncle reappeared with a bottle of whisky, a syphon and a tumbler. I said, reproachfully: 'You didn't forget the writing-paper, Uncle Demetrius?' He replied: 'No, it's in my pocket. Now you start on your supper, while I get this boring little job done.' He sat down, poured himself out a drink and began to write. I peeled a few shrimps. They were extremely tasty and my appetite came back to me all of a sudden. Indeed, I was so busy peeling and eating that I didn't notice that my uncle had finished his letter.

'Would you like to hear what I've said? I'll read it to you. Your sticky hands would make a mess of the paper.'

"My dear Letty, Francis has spent the afternoon with me. He has been a very good boy. As I hear the Eglintons are away for the night, I thought he might as well have supper with me as eat the left-overs at Albert Terrace. He will be with you again before dark, or soon after. By the way, I ought to tell you that while I was transacting a little business in the town, I sent him on the pier and told him to wait for me there. He complied with reluctance, but I assured him that, as he was in my custody, our father's ban on the pier was not operative. I understand he had the felicity of seeing Seymour, Claude and Nicolette as they were returning from their steamer-trip. Francis was not unnaturally embarrassed by this meeting, because I had told him that I wished no one to know of my being in Whitgate this afternoon. I mention this, just in case Seymour tries to be funny at the boy's expense.

Well I *am* here, but my plans are so undecided that Mapp's Club must for a while remain my address.

My fond greetings to any members of the family who may wish to hear from me. I shall probably be writing to Augustus in a day or two—I hear he is due back on Thursday—and in the meanwhile I have the honour to remain, Your devoted brother Demetrius.

P.S. I have promised the bearer of this letter a shilling. Please give it him and debit my account."

I thought it a wonderful letter, and I believe my uncle, thanks to the drink he had taken, thought so too; for when I asked him to read it aloud a second time, he would have done so, had not the grandfather clock in the restaurant struck the half hour. (It was ten minutes fast.) He said: 'I'd no idea it was so late. I must get this

off and relieve all the anxiety they ought to be feeling about you.
Timothy! Timothy!' The waitress came up and said: 'He's round
at the front. I'll send him out to you, sir.' She went inside and,
when Timothy appeared, I recognised him as the young lout who
had tormented me the day I had tried to print *Sir Francis Froxwell*
on the name-plate machine near the pier and Mr Jimmy had first
come into my life.

I hissed: 'Oh, don't trust *him*!', but the youth showed no sign of
having ever seen me before. Indeed, he seemed so much in awe of
my uncle that he promised to run all the way to Albert Terrace and
back. My uncle said: 'I don't care how long it takes you to come
back, but if you don't get there by a quarter to eight, Miss Froxwell will probably only give you twopence! Off you go!' Then he
turned to me and asked: 'Why did you say "Don't trust him"? Had
you ever seen his ugly little face before?'

I told my story with one or two suppressions—the 'Sir' of 'Sir
Francis Froxwell' being among them—and then, as I approached
the happy ending, I became so embarrassed that Uncle Demetrius
was sufficiently interested to drag the truth out of me.

'So that was how you first met Mr Waring? Go on, tell me about
your other meetings with him.'

I gave my uncle much the same account as I had given my
grandfather, but with greater detail. I ended up by saying: 'It
was so lovely here . . . I was enjoying everything so much till Mr
Ledward—oh, I hate him, I hate him!—saw us and told Granddaddy. Why did he interfere? What is it he knows about Mr Jimmy,
Uncle Demetrius?'

'Well, you see, the trouble arose from something unpleasant
that happened at the school where Mr Jimmy, as you call him, was
a master. The father of the boy who was concerned happened to
be one of Ledward's clients.'

'Did Mr Jimmy teach him to smoke or swear?'

'No, no, it was much more complicated than that. I doubt very
much if you could understand it, even if I explained it, which I'm
not going to do. You're too young, for one thing, and there isn't
time tonight. You know I've had a letter from Mr Jimmy? Well,
your story tallies with everything he says in his letter to me. Would

you like to hear just a little of it?' He felt in his pocket and said: 'Yes, here we are.'

"I know I cannot expect you to approve of my friendship with your nephew, though I can honestly say that the only thing about it with which I reproach myself is the pain I think he suffered when it had to end. I am convinced that my influence on him was good. I was able to help him quite a lot with his work—would that all one's pupils were so eager to learn and so agreeable to teach!—I got him out into the fresh air, I was able to ease his mind of one or two worries and I was beginning to show him how to conquer his shrinking from life. Since I had his letter informing me of your father's ban on our acquaintanceship, I have neither seen him nor written to him, except for a letter which I shall send him tonight, so that he may know that I have written to you. I am not asking you to urge your father to reconsider his decision—that, I know, would be useless—but I cannot help hoping that some day perhaps, when the choice of Francis's friends rests with you, you will take a more indulgent view of my painful past than is possible for the older generation. However, that time may be very far away. Meanwhile . . ."

'I shan't read you the rest. He doesn't write like a villain, and I can't afford to throw stones from the windows of my glass house. Now, Francis, you've just got time for one more go of shrimps and another drink, before I have to pack you off to bed.'

I refused the shrimps but said I should like some more lemonade.

He ordered my drink and, while we were waiting for it, I gazed up through long pendulous leaves of the tree of heaven into the black labyrinth of its serpentine branches, losing myself in their writhings, as if they were the visible emblems of my tangled thoughts. It was a moment of mystery and peace, and the stillness was emphasised rather than broken by muffled snatches of song from the pub next door. My uncle too was in a reverie; the waitress, when she brought my lemonade, had to ask him twice if he required anything further. He said: 'No, thank you', poured the drink into my glass and then, as an afterthought, topped it up with whisky. When he saw my look of consternation, he said: 'I want you to drink a toast to my happiness, and a soft drink isn't any use for that. You must get it down, however much you dislike it. I've only given you a spoonful or two.'

I raised the glass to my lips, but he said: 'Wait till I'm ready. There, we stand up, we clink our glasses together, and when we drink, *I* say: "To your very good health and your happiness, my dear Francis"—And *you* say . . . whatever happens to come into your mind.'

It was so dark in the shadow of the tree that I could see little more than the outline of his head and face, but I felt the force of his eyes looking straight into mine, as if he wished to drill some message into my brain that would make a lasting change in its structure. I put the glass to my lips, but owing to the whisky the drink tasted so peculiar that I spluttered and dropped the glass, which struck the iron leg of the table and broke into small pieces. I stood shame-faced, not knowing what to say and expecting a scolding. But he said something in French, then finished his drink, still keeping his eyes on mine, and went on in English: 'Perhaps it's just as well. It isn't time yet for you to toast *my* happiness. Besides, the accident may have saved you from getting a taste for spirits like your poor uncle. Now it's half-past eight. I think the time has come . . .'

He paused and neither of us said anything for what seemed like several minutes. Then he held out his hand. I felt a great longing to show him some special sign of affection, but no words would come and the strain soon became so unnerving that instead of taking his hand I slumped down in my chair and began to cry. He came round to me and stroked my hair, while I was drying my eyes, and said: 'Never mind, Francis. It was all my fault for trying to make this awkward moment into a melodrama. Did you understand that French proverb I quoted just now?'

I shook my head.

'It means, "Broken glass brings good luck—*verre cassé porte bonheur*". Let's hope it does. It's a phrase that comes in handy, when one has a little accident, like the one you had. Why not try it on Claude tomorrow . . . if there is such a day?'

Then at last I knew what it was that I had to say to him. Gazing at him as intently as he had gazed at me I asked: 'Uncle Demetrius, won't you come back to us? Won't you give her up?'

He stepped back a pace, as if I had suddenly threatened him with a knife. But he answered quietly: 'You don't know what you're asking.' Putting his hand on my head, he drew my face towards his and gave me a light kiss on the forehead. Then his arm slid round my shoulders and we walked through the little garden up the wooden steps that led into the café and straight through to the door that gave on the street. As we passed the waitress he called: 'Will you get my bill, please? I should like to pay it as soon as I've seen this young man off the premises.'

I whispered: 'That glass I broke . . . you won't forget to tell her about it, will you?'

He squeezed my arm and said: 'No, I shan't forget. Now you know your way home. Take care of the motors as they swish down Harbour Road. You mustn't let Mrs Desmond-Moffat run over you.' He gave me a little push and, when I turned round, he had gone inside and I could see him in the gaslight, settling with the waitress. I loitered where I was for a minute or two but, when I found he was taking his time and looking anywhere but in my direction, I understood that we really had said goodbye.

The sky was almost black and so full of clouds that not a single star shone. From time to time sheet-lightning told of a distant storm. I had never before been out so late alone and kept to the main roads rather than take a short cut through the narrow side-streets. Although I was sweating, I shivered as if I were cold.

(6)

I reached Albert Terrace about nine o'clock. When I rang the bell, it was, as I had expected, Aunt Letty who opened the door. I was feeling so exhausted and unhappy that I was quite indifferent to any scolding she might give me. But her first words were: 'Have you had your supper?' I said: 'Yes, thank you, Aunt Letty.' She looked at me searchingly and asked: 'What's the matter? Aren't you feeling quite well?' 'Yes, thank you, Aunt Letty.' She gave me another look and for once seemed unsure of herself. I asked boldly: 'Did you get the letter Uncle Demetrius sent you?' She replied: 'Yes, but it came so late, so very late. Aunt Sophy and I have been most anxious about you. It was most wrong of Uncle Demetrius not to let us know earlier. Francis, where did you leave him?' 'At the Tree of Heaven.' 'What and where is that?' 'It's a café near the harbour. You know Paradise? Well, if you go out by the gate at the lower end, you come to a short street—I don't know its name, but it takes you to . . .' She interrupted me with a nervous impatience. 'Never mind. I know whereabouts it must be. What a part of the town for him to take you to! Did he tell you where he is going to spend the night?' 'No, Aunt Letty.' 'Are you sure, or is it one of those secrets you have between you?' 'No, he didn't tell me. I asked him, but he said he might spend the night on the beach.' 'The beach, indeed! However, I suppose that was his idea of a joke. Well, we must talk about it all in the morning. You will not be able to say goodnight to Aunt Sophy. She has gone round to see Aunt Lorna and the girls and I hope you will be asleep before she comes back. Now goodnight.' As a rule she made some pretence of kissing me when I went to bed, but this time she made none at all and went abruptly into my grandfather's room.

I got into my pyjamas and lay down, longing for sleep, but it was slow in coming. I heard the church clock strike half-past nine, then ten, then half-past ten. Soon after this I heard steps on the stairs, which I recognised as Aunt Sophy's. The thought that there was now someone on my floor composed me a little and I drifted into a doze.

When I was awake again about midnight, I heard more steps, this time on the back-stairs. I learnt later that it was Freda, the between-maid, going up to her bedroom on the top floor. She had been ordered to spend the night in an airless dungeon known as the footman's room, next to the room which was normally occupied by the Eglintons, so that she could hear my grandfather's bell, if he wanted attention. Apparently, after spending two hours there, she became so frightened of sleeping alone in the basement that she forsook her post and crept upstairs to her usual bed.

This lapse from duty, when discovered, brought about her instant dismissal without a character. 'Suppose our father had been taken ill! Shameless, selfish girl!' and so on.

I slept again, as fitfully as before, while a thunderstorm boomed in the distance. In my spells of wakefulness I kept my eyes shut, so as not to see the flicker of the lightning through the crack in the curtains or reflected in the big mirror of the wardrobe, and, despite the heat, rolled the blanket tightly over my uppermost ear. Suddenly there was so loud a crash that I gave up all attempt at trying to sleep and sat up in bed, feeling extremely unwell. It may have been all the cakes I had had at tea, or the shrimps I had eaten at the Tree of Heaven, or merely excitement, but I found myself with a great desire to be sick. I struggled against it for some time, but the need became so pressing that I knew I should make a mess of my bed if I didn't quickly find a proper receptacle. I didn't like to use the chamber-pot in my room and at the risk of awakening Aunt Sophy I ran downstairs in my bare feet to the bathroom and let myself go. I felt better after the spasm, though far from right, and it wasn't long before I had another. Meanwhile, the lightning was flashing behind the blind and it had started to rain very violently. I waited in case I should have a third spasm, but I must already have emptied my stomach, for in spite of some retching nothing more came up.

Having been feverishly hot a few moments before, I was now very cold and longed for the warmth of my bed. I pulled the plug, with more apprehensive thoughts of Aunt Sophy, and was just going upstairs when I heard what sounded like the muffled ringing of a bell in the basement. I peeped downwards over the banisters into the dark hall. The bell rang again, but no one came up to answer it. Then I remembered that the Eglintons were away for the night and, not knowing that Freda should have been deputising for them in the footman's room, I began to wonder what I ought to do. Could my grandfather have been taken ill? If so, perhaps I ought to rouse Aunt Letty, whose bedroom was on the first floor at the back. I was nerving myself for this, when there was a loud rap on the knocker of the front door. I waited another minute and the rap was repeated with still more urgency. I ran down the stairs and then along through the hall into the lobby. Something bright seemed to be shining into the letter-box. I called: 'Who is it?' and a male voice replied from outside: 'It's the police. Please let me in.' I drew the three bolts, but left the chain in place, so that when I opened the door it left a gap of less than six inches. However, that was wide enough for me to see that there really was a policeman on the threshold. When he saw me, he said: 'Don't be scared, sonny. You just open that door properly. I don't want to stand all night out here in the rain.'

I undid the chain and he came into the hall, after putting his helmet and his dripping cape on an elmwood chest that stood just inside the lobby. As I shut the door behind him, I noticed his bicycle leaning up against the area railings. He looked at me doubtfully— he had a big, round face and a thin, dark moustache, twirled at the ends—and said: 'I've come with a message for Mr Froxwell, but as I understand he is a gentleman somewhat advanced in years, it might be better for me to see one of the other residents in the house first. Are you related to the family, young man?'

I replied self-importantly: 'I am the son of Mr Froxwell's eldest son.'

'Oh, and is your father here by any chance?'

'My father died seven years ago.'

'Perhaps you have an uncle staying here?'

'My uncle Seymour is staying at Prince's Hotel. Apart from me and my grandfather, there's only my two aunts here at present . . . and of course the servants.'

'A manservant?'

'No, he's away for the night, or he would have heard you ringing the bell. My grandfather is almost stone-deaf. That's his room, there. My two aunts both have rooms at the back. I only heard you because I wasn't feeling very well and had gone to the bathroom. Can't I give my grandfather the message in the morning?'

He shook his head and said: 'I'm afraid it won't keep till then. Otherwise I shouldn't have cycled round here in the rain. I shall have to ask you to disturb one of your aunts.'

'Aunt Letty's the eldest . . . she's Miss Froxwell, you know . . . I'd better fetch *her*.'

'Yes, do. That's a good boy. I'll wait here.'

I scampered up the stairs excitedly and banged on the door of Aunt Letty's room. She must have been very soundly asleep, for it was three or four minutes before I heard her say: 'Who's that? What is it?'

I shouted: 'It's Francis, Aunt Letty. There's a policeman downstairs, who wants to see you at once.'

'What about? Is it burglars?'

'I don't know, Aunt Letty. He didn't say what it was. Shall I tell him you'll come down?'

'Yes, in five minutes.'

I ran down into the hall and said breathlessly: 'Aunt Letty says she'll be down in five minutes. She asked me if it was burglars. Is it burglars?'

He shook his head again, and said: 'No, it isn't burglars. Now, sonny, the best thing you can do is to go straight to bed. And I'm sure Miss Froxwell would agree with me. Off you go, before she comes down.'

'But won't you tell me what it's all about?'

'No. I can't do that.'

I hung about for a minute, but he turned away from me and listened to the rain, which was now beginning to slacken. There was nothing for it but to go upstairs. However, when I reached the second floor, instead of going into my bedroom, I knelt by the banisters and peered down into the hall. It was not long before I heard Aunt Letty's door opening and had a glimpse of her as she turned the corner. She carried a candle and in her white lace boudoir-cap and thick Jaeger dressing-gown she had the air of a celebrated but very elderly actress who had given a farewell performance of Lady Macbeth and was making her way, exhausted, to her dressing-room—a grotesque but not laughable figure. Then I heard her say in her commanding voice: 'I am Miss Froxwell. What is it?' The policeman said something which I couldn't catch and she replied: 'No, nobody at all, except my sister . . . and my nephew, whom you have seen. You must speak to me.' There was another low murmur, then my aunt gave a kind of cry and gasped: 'No, no . . . not that . . . that can't be true!' The policeman spoke again and she replied, but this time she seemed to be whispering and I could distinguish nothing except, at intervals, a sigh of horror.

My busy imagination had already suggested two possible reasons for the policeman's visit. He might have come as a special messenger to announce the immediate conferment of a baronetcy on my grandfather in view of the precarious state of his health. (Even I could hardly take this seriously. The behaviour of neither my aunt nor the policeman suggested that he had come to us with good news.) On the other hand, and this seemed more probable, he might have come to inform us of the death of Uncle Seymour's father-in-law, who was said to be very seriously ill. Sad tidings, no doubt, but hardly sad enough to throw Aunt Letty off her balance.

Strange to say I had no inkling of the truth—perhaps because the strain of the day had dulled my wits—till Aunt Letty suddenly raised her voice and almost shrieked: 'At Moffat Grange . . . *in her bedroom!*' Then at last I understood that something awful had happened to Uncle Demetrius.

(7)

During the hideous week which followed that night, I gathered enough from what I was told and what I overheard—the two versions did not always tally—to form an idea of the catastrophe at Moffat Grange. Some of the details only came home to me years afterwards when, in a fit of nostalgic curiosity, I ferreted them out in back numbers of the local paper. The whole truth will probably always remain unknown except to the two most material witnesses—the D.M. and her friend Captain Goodrow, who had the best of reasons to distort it.

About half-past eleven, the police had a telephone call from Captain Goodrow, telling them that an intruder had broken into Moffat Grange and met with an accident which seemed to be fatal. Would they come round at once? They did so and found my uncle's body near the fireplace in Mrs Desmond-Moffat's bedroom. He was fully dressed, except for his shoes, which were later discovered by the back door of the house.

Captain Goodrow stated that he had supper with the D.M., fully expecting to be back in Whitgate soon after nine, but while they were talking together during the meal she had suddenly decided to sell the suite of furniture in her bedroom, instead of taking it to her London flat as she had planned. The drawers contained quite a lot of her things and she asked him to help her to sort them and pack them up. They worked hard for nearly an hour and a half. (There must have been more sorting than packing; for only two small boxes, both less than half-filled, were found in the bedroom.) Then they broke off for a while—say for a quarter of an hour—to go downstairs for a drink, and then started again. They were so busy that they didn't notice any noise on the landing—the thunder might well have deadened it—and they first realised that there was a stranger in the house when the bedroom door was flung open by my uncle, who rushed in as if he were drunk, waving his cane. (Medical evidence showed that he had taken a good deal of alcohol.) He made straight for Captain Goodrow and struck him. Captain Goodrow was naturally moved to retaliate but, before he could get within reach, my uncle swayed, fell near the fireplace, gave one or two groans and then lay very still and never moved again. Both Captain Goodrow and the D.M. felt the heart and agreed that he was dead. When the police arrived, Captain Goodrow had a nasty cut on his left cheek. Both he and the D.M. were fully dressed.

The D.M.—'labouring under the stress of great emotion'— declared that she was sure my uncle had been struck by lightning. 'A bright tongue of fire seemed to come through the window at the moment he fell.' Captain Goodrow said: 'I thought he must have been knocked out by hitting his head on the corner of the mantelpiece.' It is true that there was a slight bruise on my uncle's head, produced probably by his fall, but the autopsy disclosed the cause of death to be a congenital aneurism of the brain. (The thought that this may be hereditary in the Froxwell family has from time to time given me a good deal of uneasiness.) Be that as it may, Captain Goodrow had every cause to bless it, since it probably saved him from a charge of manslaughter.

But this was not by any means the whole story. Spicy details

came out. Captain Goodrow had told his landlady that he expected
to be away for the night. Indeed he had taken a bag with him,
containing his pyjamas and toilet things. When the police arrived at
Moffat Grange, they noticed that the pillows on the D.M.'s double
bed were rumpled and that the bedding was covered by a quilt,
which looked as if it had been put there hurriedly to hide some
disorder. There were discrepancies, too, in the time-table. The car
which my uncle had hired in Whitgate had set him down near
Moffat Grange about a quarter past ten, and the police surgeon
was of the opinion that he had died not later than a quarter to
eleven. Yet it was three quarters of an hour later when the police
received Captain Goodrow's telephone-call. It was almost self-
evident that he and the D.M. had spent over half an hour in trying
to save appearances. In other words, they had done their best to
make it seem that my uncle had intruded upon them while they
packed, whereas in fact he had found them in bed together.

But by far the biggest sensation of all was a letter, found in
my uncle's pocket by the police, written to him by 'a certain Mr
Waring, Mrs Desmond-Moffat's half-brother'. It was read out in
court and this extract from it was reproduced in the paper:

'I admit to having listened shamelessly to the gossip of the staff
at Moffat Grange, and to have prevailed on one of them, whom
I prefer not to name, to spy for me. As you may know, the last
two servants resident in the house are to leave about midday on
Tuesday the 22nd. My sister, on the other hand, is to spend one
more night there—as she put it to my informant—so as to be alone
with her memories. It is a little strange that her idea of solitude
should involve the preparation of a cold supper for two, but she
has given orders to that effect. On the following morning, Mrs Rait
of the village is to call at nine and bring my sister her breakfast, do
the washing-up and prepare the soiled linen for the laundry.

'In case it should interest you to make quite sure that the visitor
whom my sister is expecting for supper has left the house by a
respectable hour, I send you, with this, a key that fits the back door.
The bolt is broken. If by any chance a new one has been fitted, or
another key has been inserted in the lock, I have little doubt that

your ingenuity will suggest some other way in. There are one or two windows on the ground-floor—for example those of the servant's hall—which are almost an invitation to a burglar.

'If I am wrong, and you find my sister in lonely meditation, you and she are welcome to sue me for libel, though I don't recommend it, as you could get no damages out of me. I assure you I haven't given you this warning for the sake of distressing you. It is true I have a grudge against the present senior partner of your late brother's firm, and it may be true that I feel for a family as prosperous as yours that subconscious dislike which the "have-nots" are always apt to feel for the "haves". But this is more than outweighed by my affection for your nephew Francis. For his sake I should like to save you from a marriage which will wound him most deeply . . .'

Then came the extract my uncle had read aloud to me while we were sitting under the Tree of Heaven.

It was this reference to me, given in its fullness to the public in the Coroner's Court, that dragged me miserably into the whole affair. My trustee, Mr Ledward, either from a perverted sense of duty or owing to some personal malevolence, insisted that my relations with Mr Jimmy should be investigated by the police. While the name of Froxwell was beginning to stink more and more in the nostrils of fashionable Whitgate, and my poor aunts were smarting under the lash of the triumphant pity of their so-called friends or the open jeers of those whom in the past they had regarded as their inferiors, I was being half bullied and half cajoled into making some kind of admission the purport of which I didn't understand. I was subjected to an embarrassing physical examination at the hands of my grandfather's doctor and a police surgeon. I was questioned at great length first by Mr Ledward and then by two officials of the police. 'How had I come to be acquainted with Mr Jimmy?' That was easily answered. 'Had he ever given me any presents?' Yes, a few. There was my triangular Cape of Good Hope, he had bought me sweets from time to time, paid for me to go out with him in a boat and so on. 'Had I ever been to his lodgings?' Yes, twice. 'Had he ever taken me into his bedroom?'

No, . . . yes, once, so that I could wash my face. 'Had he suggested my face needed a wash?' Yes, . . . I had been crying . . . someone had frightened me. 'Who frightened me? Did I mean Mr Jimmy?' No, of course not. It was a woman called Mad Bessie. She tried to kiss me. 'Suppose Mr Jimmy had tried to kiss me, should I have been frightened?' Of course not. 'Had he ever done so?' No, never. 'Had he ever held my hand?' Well, yes . . . no, not exactly held it. 'Tickled it, perhaps?' Yes, once or twice. 'Had he ever put his arm round me?' Yes. 'And patted my shoulder?' Yes. 'Had he ever interfered with my clothing?' Well, he once tied my tie for me, when it kept coming undone.

They whispered together for a minute. Then one of them—he was a bull-like man with Eglinton's blue jowl—came so close to me that his huge body was almost pressing against mine and said suddenly. 'Did he ever . . . ?'

I leapt back with flaming cheeks, in which he may have read a confession of guilt, for he said: 'So he did!' I shouted at him: 'No, never, never!' and then burst into tears, while a strange shock of enlightenment quivered through my nerves and at long last I almost understood what they were getting at.

They whispered again, then unanimously did their best to soothe me, telling me that I had been a splendid little witness and that there was nothing at all to be frightened of and how they wished all boys of my age were so clear-headed and truthful in their replies. As Mr Ledward showed me out of his office, where the inquisition had taken place, he said: 'Now the best thing you can do is to forget all about this morning. Don't ever give it another thought. Here's a shilling for having behaved so well. Go and buy yourself a nice stamp with it.'

But very much more than a shilling would have been needed to erase those memories. As I made my way back to Albert Terrace, I had no thought of calling at the stamp-shop in Thanet Street. The last stamp I had stuck in my album had been Mr Jimmy's triangular Cape of Good Hope, and rather than follow it up with one that was a gift from his arch-enemy, I would have thrown Mr Ledward's shilling down the drain. No, the money should be spent

on something perishable, like sweets or chocolate-biscuits—and
even for them I had no appetite.

Aunts Letty and Sophy were so overwhelmed by what had
happened that not unnaturally they had few thoughts to spare for
me. None the less, I felt their neglect very keenly. After all, I was
in greater need of comfort than they. I knew they had never loved
Uncle Demetrius as I had loved him. Their tears were of wounded
pride and humiliation, while I shed mine for the loss of a very dear
friend.

The date of Aunt Diana's return was still uncertain. It was
even doubtful if she had yet received the expensive telegram
which Aunt Letty had felt obliged to send her. So far as I now had
anything to look forward to at Whitgate, it was to seeing Cedric
again. But though he and his family called two or three times at
my grandfather's, I was hardly allowed a moment alone with him.
He had just time to whisper: 'My word, this is all pretty bloody,
isn't it!', when his mother came up and dragged him away from
me. Frobisher looked at me with a sad disapproval which silly little
Millicent tried to imitate. I was not even judged worthy to go to
my uncle's funeral.

It was as if I had been sent to Coventry. I felt unclean, an outcast,
and my mere presence in the library seemed like an intrusion on
that stricken household of which, for some reason, I was no longer
a member.

(8)

[Monday] 28th August, 1910.   Palmyra,
                                          Throngley Avenue,
                                          Oatingford Park,
                                          Nr St Albans.
My darling Francis,

Our sweet little Rose who seemed last week to be getting just
a little better, was taken suddenly very ill last night. We called Dr
Thompson in about nine o'clock and he said she must go at once
to a nursing-home for an operation. Her sufferings were terrible
to watch. Even Uncle William broke down and said he would will-

ingly give his right hand if she could be spared them. The operation has been fixed for tomorrow morning and the doctor warned us to be prepared for the worst, as she is so terribly weak.

I am sorry I have to send you this dreadful news when you are so unhappy yourself. Your letter of last Friday reached me on Saturday—that now seems weeks ago. Yes dear, I know how very wretched you must be at losing poor Uncle Demetrius—he was my favourite too in your father's family, always so kind and considerate to me, which I'm afraid I can't say for some of the others.

No, there is no chance at all now that I shall be able to visit Whitgate this summer. Even if all goes as well as we hope, Aunt Violet will have to spend a lot of time at the nursing-home, which means that baby Mary will be thrown on my hands—she is very well, God bless her sweet little heart. Besides, it would be wrong of me to afford the expense, with so many calls upon me. I have decided to sell my amethyst bracelet and my mother's emerald ring and the pearl necklet my father gave me on my eighteenth birthday. I shan't of course think of selling your mother's diamond brooch, which your father so kindly gave me after she died. As I told you, I have left you that in my Will and I've no doubt your wife will wear it some day. I know it seems very wrong that we shouldn't meet during the holidays, but that could only be if you came here, which I daren't suggest just at present, not only because I shouldn't like to turn Uncle William out of your bedroom—though of course he would go at once, if he knew you were coming—but because you would find us such a very sad household, much sadder than they can be in Albert Terrace in spite of the tragedy. Besides, *they* have servants and can look after you properly, while we live very plainly here, waiting on ourselves and doing most of the work, which I shouldn't like you to see, as you're not used to it any more than I was when we had two servants and you and I had the house to ourselves.

I must stop now. You can tell your aunts of our trouble, if you think fit, but of course you mustn't dream of showing them this letter. Don't leave it lying about.

Your loving Auntie Mary.

This letter reached me at breakfast-time on the 29th. It was a fresh blow, not because—as I may already have made it only too clear—I was distressed on poor little Rose's account, but because for the time being at least I couldn't look even to Aunt Mary for comfort.

I spent a melancholy morning by myself. At about half-past ten I set out for South Whitgate Sands, but turned back before I had got much more than half way. When I was within a few yards of Albert Terrace, I saw Mr Ledward leaving Number Six. I slipped into a shelter on the front and luckily he turned the corner into Thanet Street without seeing me. I wondered why he had called and whether it was my grandfather or Aunt Letty whom he had wished to see. The mere sight of him filled me with an apprehensive revulsion and I felt sure that his visit boded no good.

Just as we were finishing luncheon, the sequel to Aunt Mary's letter reached me in the form of a telegram.

Our darling little Rose passed away this morning. Tell Aunt Letty.

                                        Love, Auntie Mary.

It was the first telegram I had ever received and I couldn't help admiring both Aunt Letty and Aunt Sophy for the way in which they forbore to question me about its contents. How unlike the voluble curiosity it would have provoked had I been at Palmyra! With an expression of shocked self-importance, I said as calmly as I could: 'Aunt Letty, this has come from Auntie Mary. She wants you to see it.'

Aunt Letty took the slip of paper gingerly, as if to touch anything from the Hemming side of my family were a contamination. When she had read it, she paused, then said: 'Oh, I am sorry—indeed I am very sorry. Your Aunt Mary must be greatly distressed. I shall write to her.' She paused again, then looked at me rather strangely as she continued: 'But your Aunt—your Aunt Violet, is it not?—has still another girl living?'

'Yes, Mary—Rose's twin-sister.'

'And she, of course, is at Palmyra, too?'

'Yes, Aunt Letty.'

'I see. I think I should tell our father at once of this development.'

She went across the hall to my grandfather's room and Aunt Sophy followed her, giving me a sad, reproachful look as she half shut the door. As I waited irresolutely in the dining-room, I studied the wall-paper—a self-coloured pattern of acanthus leaves in a very deep crimson—and thought how ugly and shabby it was. I resolved that, if ever the house became mine, it should be repapered throughout. The dining-room should have sprays of pink rosebuds and pale green leaves trailing up a blue trellis on a silvery ground, while as for my bedroom. . . . But it wouldn't be my bedroom then. I should move down a floor, perhaps to Aunt Letty's room or even to the spare bedroom or the drawing-room. Aunt Diana could still keep her room, if she wished, and of course there must be a room for Aunt Mary. The thought of her made me feel suddenly guilty. Why wasn't I crying? But I still couldn't honestly grieve that Rose was dead. After all, her death was a step towards my recovery of Aunt Mary. With one of the two children out of the way Aunt Violet would have twice the time to look after the survivor, and that meant that Aunt Mary would have twice the time to look after me.

Aunt Letty seemed to be spending a very long time in my grandfather's room. Since the night when Uncle Demetrius had died, he had neither left the house nor taken a meal with us. In fact, I had only seen him once and that was when Eglinton was pushing his wheeled chair down the hall from the library. He had given me a terrifying glance and made a noise like a very long drawn out 'Oh-h-h,' ending with one of his truculent 'Aha's.' Surely now, in view of what Aunt Letty was telling him, he would send for me and say something about the trouble at Palmyra, however irrelevant the death of a Hemming infant might seem to him, compared with the Froxwell tragedy.

At that moment the parlourmaid came in to clear the table. She gave me a glance of dismissal and I went into the library, leaving

the door open, so that I might have warning of Aunt Letty's movements. But when I heard the rustle of her skirts, I realised that
she was going straight upstairs, to the drawing-room or to her
bedroom. Had she forgotten me? Had my grandfather sent no
message? There was something frightening about the way I was
being ignored. I loitered downstairs for a quarter of an hour, then
went to my bedroom. If none of them cared about me any more,
why shouldn't I do exactly as I pleased? Where was Mr Jimmy?
Why shouldn't I write to him? Or was he in prison for having been
my friend? I felt like a well-meaning ghost that, whatever it does,
brings nothing but calamity to those whom it loves.

Well, I still had the beautiful triangular Cape of Good Hope that
Mr Jimmy had given me. It was a talisman that reminded me of
the happy past and beckoned me, perhaps, to a yet happier future.
I was opening the drawer which contained my stamp-album, when
Eglinton came in with hardly a knock on the door.

'Master Francis, will you please go down to the library. The
master wishes to speak to you there.'

I went down at once and minute followed minute without the
appearance of my grandfather's chair. As I sauntered round the
room I happened to notice on a side-table the prospectus of the
Parisian finishing-school to which Lavinia was to go next term.
Would they have her there now that the Froxwells were in disgrace?

I picked it up, looked at the pictures and read such parts of the
libretto as purported to be in English: *In the photographie supra we see
the voiture-de-luxe in the experienced guidance of coachman P. Jeannot,
while Marcel the lackey, proffering a discreetly gloved hand, assists the
jeune demoiselle to alight without maladresse. The correct deportment
of the carriage should be acquired by every well elevated Young Miss,
and such instructions are regularly combined with other graces such as
the court curtsy, the bow and the judicious usage of the fan. Nor are the
elegances of the repast omitted from our curriculum. The managements
of the knife, of the fork and even of the tea-cup are practised until the
pupil attains a perfection which will equip her for the most lofty social
occasion. . . .'*

I was filled with a great jealousy of Lavinia. Why should her school be so different from mine? Why couldn't Marcel's discreetly gloved hand assist *me* to alight from a carriage without *maladresse*? How lucky girls were! Why couldn't I have been born one? One might despise them and find them odious, but they had a much better time than boys. At this point it occurred to me that, if I had been a girl, I should have had no hope of inheriting a baronetcy from my grandfather. Despite all that had happened, the Corporation would still want his land and there was still a chance that by the time of the Coronation next summer our family would be sufficiently rehabilitated for the deal to go through without comment. Of course, this would mean waiting for nearly a year—and a sad, friendless year it seemed likely to be, so far as I was concerned, without either my dear Uncle Demetrius or my dear Mr Jimmy to help me through it. But suppose, meanwhile, my grandfather were to die? My gloom gave way to a sudden, greedy excitement. With whom would the Corporation have to bargain? Presumably with my grandfather's heir, and that might be. . . .

Oh, it was unthinkable, but nothing could alter the fact that, as the only son of his eldest son, I should be in a sense the head of the family. I should be Mr Froxwell, while my surviving uncles would still remain Mr Augustus Froxwell and Mr Seymour Froxwell. My wife, if I had one, would have precedence over theirs. Aunt Sophy had made a point of this to me one day, when she had had a tiff with Uncle Augustus's wife. I would gladly have sold my wife's precedence for five shillings, so unlikely did it seem that I should ever marry, but surely that wouldn't be my only asset. My uncles and aunts might each have a share of my grandfather's money, but Aunt Sophy said that land went to the eldest son, or, if he were dead, to his son. It was my grandfather's land, not his money, that the Corporation wanted. Suppose they said they couldn't manage a baronetcy, but offered me a knighthood, what should I do?

I was so lost in this problem that I hardly noticed that Eglinton had pushed the door wide open and was wheeling my grandfather straight to the desk. He was lying back in his chair, with his head tilted upwards and breathing much more heavily than usual. I walked towards him timidly, till he couldn't fail to see me. Meanwhile, Eglinton, who seemed as nervous as I was, stood at his side awaiting orders. I said: 'Good afternoon, Granddaddy, I hope you are well'—a sentence which he was supposed to be able to lip-read. To my surprise he gave my greeting no acknowledgment, but turned his head abruptly to Eglinton and said in his most ferocious voice: 'Go! Shut the door, but . . . aha! . . . be ready to answer the bell.' Then at last he looked straight at me, with a glare in his eyes I had never seen there before. I had not expected him to smile at me—it would be a long time before any Froxwell could smile again—but his expression shocked and terrified me so much that I shivered with fear. Then suddenly, still holding me with his eyes, he asked: 'Has Eglinton shut the door?' I nodded and he went on: 'Bring a chair . . . here . . . and sit beside me.' While I was struggling to put the chair in position—all the library furniture was heavy and cumbersome—he took the Book of Life out of its drawer and opened it at the page headed 'Demetrius Froxwell'. Then, when I had sat down, he dipped a pen in the inkpot and wrote 'Deceased' after the name. His hand, like mine, was trembling and his writing was so unsteady that I shouldn't have been able to read it, if he hadn't startled me by saying thunderously: 'Do you know the meaning of the word "deceased"?' I nodded, but that didn't satisfy him, for he snatched a piece of scribbling paper from a pile kept on top of the desk and told me to write down what the word meant. With the phrasing of Aunt Mary's telegram in my mind, I wrote 'Passed away'. My grandfather hissed contemptuously: 'Passed away! What a mealy-mouthed expression for a man to use! Why not say "dead"? Why not?'

I stared at him, not knowing how to answer, and he went on: 'Yes, my son Demetrius is dead, like Beresford, your father, and Egerton . . . aha! . . . But this was a very different kind of death from theirs . . . aha! . . . This was a death which should never have occurred. He could have had that woman as his mistress, if he must. I forgave Seymour one or two entanglements and I could have forgiven this one, too. But this mad idea of *marrying* the woman . . . aha! . . . of bringing *her* into *our* family . . . at a time, too, when he had the chance of making a most distinguished alliance . . . this was real folly, unforgivable folly.'

I think he had momentarily forgotten he was talking to me and was declaiming a set speech, such as he had rehearsed many times to himself and perhaps also to Aunts Letty and Sophy. Reacting from the strain, my thoughts began to wander, seeking refuge unconsciously in some external object beyond the scope of my grandfather's anger and my own predicament. It was a relief to watch the lozenges of light cast by the sun as it struck through the stained glass on to the opposite wall. The colours flickered, as wispy little clouds trailed across the sky. I decided that, if ever I had a great house, I would have stained glass in all the windows.

A sudden roar recalled my straying wits. 'Boy, attend! *You* shall strike through this page. Come, let me see you do it. Diagonally, from this corner to that one. No, with pen . . . aha! . . . not pencil.' He thrust the pen into my hand and pushed the Book of Life towards me. I was so dazed that I did nothing, till he shouted: 'Are you waiting for me to provide you with a ruler? Here you are, then!' He opened one of the small drawers at the side of the desk, took out a ruler and passed it to me so roughly that I thought he was going to rap me over the knuckles with it. Small wonder that, even though I used it, I drew a wobbly line.

My grandfather uttered a few disgusted 'Aha's!', then, giving me a strangely vicious look that was almost a leer, he said: 'There goes the fortune that I intended for your Uncle Demetrius. I shall not apportion the items among the other funds this afternoon, but when I come to do so, into how many shares shall I divide them? Aha! Have you yet turned your mind to that?' I shook my head, but began to calculate, and my grandfather, who no doubt realised what I was doing, gave me time to arrive at the figure—Aunt Letty, one; my father's Trustees, two; Uncle Egerton's Trustees, three; Uncle Augustus, four; Uncle Seymour, five; Aunt Sophy, six; Aunt Diana, seven.

'Well, have you finished?'

I mouthed 'Seven', raising one hand and two fingers of the other.

He smiled tigerishly and said with surprising softness: 'You know that seven is not an easy figure in division?' I nodded. 'A sixth of a pound is a simple matter, is it not?' I nodded again. 'But a seventh of a pound is harder to calculate. Could you do it?' He paused, watching me, while I whispered to myself: 'Seven into twenty-four, three and carry three: seven into thirty, four with remainder two. Thirty-four pence and two sevenths of a penny. Two shillings and ten pence and two sevenths of a penny.' I was going to write down the answer under my 'passed away' on the piece of scribbling-paper, when he shouted: 'Bah! We are wasting time. Get up and stand back, so that I can see your face more clearly. Do you remember the day when you were found on the pier, in conversation with a man . . . aha! . . . named James Waring?'

I nodded.

'I sent for you and told you that he was a most undesirable acquaintance for you. I forbade you strictly ever to hold any kind of communication with him again. Do you remember?'

I nodded, and he went on huskily: 'But you thought fit to disobey me?'

I shook my head and pent up tears welled quickly into my eyes.

Then my grandfather shouted: 'You are a liar! There is clear evidence that you lie! Waring states in a letter found on Demetrius's body that you wrote to him after . . . aha! . . . in spite of my orders.'

Impulsively I stretched out for the piece of scribbling-paper, intending to write, 'I had to tell him I couldn't see him again', but my grandfather struck my hand away with the ruler, glared at me and continued with increasing rage: 'I have no need of any explanations. The facts are clear. You wrote to this man and as a result he took upon himself to meddle with the affairs of our family. But for you and . . . aha! . . . this vile connexion that you formed, your uncle Demetrius would be living today. His death is on your conscience. But you shall have more punishment than that. You see this book? You know what it contains?' As he spoke, he scrabbled through the Book of Life till he reached the page allotted to my father's Trustees. Then, with a frenzy which he did his best to control, he said quietly: 'You bear our name. We cannot take that from you, but everything else that we can take . . . aha! . . . we take . . . like this!'

He scratched a ragged line across the page and said, with almost a chuckle: 'Divide by six now . . . aha! . . . by six, not seven!'

I was so dazed by the shock that I stopped crying. This seemed to annoy him, for his voice rose as he said: 'You are no longer welcome in my house. You will go upstairs . . . aha! . . . and pack your baggage. Eglinton will see you to the station and put you on the train for London. A telegram will be sent to your Aunt Mary, telling her when you are due to arrive there, so that she can meet your train if she thinks fit.'

In my wretchedness the prospect of meeting Aunt Mary that evening seemed the only good thing life could now offer me, but I had hardly begun to console myself when I remembered that Cousin Rose had only been dead for eight hours. Regardless of what might happen, I thrust my hand forward, snatched the scribbling-paper and wrote on it in pencil: 'Hasn't Aunt Letty told you my cousin Rose died this morning?'

This time my grandfather made no attempt to strike me, and read my message three or four times. Then, like an aged snake, spitting forth its last drops of venom, he said: 'Your mother's family has never been any credit to the Froxwells. I have no doubt that you inherit from them . . . aha! . . . your taste for low company. You will have every chance of indulging it when you return to your aunt's villa-residence in St Albans. We have done with you. Ring the bell, then go to your room and pack. I tell you, go!'

The last word came out so explosively that I rushed from the room, forgetting to ring the bell on my way. But there was no need. Eglinton was standing like a sentry at the end of the passage—he must have heard my grandfather's louder outbursts—and went unbidden into the library.

When I reached my bedroom, I flung myself on the bed and broke into hysterical screams. If they were heard, no one took any notice, and after a while they quietened to a sulky whimpering, which I kept up while I struggled with my packing. This was the first time I had ever tried to pack unaided. Aunt Mary did it all for me at St Albans, the matron had helped me at school, and at my grandfather's Aunt Diana had at least given me the benefit of her advice. But Aunt Letty, when at last she came in, had no such intention. She said: 'Your train leaves at a quarter to six, and a cab will be here for you at twenty minutes past five. You must make haste.'

My tears began again. 'But Aunt Letty, will Auntie Mary be there to meet me?'

'It is her duty to meet you. She is your guardian. I have sent her a telegram.'

'But today . . . when Cousin Rose has only just died . . .'

'I'm sorry to say that our father's wishes are quite definite. He will not have you in the house another hour. Of course, if you think your aunt will be so prostrated by *her* bereavement'—there was scorn in her voice—'that she will be unable to meet you, I could send a message to Mr Ledward to ask him to make some other arrangements for you.'

I cried: 'No, no, not Mr Ledward!'

'Very well.' She moved towards the door and I followed her, saying: 'Can't I go and say goodbye to Aunt Sophy?' Aunt Letty barred my way. 'Aunt Sophy is greatly distressed by what has happened. She has gone to bed with a very bad headache. I am sorry, but you will not be able to see her again before you go.'

I may be exaggerating Aunt Letty's unkindness. Had I been older or in a mood to study her, I might have judged that her tight-lipped cruelty was a form of self-defence and that she was not entirely unmoved by my plight. But at the time I took her for a fiend. A feeble spark of defiance sprang up inside me and I shouted: 'You're not sorry at all! You're delighted. I've always known you've hated me.'

She turned her back, walked out of the room and shut the door on me.

I was still trying to squeeze my clothes into my trunk, when there was a tap on the door and Eglinton came in. He said: 'Your cab will be here in ten minutes, Master Francis. You'd better hurry.' He gave me a stony look, but I felt he was less of an enemy than Aunt Letty.

I said: 'I can't get these things in. Could we make them into a parcel?'

By way of answer, he bent down and did the job for me, while he grumbled about my inefficiency. When he had finished, he picked up the trunk and carried it down to the hall, and I followed him with my playbox. I had forgotten my rain-coat, which was in the cloakroom, and he went to fetch it. Those few moments of waiting outside the door of my grandfather's room were not the least harassing part of my ordeal. I dreaded to hear a threatening shout from within, or that Aunt Letty might suddenly appear intent on punishing me for my outburst of rudeness. It was a relief to me, and I think to Eglinton also, when we heard the sound of the cab outside the front door.

I ran down the steps almost eagerly and, while the coachman was hoisting my luggage on the box, gazed up at the façade of the hostile house. When my glance reached the level of the drawing-room window, I saw Aunt Letty peeping out at me through a gap between the lace curtains, much as I had peeped out the previous January, when Lady Lucy and the Countess were coming to tea, till Aunt Letty herself had reprimanded me and told me that such curiosity was vulgar. I longed to cock a snook at her like the street-urchin who had cocked one at me, when I had tried to print Sir Francis Froxwell on the machine by the pier.

I got into the cab and sat at one end of the seat, leaving ample space for Eglinton to sit beside me. But he settled his broad rump on the tip-up seat which had its back to the horse. In his bowler hat he looked very much the gentleman's gentleman and, choosing to think that some of the holiday-makers who saw us assumed me to be a young aristocrat travelling with his valet, I did my best not to disillusion them. None the less, as we were going down the upper part of Harbour Road and I had a last glimpse of Paradise, the harbour, the pier and the sea, I very nearly started to snivel again.

When we reached the station, Eglinton paid the cab, put a porter in charge of my luggage and went to the booking-office to buy my ticket. As he handed it to me, he said: 'The Master instructed me to give you half-a-crown as journey-money.' I took it eagerly, as I had only one and eleven pence in my pocket. Then a snobbish instinct made me say: 'Of course, I must get a magazine to read in the train.' At the end of my first term at school, I had noticed that all the boys, without exception, bought themselves at least one magazine. As a rule they chose *The Strand*, *The Captain*, *The Boy's Own Paper* or *Chums*, and I felt impelled to live up to this ruinous standard. Eglinton watched with great disapproval while I squandered a precious sixpence at the bookstall, and said: 'You'll excuse me mentioning it, Master Francis, but you'll have to give threepence to the porter who takes charge of your luggage at Victoria. That is, if your aunt isn't there when your train comes in. And I'm told she mightn't be, as she's had short notice. If she isn't, you'll just have to sit on your trunk and wait. Now here's your train. I'll give the porter his tip. It's part of your fare and paid for.'

Having seen my trunk and my playbox into the luggage van, Eglinton put me into an empty compartment. I leant out through the open window and offered him a shilling, but he said: 'No, Master Francis, I can't accept that from you, thanking you all the same. From what I've gathered, you'll need every penny you've got.' He looked at me as if he would have liked to say more, but daren't take the liberty. I stretched out my hand, but he didn't touch it—the social gap was still too wide to be bridged by manual contact—and stepped back so that he should be two paces beyond the reach of my condescension. I said bleakly: 'Goodbye', and sat down by the window. He waited on the platform till the train began to move out of the station—perhaps he had been told to make sure that I didn't slip out to commit some further devilry in Whitgate—then, touching his hat, he said: 'Goodbye, Master Francis and good luck to you!' and walked away.

When I recall the horrors of that day, it seems to me that, in comparison with what had gone before and what was to come, I almost enjoyed the half-hour with Eglinton. He made me feel that I was still someone of consequence, whatever humiliations might lie ahead. But the calm interlude ended all too soon. Before the train had left the plains of East Kent, my thoughts began to busy themselves with the future. What should I say to Aunt Mary when she met me? For the time being, I had forgotten my fear that she mightn't obey my grandfather's peremptory summons. She would ask: 'But, Francis, what was it that you did?' And what should I tell her? That I had made a friend of whom my grandfather didn't approve and written to him after being forbidden to do so? 'But was that *all*?' I could add: 'Well, he was the man who wrote the letter to Uncle Demetrius warning him about the woman he wanted to marry, and if it hadn't been for that letter—which Mr Jimmy only wrote for my sake—Uncle Demetrius would still be alive.' Put baldly like that, my explanation sounded utterly fantastic even to me. And yet, in another way, I knew it wasn't. However much I might pose as an innocent victim, the guilt was mine. It dated from that evening when Aunt Sophy told me that I had two angels, one good and one bad—or, as I preferred to think of them, a white one and a black one. In my heart of hearts I had made a choice in favour of my black angel, and this was my punishment. (And yet, if I had chosen otherwise, would Uncle Demetrius have pulled himself together, abjured the D.M. and married Lady Lucy, thus paving the way for my aggrandisement? Of course he wouldn't. But this is latter-day wisdom.)

Meanwhile, what was in store for me at Palmyra? Whatever else had been taken from me that afternoon, they couldn't take away my right to go there. Aunt Mary was almost as dependent upon me as I on her. Perhaps that was why she still bothered with me. I had gone so much out of my way to flaunt myself as a Frox-well that I couldn't suppose she loved me as she had loved little Rose.

But however much or little she might still love me, my return to Palmyra on that day of all days could hardly have been more awkward and unwelcome. Uncle William would have to turn out of his bedroom and find a lodging somewhere in the town, unless he joined Aunt Violet and Baby Mary in their bedroom. That wouldn't make him any fonder of me. Aunt Violet's feelings didn't weigh with me much—she was the most colourless member of the family—but the thought of meeting Uncle Giles again was horrible. What a chance he would have of getting his own back, when he learnt that the Froxwells had rejected me!

As if I hadn't been tormented enough already that afternoon, I began to imagine what his greeting would be. 'I hear you've a nasty pain in the tummy, my boy. You must have swallowed that silver spoon of yours. Well, you're down on earth now, like the rest of us, and you'll have to give up your high-and-mighty ideas. *I'm* head of your family now, and don't you forget it!'

Apart from him, there would be Aunt Mary's friends. Aunt Sophy once said to me: 'Your aunt seems to have some very odd acquaintances at St Albans.' I remembered them well, those common, catty, middle-aged women, who used to stop Aunt Mary in the street and pat my head and call me 'the young man with great possessions'. It wouldn't be long before they found a different name for me. And when I went back to school—that dreadful day was drawing painfully near—I should no longer have the self-confidence which a background of wealth can give to the most timid. Even there it would somehow get about that I had been disinherited by my grandfather. One of the younger boys had once said to me in a moment of intimacy: 'Oh, how I wish I had rich relations like yours! *My* mater says I shall have to *work* for my living!' And I had gloated over the gulf which lay between us.

The whirl of my thoughts gave way to a kind of drowsiness, and while I looked apathetically out of the window—the sun had set and it was too dark to see much—I gave myself up to the rhythm of the train, wishing vaguely that the journey could last till I died. When we passed Bromley, I had begun to doze and remained half-asleep till we reached Victoria. A porter opened the door of my compartment and asked if I had any luggage. He was a skinny, undersized man with a pale, beaky face and looked half-starved, but I felt dislike for him rather than pity. I realised I ought to have been watching for Aunt Mary as soon as the train began to draw up at the platform. She would have dealt with the problem of my luggage. As it was, hoping to meet her as we pushed through the crowd, I followed the porter to the van and wondered what I should give him as his tip. I remembered that Eglinton had suggested threepence, but I feared this might be the amount that servants gave. When Uncle Demetrius was seeing me back to school for the summer term he had given the porter a shilling. What a day that had been! What a figure we had cut—my dear, handsome, immaculate uncle, the flaming D.M., and I, lit up by their radiance—as we stood in the circle of all those admiring parents! It was a memory from another world.

'Want a cab, sir?'

'No, thank you. I'm expecting to be met here. Just put my luggage on the platform, will you?'

I gave him four pennies. He took them without any comment and hurried away in search of another job.

The crowd round me grew thinner, as most of its members surged into the train which had brought me from Whitgate and was now about to make its return journey thither. To my dismay, there was still no sign of Aunt Mary. I walked nervously up and down, though I never ventured very far from my luggage, looking alternately towards the end of the platform and the entrance where the ticket-collector stood. The sight of him reminded me that before I passed through the barrier I should have to show him my ticket. I felt for it in all my pockets one by one and suddenly remembered that I had left it in my raincoat, which was still on the rack in the now swiftly vanishing train. I was so appalled by this discovery that I staggered to my trunk and sat down on it, covering my face with my hands to keep back yet another outbreak of my tedious tears.

I think that during the nightmarish hour which followed, I drained the cup of human wretchedness almost to the dregs.

It was in vain that I tried to think things out calmly and find excuses for Aunt Mary's lateness—her train might have been delayed, she might just have missed the one she intended to catch or she might have been out when the telegram reached Palmyra—but any comfort I could draw from such explanations faded away before the awful possibility that she might have been killed in a railway accident.

I wondered wildly what I should have to do if she didn't arrive, say, by nine or ten o'clock. My fortune consisted of three shillings and seven pence, which wasn't enough to pay for my lost ticket—without which I was imprisoned behind the barrier—let alone pay for a cab to St Pancras, my ticket from there to St Albans and a cab from St Albans station to Palmyra. I had read that people—even schoolboys, sometimes—raised money by pawning things. But what could I pawn? My fat, gunmetal watch? My stamp-collection, with the glorious blue triangular Cape of Good Hope which Mr Jimmy had given me? Oh, dear Mr Jimmy! If only he would appear and rescue me for the third time in my life! With a desperate hope that such a miracle might be granted me, I opened my eyes and searched for him in the crowd, as I had searched for Aunt Mary earlier on—but he, too, failed me.

It was now more than seven hours since I had had anything to eat or drink and my head swam with faintness. I began to shiver. The din of the station, full of zigzagging shadows cast by the swaying lamps, the thrusting travellers, the shouts of the porters as their barrows bumped against my luggage, the roar of the engines, snorting out jets of steam and startling me with screeches from their whistles, became a pandemoniac crescendo till my brain reeled in a hellish turmoil. Suddenly I felt a stinging pain in one of my eyes—a piece of hot grit had blown into it. Water poured down my cheek, while the other eye shed tears of sympathy. Then a hand touched my shoulder and a deep, female voice boomed: 'What's the trouble, little boy? Are you lost?' For a moment I thought I was in Nelson Backs and that Mad Bessie was accosting me. Then I looked up through my unblinded eye and saw, bending over me, a large woman in a nurse's uniform.

I fainted while she went in search of help. When I came to, Aunt Mary's arms were round me and she was saying: 'My darling Francis, what have they done to you?'

VIII. SIX LETTERS

(1)

Tuesday, 29th August, 1910.   Froxwell & Ledward,
                              Solicitors & Commissioners for Oaths,
                                            19, Jubilee Chambers,
                                                     Whitgate.

Dear Miss Hemming,

The Late Mr Demetrius Froxwell

I have to inform you that the Will of the above-named has only today come into my hands. It is dated the 16th April, 1909, and was drafted by a firm of London solicitors, Messrs Rodwell and Rose of 9, Champerty Court, London, W.C. I enclose a copy for your perusal and retention. As you will see, the Executors are the late Mr Egerton Froxwell and yourself. By the terms of his Will, the Testator bequeathed £50 each to his Executors, £100 to his sister, Miss Diana Froxwell, £25 to each of his nephews and nieces who should survive him, excluding your nephew, and the same sum to Stephen Eglinton, the manservant of Mr Froxwell Senior. Apart from these pecuniary legacies, the deceased bequeathed the whole of his residuary estate to your nephew, Francis Froxwell, upon the terms of the Will of your nephew's father, the late Mr Maximilian Froxwell.

I shall be glad to hear at your early convenience if you, as sole Executrix, desire my firm to act in your behalf. In the event of such being your wish, I will at once send for your signature a document authorising me to investigate and handle the late Mr Demetrius Froxwell's affairs.

                                        Yours very truly,
                                        Gavin P. Ledward.

(2)

[Thursday] 31st August, 1910.   6, Albert Terrace,
                                                 Whitgate, Kent.

Dear Miss Hemming,

I feel I should tell you that our dear father passed away suddenly last night. You will see the announcement in tomorrow's *Morning Post*. I think you will agree with me that there is no need for you and Francis to attend the funeral.

May I take this opportunity of condoling with you on the loss of your niece?

                                              Yours sincerely,
                                              Laetitia Froxwell.

(3)

Friday, 1st September, 1910.   Froxwell & Ledward,
                                 Solicitors & Commissioners for Oaths,
                                          19, Jubilee Chambers,
                                                    Whitgate.

Dear Miss Hemming,

I thank you for your letter of yesterday, informing me that you desire my firm to act on your behalf with regard to the estate of the late Demetrius Froxwell. I shall be obliged if you will be kind enough to sign the enclosed Form of Authority and return it to me at your early convenience. I am most grieved to hear of your own bereavement and much regret having to trouble you with business matters at such a time.

You will, no doubt, have seen the announcement of the death of Mr Froxwell Senior in today's *Morning Post*. In view of the special circumstances, I feel justified in anticipating the formal reading of the Will, which is due to take place after the interment next Monday, and in acquainting you with its main provisions, though I fear they will cause you some disappointment. Apart from a few inconsiderable legacies, the Testator left the whole of his estate to

be divided equally between his surviving children, with the proviso
that the children of the late Egerton Froxwell should take between
them the share to which their father would have been entitled had
he been living. The Executors are the Reverend Augustus Froxwell,
Miss Froxwell and myself. There is no mention of your nephew
Francis Froxwell in the Will.

As you will no doubt learn in due course, the Will is dated the
30th of August—last Wednesday. I received an urgent summons to
attend the late Mr Froxwell soon after nine o'clock in the morning
of that day. On my complying with his request, he instructed me
to prepare a new Will for him with as little delay as possible. The
document was ready before three o'clock and the late Mr Froxwell
executed it at about four o'clock in the presence of myself and
two of my clerks, who acted as witnesses. Though his breathing
was somewhat laboured and his manner betrayed signs of agita-
tion, his brain was completely lucid, and there can be no question
but that he was in a fit state to dispose of his property. I stress this
point, in case some misguided person should suggest to you that it
is your duty to contest the Will. In my view, it would be the height
of folly for you to embark on such a course, which would be fore-
doomed to failure and would inevitably make heavy inroads on
the comparatively slender capital which you and I hold as Trustees
on your nephew's behalf.

I hope to write to you in the course of the next few days
regarding the estate of the late Mr Demetrius Froxwell.

I am,

Yours very truly,

Gavin P. Ledward.

(4)

[Tuesday] 5th September, 1910.   6 Albert Terrace,

Whitgate, Kent.

My dear Francis,

I only reached home on Sunday. Such a chapter of accidents.
The yacht broke down in a small Norwegian harbour, hardly

accessible by land, and it was not till last Wednesday that I received the dreadful news about dear Uncle Demetrius. I still cannot believe that we have lost him. Of course, I hurried back as soon as I could, only to meet the further shock of our father's death. I am so dazed with these blows—though it would be hypocritical of me to pretend that they distress me in the same measure—that I find it hard at present to take a coherent view of life.

But I am really writing about your own trouble. I have heard different accounts, but I am sure I know what must have happened. There is no doubt that our father was thrown off his balance by the death of Uncle Demetrius—who, in spite of their estrangement, was his favourite son—and also by the disgrace which the tragedy has brought on our name. He persuaded himself that if you hadn't written to the D.M.'s brother, after being forbidden to do so, the D.M.'s brother would never have had the cheek to write to Uncle Demetrius. Even so, I cannot believe our father would have punished you as he did, if Mr Ledward hadn't called that very morning—I mean the Tuesday, the day you left Whitgate—to tell him that Uncle Demetrius had made you his heir. That you should be both the cause (in our father's eyes) and the beneficiary of Uncle Demetrius's death was too much for him to bear. I am so very grieved about it all, and almost wish I had never gone on that cruise, enjoyable though I found it at the time. I really think that, had I been at home, I could have done a lot to smooth things over.

If Uncle Demetrius had not made provision for you, I should have suggested that the rest of us should club together to make up your share of our father's estate. But I fear the only one who might have agreed with me is Uncle Augustus. Although he's a parson, he's really the best of those of us who are left.

Well, you must try to be thankful for what you *have* received. I hope it turns out to be a substantial sum. Our father gave each of his sons a generous start in life, and as Uncle Demetrius had a good head for business, when he chose to use it, you should find quite a nice little Book of Life coming your way.

These are early days for us to be making plans, but I doubt if any of us now want to go on living at Whitgate. Aunt Letty has just discovered that not only the visitors but even the residents are becoming increasingly common year by year, and Aunt Sophy declares that for some time she has been finding the air too strong for her stomach. I myself rather fancy a flat in London. If I do move there, I hope we shall meet from time to time.

Please remember me kindly to your Aunt Mary and show her this letter.

Your affectionate Aunt,
Diana Froxwell.

P.S. I see, on re-reading this, that I have said our father was thrown off his balance. Please don't, for one moment, let that give you the idea that he was not of sound mind when he made his last Will, and that it might be possible for you to upset it. I am told that his brain was perfectly clear, even during his fatal seizure.

(5)

Thursday, 7th September, 1910.   Froxwell & Ledward,
Solicitors & Commissioners for Oaths,
19, Jubilee Chambers,
Whitgate.

Dear Miss Hemming,

The Estate of the late Demetrius Froxwell

I feel it is my duty to inform you at once that the nett value of the estate which will be vested in us as your nephew's Trustees may be much less than you have anticipated. The figures before me are still incomplete, but I shall be agreeably surprised if the total exceeds four thousand pounds. It would appear that the deceased had made heavy inroads on his capital during the last six months or so. Of course, had he outlived his father and shared *pari passu* with his brothers and sisters, the situation would have been very different.

While the Trustees have ample funds to continue your nephew's education on the basis now in force, it has occurred to me to wonder whether, for the boy's own sake, it might not be wiser, in view of his changed circumstances, to plan his future less ambitiously. I do not pretend to know what expectations he may have from your side of his family, but, unless these are generous, I feel it is only right for me to suggest that instead of returning to his expensive school (where his school-mates mostly belong to a social sphere in which he will now find it hard to hold his own) he should be sent to some good day-school in your district and later, also as a day-boy, to one of the local grammar schools, where he would learn to rub shoulders with the world in which he will in all likelihood have to move. By this means his Trustees should be able to accumulate, say, fifteen hundred pounds which will stand him in good stead when the time comes for him to embark on a career. Above all, I feel he should be taught here and now that he depends upon his own exertions for his living. From what I have seen of him, and gathered about him, I fear he has been too much inclined to rely on some day stepping into a dead man's shoes, if you will forgive such an old-fashioned expression. This is an unhealthy attitude for any boy whose patrimony is not well secured.

I now come to a more personal point. In view of my increasing responsibilities and the fact that you and your nephew are prob-ably no more likely to visit Whitgate than I am to visit St Albans, I should be glad to resign my Trusteeship, if you can find a suitable substitute. Perhaps you have a family solicitor in whom you have confidence? If not, I am sure I shall be able to put you in touch with a reliable party, resident in your neighbourhood, who would be very willing to take my place.

I shall be obliged if you will be kind enough to give these matters your early consideration. As time is short, I have already taken the liberty of writing to the headmaster of your nephew's school, and he informs me that, having regard to the fact that your nephew has already shown himself to be something of that schoolmaster's bugbear—'a problem child'—he is quite prepared to waive any claim for fees, should your nephew not return for the Autumn term. I understand he has a long waiting-list.

I am,

Yours very truly,
Gavin P. Ledward.

(6)

Friday, 15th September, 1910.   The Vicarage,
                                          Broadforsters,
                                       Nr. Whitgate, Kent.
Dear Francis,

I'm writing to you with one leg up on a stool as I sprained my ankell yesterday on the common—I tripped in a rabbit-hole. So I have to rest it, otherwise I shan't be ready for school and it would be awful to go there a few days late with all the other new boys knowing their way about and looking down on you because you don't. I'm looking forward to it in a way and in a way I'm not, though I think I shall soon get used to the change.

I was going to write to you before, there has been so much news, but Frobby caught me at it and told Mother and she said I wasn't to write to you at present, but Daddy heard and said that wasn't a Christian attitude and that I could write if I really wanted to. So I'm writing now Mother and Frobby are out and I shall get Millicent to post this before they come in so that they can't ask me to show them what I've said. (It passes the time.)

I do wish I knew exactly what you did to make G. Daddy so angry. I can't think what it was unless you made secret friends with the D.M. It *was* bad luck getting nothing in G.D.'s Will, and it doesn't seem so unfair as some of them think, Uncle Demetrius leaving you what he had, though Lavinia says he'd spent nearly all his money on the D.M., so you won't get very much. She came to lunch here yesterday with Aunt Lorna and Esmeralda and Oenone. I was chasing Oenone, she'd been a bit cheeky, when I had my accident. Lavinia is going to her finishing-school in a week's time and Esmeralda is absolutely delighted because there'll be plenty of money now for her to go too when she's old enough, and Oenone says by the time *she's* ready there'll be a better one and she's going to that. Lavinia says you're not going back to yours but are going to be a dayboy. Well, you know, I've been a dayboy myself and though it's nice in some ways I've always thought there was somthing common about it. Though of course it doesn't matter at all if you go as a boarder to a good public school, which as you know is what I'm going to do. Well, even if *you* don't go to a public school you can always say you were a boarder at a prep-school for a term and a half and you needn't let on you didn't like it very much.

I must say it's a nice feeling to think we're really *in the money*. Daddy says that's a terrible expression and I mustn't ever use it. I shouldn't be surprised if he doesn't resign his living, not just yet, but say in about a year, and we all move somewhere else. Mother would like to go to Bournemouth but Daddy prefers the country and wants some fishing handy.

Oh, what *do* you think! He's going to give Frobby and me and Millicent a Book of Life each. It's something about death-duties. They say THAT FILTH Lloyd-George wants to put them up, as if they aren't bad enough as they are. Unfortunately we can't draw out the money till we're twenty-one. Tippical, isn't it! And all the dividends go to pay for our education. Frobby says when he comes into his share he's going to start some kind of mission. You bet I shan't waste mine on that kind of thing!

I don't think I like Mr Ledward much, do you? Lavinia says she heard Aunt Diana say he's got swelled head through being made G.D.'s Executionery or whatever the word is. After all, he started as junior clark in Uncle Egerton's office. He came to lunch last Sunday with his wife, she's *very* common and uses lots of scent— Lavinia says she *has* to use it to hide a nasty kind of smell she has— and the son who's about your age but much taller than you and pasty-looking with a sort of squinte. He's a slimy tipe and always called Daddy Sir and even tried to suck up to Millicent. I shan't have Mr Ledward as my solicitor when I'm grown up and if I were you I should turn him out of being your Trustee.

I haven't seen much of any of the aunts except Aunt Lorna and she's only one by marriage. Lavinia says she's quite sure Aunts Letty and Sophy will go to Bournemouth as soon as it's decent, whatever that may mean, and buy one of those red-brick villas like you see at South Whitgate and they've always said were very common. She thinks Aunt Diana will go to a flat in London. She might marry, as she met a man she rather liked on her ychating-cruse.

Well, that is all I can think of for now and in any case this is far
the longest letter ever written by

                              Your affec. Cousin, Cedric Froxwell.

P.S. Oh, I forgot to say this. You know that shilling Uncle Demetrius
asked Aunt Letty to give the errand-boy who took the letter to No.
6 saying you were going to be late the night Uncle Demetrius died,
and she gave it. Well, Lavinia says Aunt Diana says Aunt Letty is
going to claim it out of your estate!

THE END

ALSO AVAILABLE FROM VALANCOURT BOOKS